D1273295

White Dog

Books in English by the same author

THE COMPANY OF MEN

THE COLORS OF THE DAY

THE ROOTS OF HEAVEN

LADY L.

A EUROPEAN EDUCATION

THE TALENT SCOUT

NOTHING IMPORTANT EVER DIES

PROMISE AT DAWN

HISSING TALES

THE SKI BUM

THE DANCE OF GENGHIS COHN

THE GUILTY HEAD

White Dog

Romain Gary

Jonathan Cape Thirty Bedford Square London

FIRST PUBLISHED IN GREAT BRITAIN 1971
© 1970 BY ROMAIN GARY

JONATHAN CAPE LTD, 30 BEDFORD SQUARE, LONDON W C I

ISBN 0 224 00539 1

PRINTED IN GREAT BRITAIN
BY LOWE AND BRYDONE (PRINTERS) LTD., LONDON
BOUND BY JAMES BURN AND CO. LTD., ESHER, SURREY

Part One

Part One

He was a gray dog with a mole like a beauty mark on the right side of his muzzle and tobacco-colored hair around his huge, shining truffle of a nose. It made him look like the inveterate smoker on the sign of *The Smoking Dog*, a *bar-tabac* in Nice, who greeted me on my way to school in the days of my Mediterranean childhood.

He was watching me, his head cocked to one side, with that unbearable intensity of dogs in the pound waiting for a rescuer. He had the powerful chest of a fighter, and, many times, later, when my old Sandy teased him, I saw him shove away the other dog with the effortless power of a bulldozer.

He was a German Shepherd and he came into my life on

February 17, 1968, in Beverly Hills. I had just rejoined my wife, Jean Seberg, who was making a movie. That day, a rainstorm hit Los Angeles with the kind of larger-than-life fury you soon come to expect in America, where everything tends to be more dramatic and violent than elsewhere, with both nature and man trying to outdo each other at the art of showmanship. In a matter of minutes Los Angeles was transformed into a lake dwelling, with humbled Cadillacs crawling pitifully along through rapids; the city now had that incongruous, surrealistic air of things intended for quite another use. I was worried about my dog, Sandy, who had taken off the previous evening for a night on the town somewhere around Sunset Strip. The Strip was not the best place in the world for a simple, credulous soul. Sandy had remained a virgin until he was four, thanks no doubt to the strongly moral influence of our highly principled family, but recently he had lost his head over some cheap trash from Doheny Drive. Four years of solid middle-class upbringing had flown out the window. The poor dog was quite unable to cope with the insidious seductions of the Hollywood set.

We had brought along from Paris all our menagerie. There was a Burmese cat, Bruno, and his Siamese friend, Maï; actually, Maï was a male, but for some strange reason we had always thought of him as a she, probably because of the wealth of fond caresses he showered on us. There was also an old female alley cat, Bippo, of a misanthropic and nasty nature: she would scratch you, hissing at any attempt made to stroke her and would stare at you with an I-know-you-all look. I have never met a better informed cat. There was also a toucan, Billy-Billy, we had taken on in Colombia, and I had just offered to Jack Carruthers' private zoo in San Fernando Valley a magnificent python, twenty-three feet long, named Pete the Strangler. He had crossed my path in the Colombian backwoods at the same time as the toucan, and each of us was so impressed by the appearance of the other that it had become a kind of friendship, based on mutual lack of understanding. I had been compelled to get rid of Pete because no one else would look after him when, seized by one of my irresistible urges to run away from something —which I can only describe as the claustrophobic predicament of being trapped lock, stock, and barrel within a human skin, a very inhuman situation—I would dash across continents in pursuit of . . . what I don't know. Something truly different, anyway. I may as well say here and now that I have never come across anything truly different, except for some quite remarkable cigars in Madras, one of the greatest and nicer surprises of my life.

From time to time, I would pay a visit to Pete. Jack Carruthers had built a special enclosure for the python, out of respect for writers. I would go in, squat on the pebbles, and face the other creature. We would stare at each other in absolute astonishment, often for hours, deeply intrigued and wondering, awed and yet incapable of giving each other any kind of explanation about what had happened to us, and how and why it had happened, unable to help each other with some small flash of understanding drawn from our respective experiences. To find yourself in the skin of a python or in that of a man is such a mysterious and astonishing adventure that the bewilderment we shared had become a kind of fraternity, a brotherhood beyond and above our respective species.

Sometimes Pete would fold into a perfect triangular position, with only his slightly oscillating head emerging from this rigid geometry—pythons don't roll up in a ball, they tend to be squares—and in the first days of our relationship, I interpreted this as some sort of cabalistic sign, an attempt to communicate with me, as I happen to be one of those seekers who forever look for secret meanings and messages waiting to be discovered and decoded, buried within life's apparent meaninglessness and chaos. I have since been told that the triangular position is assumed by pythons in self-defense in the presence of all things strange, suspicious, and possibly dangerous. Thus I learned that Pete the Strangler and myself did have one thing in common: an extreme wariness in dealing with people.

About noon, when celestial floods were rampaging through the streets, I heard a familiar baritone bark and went to open the door. Sandy is a big yellow dog, with a broken left ear, a not-too-apparent descendant of some far-off Great Dane. The heavy rain and the mud had given his coat the appearance of crushed chocolate. He was standing at the door with his tail down and his muzzle low, the picture of guilt and shame, acting out the return of the prodigal son with a kind of perfect phoniness. He had been warned never to go out without telling me and so I shook my finger at him and repeated the words "bad dog" several times, with all the severity of the adored and feared Lord and Master, at which he duly reacted with a deep sigh, assuming an even more wretched and miserable air. Then, the ritual fulfilled, he tilted his head back to tell me that we were not alone and that I should moderate my transports in the presence of a stranger. He had brought home a guest. His companion was a graying German Shepherd, aged about six or seven, a beautiful animal whose strength and air of intelligence were striking. I noticed he had no collar, which is very unusual for a dog in America.

I brought my lowly cur inside, then wondered what to do with his high-bred gray friend. He was waiting in the rain and his wet fur made him look like a seal. He was wagging his tail; his ears were pricked up and he was watching me with that attentive intensity of dogs eagerly expecting an order. He was waiting to be asked in, claiming the sacred right of refuge, that ancient law that millenniums had so firmly established between dog and man, those old companions of misfortune.

It is fairly easy to form an opinion of a dog's character, except with Dobermans, whom I have always found unpredictable. My gray guest was good-natured, tolerant, and even fatherly in his endurance of my six-year-old son Diego's tail-pulling whims—and beautifully house-trained. Moreover, anyone who has lived among dogs knows that when an animal you trust shows friendship for another, one can almost always rely on his judgment. My Sandy, though a bit of a romantic, is a gentle soul, with a rosy, loving outlook, and the spontaneous sympathy he showed to this colossus saved from the flood was for me the best recommendation possible. I informed the SPCA that I had taken in a stray German Shepherd, and left my telephone number, in case his master showed up. I was relieved to note that my guest treated my cats with the respect due to these scornful deities and showed himself to be a well-mannered animal of a pleasant and humorous disposition.

During the next few days the German Shepherd proved to be a great success with my friends, who at first were rather taken aback by his fearsome appearance. I had called him Batka, which means "little father" in Russian. Besides his wrestler's chest and his big brown-gray mug, Batka had canines which looked like the horns of those little bulls they call *machos* in Mexico. Yet he was very good-natured; he would sniff the visitors carefully for the purpose of future identification, and then would shake hands as if to say, "I know I look frightening but I'm really a good fellow." At least, that's how I interpreted his efforts to reassure my guests, but obviously a novelist is more likely than normal people to be wrong about the nature of beings and things, because he has a tendency to *imagine* them. I have almost always invented everyone I have met in my life and particularly those who are close to me and share my life. For a man accustomed to dealing with imaginary beings and to whom invention comes quite naturally, it

7

makes human relationships much easier and it saves you a lot of trouble. You no longer waste time trying to get to know people; you don't have to bother and pay attention. *You make them up.* Afterward, when you get a surprise, you bear them a terrible grudge. They have deceived you. You have lived with an imaginary being and when reality suddenly sets in, you feel cheated. They were not worthy of your talent, so to speak. More often than not, when comes the moment of truth, you emerge from your comfortable unreality feeling a real bastard.

Nobody claimed the dog, and I had begun to consider him a member of my family.

The house I occupied on Arden had the usual Beverly Hills swimming pool, and the maintenance company sent me a workman twice a month to check the filter. One afternoon, while I was writing, I heard a sudden, long howl from the direction of the pool, followed by angry, staccato barks. This is how dogs signal the presence of an intruder and the imminence of the attack they intend to carry out within the second. It is often only a canine equivalent of our "Hold me back, someone, or I'll kill him," but with true, well-trained watch dogs it means business. I know of nothing more nerve-racking than these sudden, violent outbursts of rage. Their purpose is to paralyze you, and to keep you there without making a move, or else. . . . I ran out onto the patio. A black worker who had come to check the filter stood on the other side of the iron gate. Batka was hurling himself against the gate, foaming at the mouth, in a paroxysm of hatred. It was so frightening that Sandy had crawled whimpering under a bush with only his limp yellow tail showing.

The black worker stood completely motionless, his face shining with sweat. A young man, and somehow the expression of fear is always more painful when you see it on a young face. He was safe behind the gate, but this was more a matter of shock than of danger. The good-natured gray giant, always so nice with our visitors, had changed into a primeval fury howling like a starved beast who sees the meat but can't reach it.

There is something deeply demoralizing and disturbing in those sudden transformations of a familiar being, man or animal, into a total stranger. It is one of those painful moments when your reassuring little world flies to pieces. A discouraging experience, for lovers of comfortable certitudes. The quiet dog had turned before my very eyes into a wild monster, and I have seen this happen with humans too, when those I used to think of as *people* would suddenly turn into a savage mob.

I was being brought face to face with the fundamental brutality which lurks deep within nature. We try hard to forget this menacing presence between its murderous manifestations. What used to be called humanism or idealism— the same thing—has always been caught in this dilemma between love of animals and horror of beastliness.

I tried to pull Batka back and drag him into the house, but the damn dog really had a sense of duty. He didn't bite me, although my hands were covered with his saliva, but kept throwing himself at the gate with bared fangs.

The black American stood petrified on the other side, holding his tools. I remember with painful clarity the expression on his face, because it was my first sight of a black man confronted with animal hatred. He looked sad, the way certain men look when they're afraid. During the war, I often saw that expression on the faces of my comrades. I remember a certain dawn before a low-level bombing sortie which had all the marks of no return, when Colonel Fourquet had said to me, "You look sad, Gary." I was afraid.

I told the young man to leave, I wasn't going to have my pool cleaned that week, forget it. . . .

Next morning the same scene exactly was repeated when

a man from Western Union brought me a cable.

In the afternoon some friends came to see us and Batka welcomed them most graciously. They were white.

I remembered then that the man from Western Union was black.

█ █

I began to feel the unease known to all those who sense a
harsh truth growing around them, more and more obvious,
but who stubbornly refuse to face it. A coincidence, I told
myself. I'm imagining things. I am obsessed by the Problem.

My feeling of unease became something akin to panic
when Batka almost got at the throat of a delivery man from
a Canon Drive supermarket. As I went to open the door, the
dog was in the kitchen, but he bounced past me and leaped
at the man's throat, while keeping the crafty, treacherous
silence that a surprise attack requires. He missed by a
second: I barely managed to slam the door with my knee.

The delivery man was black.

That very day, I put the animal into my car and drove

him to Jack Carruthers' zoo, *Noah's Ranch,* in San Fernando Valley.

I have known Jack for years and since our first meeting in the fifties, the old movie stand-in, who had fallen from more horses than almost anyone in the trade, had become an expert in training animals for the screen. His ranch also prided itself on its snake pit, where you can find all the most representative venomous snakes in America. Jack and his assistants extracted the venom needed for serums. The snake pit is a place I carefully avoid when I go out to the ranch; as you look at all the wriggling, crawling things in it, you soon feel you are watching the unconscious of our own species, Jung's famous "collective unconscious"—and that is a pretty depressing sight.

Jack was seated behind his desk, wearing his blue overalls and his eternal baseball cap. A big man, who looks calm and collected in that old-fashioned American way that becomes rarer and rarer today. His body has the kind of massive rigidity you often notice in aging men whose limbs and muscles lose their elasticity while keeping their strength. He had been a stunt man for something like forty years and his bones had been a nightmare to insurance companies. He always wore leather straps around his wrists, and on his right forearm there was a tattoo of a horse's head.

He listened to me without a word, chewing one of those filthy cigars America has condemned itself to by breaking with Havana.

"What do you expect me to do?"

"I want you to cure the dog."

"Noah" Jack Carruthers is what is known as "a quiet man." The quietness is of that slightly ironic nature which comes from an inner strength too sure of itself to be in need of assertion through the usual physical clichés of hard-boiled showing-off. Only the strangely motionless stance of that massive body carries a hint of controlled aggressiveness, a kind of deliberate physical withholding. But that may be the self-reflecting observation of a man who is used to keeping himself carefully on a leash. I have come to accept once and for all the fact that I shall never succeed in suppressing entirely the inner savage animal that I carry everywhere within myself, like so many French motorists at the wheel of their instrument of power.

Everybody likes Jack in Hollywood, in spite of his cold, rather stand-offish way of not quite welcoming you. They like him because he is a man who understands that the canary you entrust to his care is not replaceable by any other canary and that a gentleman who has just brought his boa constrictor to board, begging you to take the utmost care of the beast, is parting with a much loved creature—much loved, perhaps, because the boa is the most different thing from himself he has found, which makes love possible.

"Cure the dog?"

Jack stared at me with his ice-blue eyes.

"Meaning what?"

"This dog has been trained especially to attack blacks. No, I'm not imagining things. Every time a Negro comes near the door, he goes mad. Vicious. With whites, nothing happens. He wags his tail and shakes hands."

"So what?"

"What do you mean, so what? It can be cured."

"No. Your dog's too old."

A little mocking twinkle gleamed in his eyes.

"As far as the old generation is concerned, forget it. You ought to know that."

"Jack, everyone knows you've done wonders with so-called vicious animals."

"Depends on how old they are. And how vicious—or rather, *viciated*. You just can't do much about things that have become second nature. It has very little to do with nature, mind you. Anyway, your dog is too old. You can't undo a lifetime of deliberate, professional conditioning."

"It's a matter of patience. It can be done."

"No. It's too late. He must be around seven. He's got the habit, you can't change that. It's inbred now, deep in, deep down. That's it. He's learned what they made him learn and that's the kind of dog he is and always will be. Period."

"We can't leave him like that."

"Okay, put him to sleep. That's what I'd do."

"It seems to me it's the people who trained him who should be put to sleep and——"

Jack began to laugh. He's one of those lucky guys who can get the whole world off his back in a ha-ha-ha.

"I'm not even sure I can keep your pooch here. I've got two black helpers. They won't like it. Well, okay, leave him for the time being, we'll see."

I say goodbye to Batka. He watches me, pricking up his ears and cocking his head a little to one side, with that intense, absolute concentration of animals whose minds have reached the limit of instinctive comprehension, while actual understanding, in terms of human reasoning, remains beyond their grasp. I come back and sit down with him and stroke his gray head. See you soon, little father. Don't worry. We'll lick them all. We'll make it all right, somehow.

I drive through Coldwater Canyon with enough stones in my heart to build a few more cathedrals. The broad avenues between the proud, tall palm trees are deserted: only the cars are inhabited. I go around and around in circles in this motorized emptiness, then follow Wilshire Boulevard, where there are sidewalks and people. A sidewalk here is an oasis.

I end up at a friend's house. His days are numbered, after three major operations. A well-known screenwriter, he was one of McCarthy's "victims" during the witch-hunting days in the fifties and was kept from working for ten years, until his health was gone and a sort of mild yet unshakable sadness set in. I found him busy working at a model city he is building with all sorts of clever do-it-yourself kits. He has been putting his fucking utopia together for two years now, interrupting this crazy, dedicated work only to dash off one of his science-fiction scripts for TV. All that is left of his hope, love, and belief in man's future goes into the building of his ideal city. "The City of Light," he calls it. He puts it together, then demolishes it, rebuilds it again and lovingly polishes every detail, then starts from scratch again, never satisfied, working in a shed at the bottom of the garden, beyond his pool. The whole thing is a combination of plastic and steel with an agonizing dream of beauty and perfection, and it is stronger than the illness that is eating him away. A total dedication to something that cannot be and never will be, a desperate trust, a craving for the absolute that nothing can shake. A devotion to a magnificent unreality that could end up in reality someday, if there were only more lunatics like him. I give him a hand with his Palace of Culture with a beautiful view over the sea, but after half an hour I've had enough and leave him to his masturbation.

The car radio announces riots in Detroit. Two dead. Since Watts and its thirty-two dead, this country is haunted by the thought that America is a land where a record never remains unbroken. Still my belief in this people's future remains unshaken and unshakable. Americans are notoriously bad at not solving problems, in the sense that they are incapable of living with thorns in their side. It may well be due to the absence of what can be called a "tradition of acceptance and forbearance," so evident in European history, a mixture of absolute power of kings with catholic submission. Whatever the reason, this refusal to accept misery and suffering as part of our human fate is more striking in America than in any other nation I can think of. The consequences are sometimes destructive to the individual: it makes the national character more prone to neurosis than elsewhere and it partly explains why this country is more vulnerable to drug addiction than Europe: heroin and amphetamines are really nothing else but an instant solution to all problems, an all-solving gimmick, an illusion of absolute remedy. The psychological makeup of a European makes him less exposed to that kind of "solution" because, in terms of culture and history, he is better adjusted to the impossibility to adjust, that is, to coexistence with the unacceptable. The American can't abide things that don't work out. I do not believe that the conflict between white and black can continue unresolved in this country simply because indefinite acceptance of such a situation presupposes a radical change of the country's national characteristics. I see no example in history of America giving up on itself.

When you think of mankind, you can console yourself with faith, hope, with Shakespeare, antibiotics, or with our footprints on the moon. But with a dog, there can be no alibi. Every time I went to visit Batka in his cage, I could see a silent question in his eyes: "What have I done? Why am I locked up behind bars? I have always done as I was taught. Why don't you want me with you any more?" There was no possible answer to this basic innocence facing me, except a reassuring caress. I always left the cage in a state of self-hatred, and here I must quote a famous line from Victor Hugo. I had looked for it a long time with no luck until one day Monsieur Hélou, now President of Lebanon, gave it to me: "When I say *I*, it is *you*, all of you, I am talking about."

The dog had been in Jack's hands now for almost two weeks and I had been visiting the animal every day: I wanted to know how *I* was doing, if something could be done about *me*, about that hard core of primeval savagery in all of us.

It was seven o'clock in the morning. Except for the night watchman, Fred Hokum, there was not a trace of a human presence in the Noah's Ark. Heavy drops of dew hung on the leaves and flowers like some shining fruit of dawn. Dr. Dolittle's giraffe was watching me. Its soft, languorous eyes and its long airy feminine eyelashes would fill with envy the ladies in Elizabeth Arden's *salons de beauté*. Batka greets me standing on his hind legs, wagging his tail and showing his teeth in something very much like a smile: he had caught my smell before seeing me. I press my cheek against the wire netting and feel his cold nose and hot tongue. It is not difficult to recognize an expression of love in a dog's eyes, and I think of my mother, because of this faithful dog and because of love. But my mother had green eyes. I also think of a beautifully idiotic opinion expressed by one of my friends, an excellent novelist, in his usual English persnickety supercilious way, a mixture of condescension, exquisite feelings, and psychological dandyism: "I don't like dogs," he told me, "because I don't like the kind of boot-licking love they offer you." You never can tell where dignity is going to get screwed up next.

I didn't have the key to the cage, so I sat there on my heels, while Batka watched me lovingly, his muzzle resting on his paws and it was one of those moments of peace and communion, feeling good together, I mean, sharing something, a quiet happiness.

The sky of dawn was still fresh and pure, filled with that California blue which always carries the suggestion of orange groves, palms, eucalyptus trees, and canyons ringing with a million voices of insects and birds, that shining hour before cars' and factories' exhausts begin their daily murder of air and light, when the yellowish rotten smog raises into the sky its flag of pestilence.

I intended to leave unnoticed after my little daily communion with dog and nature. I had nothing to say to anyone. But as is often the case with happiness, I had lost all notion of time, living outside of myself, sharing something, I don't know what, with light, trees, and with the sweetness of the air. It was one of those moments when a man can still feel almost a part of nature.

It must have been about ten o'clock when I saw the black keeper walking toward the cage. Like everybody in the zoo, I called him Keys, for the hundreds of keys that dangled from a belt around his waist and had earned him the title of "master of the keys" and control of all the lion dens, snake pits, alligator pools, monkey houses, kangaroo cages, and all the other compartments in "Noah" Jack Carruthers' ark. He was still about fifty yards away from us when Batka pricked up his ears, got up quietly, and froze in total immobility. Then, his ears back, he leaped forward and hurled himself against the bars with a long, frustrated, hateful growl. I felt drops of saliva fall on my face. Besides the Pavlov reflex image of slaves fleeing through the cotton fields that instantly sprang to my mind from the long-gone days of history, there was again the shock brought on by this sudden disintegration of the familiar, the instant transformation of a friendly nature into ferocity and beastliness, with the familiar suddenly becoming the unknown. . . .

Keys walked by the cage without a glance at the dog. He was smiling, with sunshine and smile sharing his face, a thin young man in a short-sleeved shirt with a little moustache perched over his lip like a butterfly. A vague resemblance to Malcolm X. But then I always see a trace of that fallen fighter on black American faces.

"Hello there," he said to me. "Nice day."

"Hello."

I was squatting on my heels, avoiding his eyes while Batka was throwing himself against the steel netting of the cage with strangled howls—the howls would stop suddenly while the animal looked sideways at Keys, baring his fangs, his mouth foaming, his head turned one way and his eyes squinting toward the black American. Then he would throw himself once again at the steel netting, repeating his savage hunting call for blood. The black man was smiling.

I said, "No progress."

Keys pulled a pack of Chesterfields from the pocket of his denims and tapped out a cigarette. He took it between his lips directly from the pack, lit it with a lighter, and looked calmly at the dog.

"Yeah," he said. "White dog."

I remember the sudden flush of irritation, the indignant reaction of—how am I to define it?—of my self-respect. It was really a little too easy.

"Now come on," I said. "That's not funny and it's cheap."

He watched me for a while with that calm, total self-control of someone who *knows* and who doesn't have to prove it to you or convince you.

"White dog," he repeated. "You know the kind?"

His searching eyes kept drilling deep into me as if I had two or three centuries of history hidden somewhere on me.

"No, you don't, of course. Well, man, you haven't lived. He's a white dog all right. He comes from the South. Down there, those doggies especially trained to help the police against the black people are called white dogs. That's what *we* call 'em. They're given a thorough training. The best. They're not watch dogs. They're attack dogs."

I was dying inside. Because I was the one who had trained that dog. The famous line from Victor Hugo was a reciprocal: "When I say *you*, I'm speaking about me, of course." There's a nice song, "Tea for Two and Two for Tea," and you could make another song with the words "I am you and you are me," and there is even a word for it: brotherhood. Brotherhood. There's no way out of that. No emergency exit.

Outer Mongolia, I thought. That's where I'd like to go: Outer Mongolia. It is the word *outer* that I find irresistibly attractive, of course. Get the hell out of it all. A complete outsider with clean hands.

"In the old days, they trained them to track down runaway slaves. Things have changed. We don't run away any more. Now those dogs are used against us by scared cops."

The dog was strangling himself. So was I, silently.

"And with a watch dog like that, your white wife can sleep in peace, if you happen to be away. No one will come and rape her."

Keys turned toward Batka and inhaled the smoke slowly. He watched the animal with an expert eye.

"A beauty," he said. "Wish I had one like that. He's a fine animal."

He shook his head.

"But he's too old. About seven, I'd say. You can't change them at that age. It's set in real deep. Too bad."

He remained silent for quite a while, watching the dog almost dreamily. He was thinking something over. Today I am convinced it was at that moment that he first thought up his little scheme and that the dreamy expression on his face, that speculative look, was the look of a man surmising his chances.

"Be seeing you," he said, and walked away slowly, with the keys ringing around his waist, and I remember thinking of troika bells, with my mother and me driving through the Russian snow, one of the recurring memories of my childhood.

Batka calmed down immediately and busied himself with a flea.

I went into Jack's office, but found no one there. Jack was on a studio set, supervising his star chimpanzee who was acting in a TV picture, an ape version of *Romeo and Juliet*.

I went home. Jean was out. She was attending a meeting of the Urban League; it was a matter of training young Negro kids for future unemployment. I spent the afternoon alone on the patio, with twenty million American blacks on my back, wondering what to do with them. Slowly, the cowardly idea of writing a book began to stir in my head, my usual way out of the suffering of other people. You don't write books to help people. You write books to get rid of them. To help yourself.

In the afternoon, there was another meeting, this time at the home of a drama coach. It's aim was to enlighten certain whites, as to the degree of hatred for whites reached by black children and to get from them funds necessary to keep in operation a Montessori "school without hate."

I had refused to attend. I have been so overexposed to history since my early teens that the very idea of signing a manifesto, of making another purely verbal protest, denouncing another intolerable social situation just to relieve my conscience and to feel better, to feel a fine human being, fills me with shame. I cannot resist human suffering: I fill my books with it and they bring me a great deal of recognition, esteem, and material comfort. You either give up everything and share the suffering, or you just tend to become an exhibitionist of your noble *de luxe* conscience. You achieve a kind of aristocracy on other people's backs. You become a professional of indignation, you keep signaling your nobility, and your social awareness turns into a kind of elegance.

Since my early youth, I have been stricken with elephantiasis of the skin. I mean, my skin has grown far beyond my own, and it hurts me in and through the skin of other people. I was determined to put a stop to that: there are a million ways of becoming a whore and one of them consists of getting rid of injustice and suffering by merely writing best-selling books about it.

I must also confess that I felt a strong dislike for the acting coach in whose house the fund-raising display of black children's hatred was to take place. I saw in him a typical California phony. He was one of these progressives who are up in arms against our society, while speculating in real estate. Besides, I cannot stand people whose political beliefs stem not from social awareness but from secret psychological flaws. Young people claim, with good reason, that certain disciples of Freud are wrong in seeking to adjust them to a sick society. Yet the reverse operation, the attempt to adjust society to your own sickness, does not strike me as a solution either.

And some of the artistic methods of this particular acting coach gave me nausea. At a gathering of his "class" I saw him order a young actor to give him a long wet kiss on the mouth. The actor was perfectly heterosexual and married, but this was part of the "method." The purpose of this kiss against nature was to get rid of inhibitions, in this case the "inhibition" the young man felt when it came to mixing his saliva with that of another man. A process of "liberation," I was told. Well, I don't know. I guess something is wrong with me, but it seems to me it was the coach who had a problem, not the student.

I didn't show up at his place, but I was given a detailed account of the pathetic little demonstration in which a few black kids aged seven to nine conscientiously played their well-rehearsed roles. Their parents were present. And here follows a dialogue between the kids and a white lady who was a friend of the family and in whose home the black parents and their five children were living. I guarantee the authenticity of this word-for-word transcription. But first imagine the two black kids standing there, surrounded by fifty thoughtful white adults.

"Am I a honky, Jimmy?"

"Yes, Ma'am, you are a honky."

"Am I a blue-eyed devil?"

Here a footnote for my benefit: *In the teachings of Black Muslims and their prophet, Elijah Muhammed, people with blue eyes are fiendish enemies.*

"Yes, Ma'am, you are a blue-eyed devil."

"Do you hate me, Jimmy?"

Here, the report reads: *A long moment of hesitation. The*

child blinks worriedly. He glances toward his parents, swallowing hard. . . . Well, the poor kid had been smothered with kindness for months by the "blue-eyed devil" in question, and he had a problem. The problem has a name: an act against nature. The report further notes: *Deep sigh from the child.*

"Yes, Ma'am. I hate you."

A hesitation.

". . . sort of."

The report ends there. It does not say whether, after his performance, poor little Jimmy, dancing on his hind legs, was given a sugar and a pat on the head. I bet the parents breathed easier after that. The kid didn't let them down.

Goddamn masochism, exhibitionism, showmanship, and also good old conning, that typically American art of exploiting the credulous immortalized by Mark Twain, a way of *gaming whitey* smacking of the old Mississippi days of magic medicine, the tar-and-feather days. You almost hear that old steamboat's whistle. For it is obvious that Jimmy didn't hate anyone, that the whole thing went against his grain; he had to force himself, and even so felt compelled to add "sort of" after "I hate you." That "sort of" is America's greatest hope.

The people who had organized this little demonstration, whatever their good intentions, proved only one thing: that the greatest spiritual force in history is Stupidity.

"Yes, Ma'am, I hate you . . . sort of."

And they pass the hat around. Out of the goodness of your hearts, ladies and gentlemen. . . . They pat Jimmy's militant head. Candy.

But again, as Seberg says, all the hope for America lies in these two words: "sort of."

Thank God, I wasn't present. I would probably have bitten someone.

Which reminds me that it's high time I bought myself

a stronger leash. The one I have is wearing out, I've been using it so long and so often. One of these days it's going to break and I'll end up in a dog pound, with no owner coming to my rescue: they say God is dead. . . .

After reading this report, I had to go for an hour's run through Beverly Hills. My friends think I run to keep in shape. Not at all. I run to work out the hate, anger, and resentment, the love and the fury, to tire out the animal in me, and then I put him back on that leash and come back home, pleasantly emptied, in that state of physical fatigue which takes care of all your inner boilings. It was ten in the morning when the phone rang. Jack Carruthers was on the line.

"Can you make it here right away?"

"Why? What happened?"

"Just come along, okay?"

I did.

He was all there, behind his desk, with his crushed nose, his gray crew-cut, and the little circle of bare skin where his broken skull had been patched up with a steel plate. He looks Prussian, the way people do when their faces have been flattened by all the beatings they've taken. The baseball cap had slid back with its peak high, an aggressive erection. He lights cigarettes and puts them out immediately, which he calls "not smoking." He has a typically American proletarian distinction, a kind of physical nobility of build and movement. He didn't say hello, just stared at me with extreme distaste.

"All right now. I want your permission to put him to sleep."

"Why, all of a sudden——"

"Come on, I'll show you."

The old dog was lying on his side, panting heavily. His mouth was bleeding. He saw me and wagged his tail feebly a few times, without raising his head.

We went into the cage. Jack leaned over the dog and felt his ribs. The dog had a spasm of pain.

"You've made me lose my best man."

"Keys?"

"Yes. He'd go by the cage twenty times a day, and every time it was the same damn thing. All hell breaking loose, rage, blind animal rage. That dog has been remarkably well trained. A good pedigree. Keys didn't seem to pay much attention, except that he seemed to be hanging around the cage a bit too often. I guess he wanted to fill himself with it. The howls, I mean, the rage . . . His Master's Voice . . . you get it? Every morning, he comes here to . . . to refresh his memory, I bet. To wind up his hate machinery."

The dog licked my hand and left traces of bloody saliva on my fingers. My hand hesitated. I pulled it back. . . . The dog was looking at me, waiting for his reward: "You see, I did what they taught me to do. I'm a good dog."

I stroked the faithful head.

"So, this morning, Keys put on a protective suit and went into the cage. He had it out with the dog. I heard both of them howling and I'm telling you, I don't know which one howled loudest, the dog or the man. He almost killed him. . . . Sure, sure, you don't have to say it, I know it isn't the dog he's getting at. Only *them*, you see, he didn't have them at hand. I wish he did. The dog paid for his masters. Then——"

"Noah" Jack Carruthers laughed. A quiet, good-humored laugh.

"He hit me. Tried to knock me down. . . . Yeah, I know how he felt. I just happened to be there, with my white face. When I helped him to his feet, he took off all his keys one by one, put them down on the desk, and left."

"I'm sorry, Jack. Really sorry."

"Me too. There are millions of people who are terribly sorry in this country. Being sorry doesn't change a thing.

Now listen. You can't change that dog, it's in him and it's there to stay. The best thing you can do for him and for everybody is to have him put to sleep. He's been ruined. . . . Well, you see what I mean. *Viciated.*"

He looked at the animal.

"They don't have the right to do that to a dog."

"Jack, I wish I could get my hands on the guy who————"

"Well, I don't think you'd have any success in changing him either. It's just a generation like that, it will go away by itself, nice and proper. That's what generations are for: for disappearing. Except I'm not sure the blacks, or this country, for that matter, are willing or can afford to wait."

He fixed his pale blue eyes on me and they didn't make me feel very popular.

"So it's up to you."

"I won't have him put away. That's final."

"Right, then take him with you. I won't have him here."

He narrowed his eyes a little, and wrinkles suddenly spread all over his face. Then he smiled his usual half-smile, a strange unfinished thing, that always stopped halfway as if hitting upon an obstacle, like all the expressions on this patched-up face with its numerous paralyzed spots.

"Why don't you place the dog with a kennel where they don't employ Negroes? There are quite a few of them around. I'll give you an address."

"Screw you."

He nodded approvingly and went off, throwing away the cigarette he had just lit.

I sat there on the ground in the damn cage next to White Dog. That's what they all called him now. White Dog. Sounded like some kind of constellation up there in the sky.

I let time pass, I let pass as much of it as I could. One hour, maybe two, I don't know. I had made up my mind, but I used the finality of the decision I had reached as an excuse to put it off.

I go to fetch the leash from the car and phone Chuck Belden. How are you, Chuck, and could you let me have your gun? I'll give it back tonight.

I go back to get Batka. He hobbles after me with his tongue hanging out. He tries to jump onto the front seat, but can't make it. One or two broken ribs, I bet. I help him and we drive along Ventura Boulevard, then through Laurel Canyon. At the red lights, people smile at the good dog settled quietly next to the driver, inspecting the road. At Van Nuys, I run a light to avoid stopping next to a truck whose driver is a black man. . . .

I shut Batka in the garage.

Chuck brings me his Army Colt about four in the afternoon. I pour myself a Scotch, but think better of it. I have no tolerance whatsoever for alcohol and haven't touched the stuff for over thirty years. I can't allow myself to drink a glass of Scotch and then cruise around town with a loaded gun close at hand. With me, liquor makes the leash snap and I lose whatever control I have over myself.

So I empty the glass into the begonia pot and get behind the wheel. Batka loves to be driven around, watching other dogs with a superior air. I close the windows and we ride through Hollywood, driving toward Griffith Park where I used to go for my early morning runs before going to work in my consular office at 1919 Outpost Drive.

Ten years ago those scrub-covered hills were a favorite place for lovers of nature and simply lovers; today, people take a drive through this wilderness but rarely leave their cars. The crime rate is rising constantly in L.A., as in all big cities, and though you only have one chance in a thousand of being mugged, each of us imagines destiny as a personal, exclusive relationship and feels a specially selected target.

The park is empty.

I stop the car near the Pilgrim's Cross and let Batka out.

I take the gun.

Batka looks at me. He knows. Instinct, or some *other* kind of intelligence.

He hangs his head low.

I aim carefully behind the ear.

White Dog looks at me again and waits.

My hand shakes. I am crying. Tears drown everything around me, the world is a gray swimming mist. I press the trigger.

I miss.

The dog hasn't moved—didn't react to the shot.

I feel as if I have tried suicide and failed.

White Dog raises his eyes toward me, then lowers his head again and waits.

You don't believe me, I know. Well, get the hell out of this book then. This is God's truth and it's for true believers.

I turn away and vomit.

"Come now, Sir, so much fuss over a cur. . . . What about Biafra?"

"Yeah, sure, I know. Biafra. Doing nothing for Biafra, that's some excuse for not doing anything for a dog."

There's a new kind of logic around. Because of Biafra, because of Vietnam, because of hunger, slavery, and wretchedness almost everywhere in the world, you feel excused from helping a blind man across the street.

The gun is slippery in my wet hand.

"Come here, White Dog."

He gets up, looks at me, takes a step and sniffs the barrel of the gun. . . .

Merde, no, never.

Why should I care about the blacks? They're just people like you and me. To hell with them. I'm not a racist.

And as for putting a bullet through Batka's head, there is a name for that, Mr. Romain Gary, Sir: capitulation. It's never happened to me yet. You don't give up when you hold a loaded .48 in your hand.

The hills around me, the scrubby bushes entangled like barbed wire are already fading away and the evening mist is softening the thorny landscape. But the softness stays outside.

I light up a Havana cigar, expensive enough to feed an Indian family for ten days.

I'm feeling better.

I pat Batka's head reassuringly.

"We'll make it, somehow. We'll be all right."

He wags his tail and barks cheerfully.

"We'll see this thing through and we'll make you a nice, loving, democratic beast."

He offers me his paw.

Pity there isn't one of those nice clean walls around. I could have scribbled a few of those proclamations of faith in humanity that all walls, particularly prison walls, are so good for.

"A new world is in the making!"

When it comes to clinging to a hope, I am unbeatable. A real champ.

"Man shall prevail."

I know I am cheating, I am conning myself, but I have only one philosophy left: anything goes, when faith in Man and trust in his future dignity are at stake. When it is a matter of preserving that essential investment, cheating, despair, and cynicism have always been a sacred law of the species. Truth can be *made*. It can be made to materialize against all logic and odds, through the very act of serving it with total, obstinate devotion.

I don't believe a word of it, of course, but the important thing is that it works. I experience a euphoric boost of energy, a strengthening of my moral fiber, I feel myself again, by which I mean a sucker no one can cheat of his faith . . . in what? In *you*. I give Batka a friendly wink: it can be done, with a little good will and patience. We shall overcome. I open the car door for him and the dog jumps next to me. We're off. The little psychodrama is over.

I pull up at Schwab's and phone the zoo. No one answers. I look up Jack's number in the book and give him a full account of the Griffith Park "happening."

"Why're you telling me all this, may I ask you?"

"Keep the dog until I leave the States. I'll take him with me."

"Listen, Gary, get off my back. Forget it. Put the cur in a clean-living kennel with no niggers. I know a terrific one in Santa Monica. Strictly *de luxe,* all white. Even Mayor Yorty couldn't do better."

"All right, give me Keys's phone."

"What for?"

"I'll talk to him."

"He's a Black Muslim, you know. All you can do is help him get his ticket to Mecca. I'm told the Muslims qualify for one if they present Elijah Muhammed with five blond scalps, or five pairs of pink ears."

"If he goes back to work at your place, will you take the dog back?"

"It's a deal. I have two hundred snakes full of beautiful venom and no one to milk them. Keys is a venom expert. The best. Anyhow, I don't have his phone number here. Call me tomorrow at the office."

I lock Batka up for the night in the garage, with a royal helping of dog food.

I don't breathe a word of this to Jean. This is not exactly the right moment to tell her White Dog is here.

There is another meeting of black militants in the living room.

Seberg has belonged to every possible civil rights organization since she was fourteen and living in Marshalltown, Iowa. Her idealism is of that typically American kind that cannot leave a problem alone without solving it, a trait of American character totally misunderstood in Europe, where it is always cleverly interpreted as hypocrisy. It creates a serious problem for our marriage. There is a twenty-four-year difference between us and I have done all my fighting, bleeding, and swallowing of defeats and disillusions between the ages of seventeen and thirty—I was in all of it. Mussolini's invasion of Ethiopia, Munich, Spanish Civil War, Second World War—and it is more than I can bear to start it all over again and to witness her own daily defeats, indignations, tears, anger; a kind of continuous flashback into my own past.

As soon as I appear in the living room, they all shut up. They can feel it. It shows, I mean, you only have to look at me to feel a certain coldness. Some of the people present, both black and white, are true fighters and as earnest and sincere as they come, but I learned long ago that the favorite hideout of con men, racketeers, and parasites is in the shadows of a good cause. It offers perfect cover and excellent opportunity.

In the case of that particular meeting, I was soon proved right.

A few weeks later, one of the bastards present, who happened to be wearing a black skin, turned up at the house with a nice attempt at blackmail, with no doubt that noble excuse of *gaming whitey:* an attitude which is quite rightly considered by some blacks as "Uncle Tomism in wolves' clothing." "Miss Seberg, we have a letter you have written; it can badly damage your reputation. . . . In this letter, you agree to carry a message of greetings and sympathy to the African revolutionary students in Paris. . . . There are even the names of two black power leaders among the signatories. . . . If this letter gets published, your movie career in America. . . ."

Jean told him:

"Publish it and drop dead."

Afterward, she cried a little. Miss Seberg is still at an age when she can be disappointed in people.

I get Keys's phone number the next morning and call him up. A sweet little girl's voice tells me Daddy is out.

"You don't know where I could find him?"

The child sounds worried:

"Is it about an animal?"

"Yes, it's very important."

There are whisperings at the other end.

"Daddy's at the Pancake Studio on Fairfax."

I look up the Pancake Studio in a phone book and find Keys settled in front of a mountain of pancakes dripping with maple syrup. He's wearing one of those Muslim skull-caps which look as if they have been cut out of a carpet bag. "Hi," he says, "hi," very polite in a cold, absentminded way, and points his knife at the chair. His teeth are very small, very white and sharp, very closely set, and the effect is that of twice the quantity of teeth in any ordinary God-fearing mouth.

"Listen, about that dog——"

"I know, I know. I'm sorry about that. I lost my head. My ears got mad."

"Your ears, huh?" I repeat, trying to suppress the expression of idiocy on my face.

"Yeah, I have sensitive ears, you know. They couldn't stand those howls, so I beat the dog up, the way you smash something that makes too much noise. . . ."

He thinks things over, his knife and fork busy with the pancakes. Once more, I caught that expression of scheming, there's no other word for that thoughtful look with a trace of slyness, and I was to remember it later, and doubt now that I shall ever forget it.

"Bring him back. I'll take care of him. It's going to take time, mind you. But it can be done."

He lowers his eyes toward the mountain of pancakes

basking in a kind of golden sunset and cuts it carefully in four.

"Yeah, I'm pretty sure I can manage it. It'll cost you a little more, of course. It'll take a lot of my time."

"Do you want me to talk to Jack?"

"He won't mind, as long as I take care of the snakes. Bring the dog around noon."

He was eating his pancakes with such relish that it made my mouth water.

"He's a beautiful animal. It'd be a pity to give up on him."

He watched me thoughtfully and grinned in a display of pearly-white sharpness; a quick, thin knifelike stroke of a smile.

I take Batka back to the kennel and give Carruthers the
good news of the imminent return of his loved one. The
snakes will once more be milked of their venom for the
good of humanity. I find Jack drinking his morning coffee;
he's leaning against the bars of the monkey colony. A little
black hairy thing is trying to dip its finger into the cup, over
his shoulder. Jack holds his buttered toast out to him, the tiny
monkey bites into it, and Jack eats the rest.

"The kangaroos have been a real pain in the ass this
morning," he informs me. "The mother has beaten up papa,
good and proper. I don't know what's the matter with that
family. Kangaroo psychology, my friend, sometimes I just
give up on it. They say Australians are like Americans,

but with kangaroos that's not true at all. What's the matter with that bitch? There's no other female in her fellow's life, so what the hell? It's a damn nuisance, because this afternoon they're to give an exhibition, a boxing match for the benefit of Korean orphans, and the old man is scared shitless and in no shape to fight. He's terrified of her. You know, all kangaroos are a bit nutty. One I had a few years ago would faint every time I presented him with a female in heat. He'd sniff the air with quick little sniffles, like a rabbit, and then he'd pass out. . . . An emotional type. The female would get so indignant that she'd jump on top of him with both feet. Psychology, my friend, it's nothing but a bag of troubles. Want some coffee? Sure? So Keys is coming back, huh? And he's going to take care of the mutt?"

"Keys is a great guy."

"Noah" Jack Carruthers sips his coffee dreamily.

"Yeah," he says, with a total lack of conviction.

His very pale eyes go over me, then he glances away.

The monkey stretches out his arm and snatches the rest of the toast from Jack's hand.

"Yeah, the snakes love him too," Jack says. "Keys is a real charmer."

He empties his cup onto the grass.

"Never seen a son-of-a-bitch more full of hate than that one," he says with obvious respect. "It's a real pleasure to have him around. Okay, I better go and try to boost the morale of my kangaroo."

He stares at me again.

"Just why are you doing all this?"

"What d'you mean?"

"I mean the dog."

"I want to do what I can for him, that's all."

"You bet. What is it you're trying to prove, exactly?"

"I'm not trying to prove anything."

"Oh, come on. It's always the same, with you intellectuals.

You always make . . . I don't know, some kind of a general issue out of everything. Are you trying to prove it's curable?"

"It *is* curable."

"Sure, it is. But you've got to begin in the cradle. It would take fifty years. That's not a solution, that's forbearance. Anyway, with Keys——"

"What, with Keys?"

"You're in good hands. The best. He knows about venom . . . an expert. Be seeing you."

He wanders away with that slow rolling walk of cowboys, sailors, and lonely men.

The monkey is clinging to the bars, holding out its tiny hand, yapping.

IV

Back at Arden, Celia, our Spanish friend, tells me that a *Señor muy simpático* has been there twice to speak to me, didn't leave a message but will be back later, *una cosa muy importante.*

It is three in the afternoon. I am out on the patio, by the pool, chewing gloomily on a wet cigar-butt.

Seberg is out raising funds for the Montessori school she has been helping to survive for a year or so. One of the goals this school has set itself is to give black children an education "without hate." Yes, folks: it's here, written in big letters in their brochure. An education *without hate.* Now, if this is what makes the school so very special and different from others . . . I suddenly feel a great urge to attend that school myself. The very idea of the need for a school *without hate* fills me with precisely that: hate.

The black-white situation in America has its roots in the core of almost all human predicaments, deep down within something it is high time to recognize as the greatest spiritual force of all time: Stupidity. One of the most baffling paradoxes of history is that all our intelligence and even our genius have never succeeded in solving a problem when pitched against Stupidity, where the very nature of the problem is, precisely, what intelligence should find particularly easy to handle. Stupidity has a tremendous advantage over genius and intellect: it is above logic, above argument, it has no need for evidence, facts, reasoning, it is unshakable, beyond doubt, supremely self-confident, it always knows all the answers, it looks at the world with a knowing smile, it has a fantastic capacity for survival, it is the greatest force known to man. Whenever intelligence manages to prevail, when victory seems already secured, immortal Stupidity suddenly rears its ugly mug and takes over. The latest typical example is the murder of the "spring of Prague" in the name of "correct Marxist thinking."

There is another reason for my sadness, much more personal, and it throws a rather comical light on myself. Since my arrival in Hollywood, my house, that is, my wife's house, has become something like General Headquarters for a "save the world now" army, and I am up to my nose in Vietnam, Biafra, Greek dictatorship, plus some twenty million American blacks, not to forget the Indian, Mexican, and Puerto Rican minorities, police brutality, how to fight the drug problem, and the environment, of course, yes the environment; I almost forgot that one. Now, it so happens that I have a personal problem, have had it for some time. I am in danger of becoming a professional beauty.

I have written some fifteen books, all dealing—fiction or personal memoirs—with various forms of human predicament and agony, *almost all best-sellers*. See what I mean?

There are many ways of becoming a professional beauty, not to say a whore, and one of them is to write noble books, to take inspired, humanistic positions on all the right causes, keep signing those manifestos. You become a professional of other people's suffering and you end up by no longer quite knowing if you are working for humanity or on your own moral beauty, on your own image and, no disrespect intended, for he was a great man *as well*, but who can deny that Lord Bertrand Russell, bless his truly noble soul, did become a professional beauty, and that this self-creation, this tirelessly painted self-portrait, in all its generosity, in all the pure gold of true belief and intention, in the last analysis, was a more successful achievement than the actual, practical help he succeeded in giving the world, more evident than the social changes—which ones?—that he brought about.

Every time I see another black face in my living room I feel the presence of a best-seller lurking. Another indignant, fighting-mad book that will do a lot for me and nothing for the world, nothing in terms of solution, changes, help. My home on Arden is bursting with liberal American good will and idealism. There are moments I feel it may rise from the ground and fly to heaven. Noble souls, black and white —with a few of the usual con men and informers thrown in, as if to underline with the blackness of their souls the purity of the others—have the run of the place night and day, and when Seberg is out working at the studio, they keep the sacred fire burning waiting for her return. I have never seen so much moral beauty per square foot, and for the first time in my career, when at last I manage to lock myself up with my wife in our bedroom, I find myself having *scruples*—yes, what kind of a brute am I, what with Vietnam and all those starving Biafran children staring at me. See what I mean? A rapist, that's what I have become at the age of fifty-four, a rapist.

For forty years of my life I have been dragging all over

the world with me my hope and my liberal beliefs, as intact, unshakable, and unbreakable as immortality itself—perhaps, indeed, the only taste of immortality given to man. And in spite of all my efforts to give up once and for all and to attain that peace of mind and soul which comes when you sink to the bottom of despair and disillusionment and rest there peacefully in the comfortable mud of indifference, I keep popping up to the surface again, physically and physiologically incapable of giving up hope, of giving up, period. All my attempts at cynicism always end in dismal failure, a goddamn, unsinkable liberal, the kind you find hung by the neck from every branch of hope. In my totally misunderstood novel *The Guilty Head,* I showed myself under the disguise of Genghis Cohn, trying to attain cynicism through self-mockery and self-parody, trying to get rid of sensitivity and vulnerability until my hero's very life became a whirling dervish's dance, a clownesque Atlas attempting—and failing—to shake the world off his back.

My impatience with liberals is nothing but impatience with myself, a scorpionesque assault on my own hope, not unlike those Negroes in whom hatred for their condition turns into a hatred of other Negroes, a well-known form of "transfer," as with Jew-hating Jews.

I withraw into a corner, listening to Abdu Murad, a young dentist who got rid of his former all-American Thomas Nettleton self. White skullcap riding that pseudo-African hair-do that has achieved nothing except to start a fashionable trend in wigs in Paris *haute coiffure* and *haute couture,* a beautifully embroidered *yashmak,* and why does he think it makes him look different, considering that this typically American taste for parading in disguise, as with all the Knights of Columbus, shriners, and all the incredible get-ups to be admired at political conventions, is really conforming to Americana?

"I don't want any more of your psychoanalytical bullshit,"

he is yelling. "Sure, whitey's hatred for blacks is nothing but transferring his guilt and hatred for himself, but I don't want to untie the Gordian knots, I want to cut 'em!"

Some young white guy whom I always seem to find around my house, but somehow we never get introduced, and who is so cool and self-controlled that from time to time his whole body begins to shake and rivulets of sweat run down his forehead, raises a calming hand:

"All I mean to say is that this is essentially a psychological situation, rather than a social one."

A typical French intellectual's discussion: my home has become the Hollywood branch of the *Café de Flore* in Saint Germain des Prés.

Perhaps the true reason for my exasperation is the number of various leeches and parasites who gravitate toward my wife. My beady eyes follow them through the room, and whenever they come around in that "it's not just your wife, I like you too" way, I bare my teeth and almost growl. God knows there are some wholly committed hard workers here, but let me tell you that this colorful Ahmed Islam Marabout, or whatever name he chose last week to go with his newly shaved head and flowing white *gandurah* robe, is nothing but an honest-to-God-long-live-America-con-man, milking both white and black, and Seberg knows it as well as I do. And that is even why she's particularly kind to him; she feels guilty because she has found him out, she tries hard not to make him feel like a son-of-a-bitch. I get an irresistible urge to tell him that his new Organization is nothing but a sham, and its purpose is not to help blacks in their struggle, but to grab whatever they can for its three members, while competing for recognition and foundation grants and jockeying for position against other similar pseudo-groups on the fringe of the true civil rights-movement. The idea is to attract big names and personalities capable of impressing the various foundations and federal authorities. We had this same situation in the French Resistance during the German occupation; it is the shadowy price authentic sacrifice and dedication pay for shining too brightly.

"You know, Gary, somehow we never had a real talk, you and I, why don't we go have dinner someplace?"

The lower nerve on the left side of my face is dead and it gives my smile a crooked, mean, sarcastic touch. Sincerity, in fact. The guy wanders away quietly.

I have never put my nose in Jean's financial affairs. But as with every movie star, I guess, there are always a few ravens around her, who play—and usually win—by betting on her double feeling of guilt: her guilt as a movie star, probably one of the most scorned because the most envied of human beings, and her old Lutheran guilt with its inbred poison of original sin.

This is one of those moments when I wish I were more conventional, more of a bourgeois, so that I could avail myself of the French marital code dating back to Napoleonic days, claim the husband's rights of lord and master, such as they are still spelled out by the law, and kick out of *my* house one or two black hustlers who are mercilessly preying on the black man's hurt and on the white man's guilt.

No use deluding myself: I don't feel any more at ease here in this country than back home in France. Too much of my life has been spent in America and I am no longer able to savor the blessed feeling of being a stranger here.

I phone my publisher in Paris and wangle out of him a writing assignment in Japan for one of his lousy magazines. I had already been to Japan and had felt so lost and alien there to everything and everybody, the whole country and its people had made on me such an impression of strangeness, that I can truly say without bragging that I knew total alienation there, and it was wonderful. I was careful not to take chances, I stayed in Japan only two weeks, but during all that time, brief as it was, I felt a complete outsider, not part of anything, truly alienated. Alienation, today, as you probably know, is the greatest problem of all. How to achieve it, I mean.

There's a terrific language barrier in Japan, and it makes everything easier for you. You simply can't communicate with anybody. Lovely, generous country. Tears of gratitude come to my eyes.

So I wind up my decision-making machinery and prepare my suitcase, ready to run away somewhere where I won't hear my wife tell me with tears in her eyes: "Okay, so Mejid is a bastard, but don't forget it is we whites who made him a bastard." My old belligerence gets hold of me again and it is of that painful self-eating nature, which finally leaves you yourself as an enemy.

It's six P.M. and they're all gone at last. Maï is miaowing for attention. This sweet Siamese beauty who always keeps me company settles on my shoulder and talks to me in her squawky multi-tonal voice, sharing with me the latest news and secrets of the cat world of tasty birds and lizards and of all kinds of strange goings-on at night, a rich folklore full of green eyes and whiskers and dark courtships and moonlit lovers—a whole cat philosophy passes me by because of my shameful ignorance of foreign languages, a true philological disaster.

Seberg comes back and hangs rather guiltily around me. I remain stony-faced, and display such extreme courtesy and good manners, such civilized behavior that she begins to cry and I turn almost Lutheran with remorse. But then put yourself in my place: How can she worry about twenty million black Americans when she's got *me*? That should solve all her problems.

The doorbell rings and there are two kids outside, a boy and a girl, seven or eight years old. They are adorable with that fairy-tale blond look of American children who always take me back where I really belong, on the threshold of the "and they lived happily ever after" world.

"Excuse us, Sir. Is Fido here?"

"No, Fido isn't here."

I make a rush to the refrigerator and come back with some juicy brownies. My diet forbids me these delights, but I always keep some in the house to satisfy at least my visual craving.

"No, thank you, Sir."

Great. I stuff a brownie in my mouth.

The children stare at me with the kind of five-years-hard-labor-and-no-parole expression children are apt to assume.

"He's lying," the baby doll says.

"Mister, the SPCA says Fido is at your house all right."

I begin to realize who Fido is and give the kids one of those big, friendly grins that would make the wolf in Red Riding Hood turn pale with envy. It's then that I notice the Chevrolet, and the man who finishes parking it in front of my house gets out and walks toward me. Old, wrinkled, tall, thin, and all dried-up in that healthy and preserved fruity way evocative of a lifetime of sunshine. His salt-and-pepper hair and pleasantly rugged face remind me of the grandfather we used to see forty years ago leaping over a fence in those ads for "Kruschen Salts, eternal spring, keep your blood pure." I am delighted to see the old boy is still alive and full of beans. He walks across the lawn in that lazy, lanky American way which is always missing in those "spaghetti westerns." I like him immediately. For sheer physical distinction, you can't beat those Americans. They seem to have been invented by horses. A good seventy years old, you can almost count the seasons in the lines of his open, cheerful face. It speaks to you of a happy life of retirement with a good pension and some good savings, the Blue Cross and all the mortgages paid, of fishing and duck-shooting, all of it in a red-checkered Pendleton shirt. The relaxed, benevolent presence of that guy speaks of a civilization that reached its peak forty years ago and has solved almost all its social problems—except those you can live with comfortably as long as you can afford to ignore them. He comes between the two kids, puts his arms around their shoulders.

"Good afternoon, Sir . . ."

I love that southern accent, with its echo of leisurely ways, of fields and white-columned mansions, of rocking chairs, porches, slow rivers, and ponies on the lawn.

" . . . They told us at the SPCA you took in a dog three weeks ago that may well be ours. A German Shepherd with a mole on his muzzle and some funny rusty hair around the nose. Our trailer burned out in Gardena while we were out and the dog panicked and got away and we had to move on so . . ."

"Fido is the name," the little boy says.

I hear footsteps behind me. My wife. I hope she will keep out of this. Seberg is a very poor liar.

"Won't you come in?"

They come in. Those damn kids don't take their eyes off me: instinct. They smell a rat.

I give them a nice, warm smile simply bursting with good will and honesty. I have been expecting this encounter and I am ready for it. As a matter of fact, I am enjoying every moment of it. I can feel the villain within me rubbing his hands gleefully.

"Your dog had a collar, of course?"

Kruschen Salts shakes his head.

"No. The dog had put on weight and the kids took the collar off, it was choking him. We were just going to fix him up with another one when this happened."

I raise my hand reassuringly.

"Never mind. I'm sure it's your dog all right. It's all there,

D

the mole, and those funny tobacco-colored hairs, one of those cigarette fiends, ha-ha-ha . . ."

The blond angel's face lit up.

"That's Fido, sure thing," the boy says.

I give out a deep sigh and shake my head sadly.

"I am *terribly* sorry. I don't have the dog any more. I called the SPCA and even put an ad in the *Examiner*. . . . Nobody showed up and I couldn't keep the dog here. There were some problems that came up . . ."

I clear my throat meaningfully, but Kruschen Salts is not interested.

"We were on vacation here," he says. "My son and wife came to Los Angeles to see if they liked it here, and then to look for a house. He went back to Alabama to settle things before moving here for keeps."

"Nice place, Alabama," say I in a dreamy way. "Been there a couple of times myself. Loved it. Great."

Grandad Kruschen's bright smile could light up the room.

"The greatest," he says.

"But then California isn't bad, either," I say.

He nods.

"Sure. And there're more opportunities here. My son's just retired from the police, after twenty years. He plans to go into business for himself. He wants to open a kennel. He's a professional dog-trainer. Police dogs. Yes, he was in the State Police. I used to be a sheriff, myself."

I give him a friendly wink. I feel I'm giving a truly fine performance.

"Runs in the family, huh?"

"Yes, my own dad was deputy sheriff and . . ."

He'll be showing me those snapshots in a second.

Seberg's very sharp voice rises behind me.

"If you give them back the dog, I'll leave you," she says in French.

My smile grows wider.

"Keep your mouth shut," I tell her, with an exquisitely polite air. "*Je joue au con.* I'm playing dumb."

Kruschen Salts is delighted.

"You are French?"

"Yes, I was born in Verdun, which is what they called the miracle of the Marne."

"I was in France in 1917," he says. "Volunteered. The trenches, Madelon, Marshal Foch. . . . It doesn't make me any younger——"

"He doesn't miss a cliché, the old *schmuck*," says Jean, who had picked up some Yiddish when playing Joan of Arc for Otto Preminger.

"I don't have the dog any more. Terribly sorry."

I give him again one of those searching looks full of things that are better left unsaid.

"A remarkably trained dog," I murmur. "You certainly did a great job on him."

The sarcasm is way off the mark. I expect him to behave like one of those cliché southern heavies in the movies, but the fact is that I am dealing with a completely honest, decent, and straightforward person—and that is exactly what makes the whole thing so horrible. If only he could be a villain, I would feel a lot better. But the impression of American niceness, even goodness, the son-of-a-bitch radiates, leaves *us* no alibi, no excuse. His conscience is clear, his eyes unflinching. Any accusation of wrong-doing, of guilt, of an act against humanity in the training of that dog to attack black men and black men alone, would appear to him as sheer lunacy, the sick ravings of a distorted mind. Here is a perfectly honorable man, and all my barbs not only fly past him unnoticed but they come back and make me feel like a neurotic intellectual confronted with a picture of the quiet moral strength and self-assurance that have built the world.

"Yes, Sir, he's a fine police dog," he says. "As good as they come. My boy trained him. He's been training them for twenty years of his life, he's a real professional. That's why he's moving out here, to L.A. There's a lot of crime here, so there's got to be a market for good watch dogs. My boy's always liked animals, ever since he was a kid, raccoons, snakes, everything that came his way. Fido has three generations of attack dogs behind him, all in the Police Canine Corps, all trained by my boy. When they get past eight, the dogs are retired, they're put up for sale. They're much in demand. My son got that one when he was seven, the best dog he's ever trained, he says. With a dog like that in a house you've got nothing to worry about."

"*Tu parles, Charles*, you bet, my pet," says Seberg in sudden reminiscence of a famous line of her dialogue with Belmondo in *Breathless*. I fill him in.

"Please excuse my French wife, she doesn't speak a word of English. She asks if you would care for a drink."

"*Et avec tes oreilles, tu ne fais rien?*" Seberg growls. "And with your ears, you do nothing?"

This is a key phrase in our relationship. I owe it to the actor Mario David.

I ran into him one day at the Madrid airport, in the cafeteria, where he was having dinner. I rushed toward him, overflowing with friendship, upset his bottle of wine, tried to catch it, broke a glass, stepped on the waiter's foot and, losing my balance, hit Mario in the eye with my elbow. As I was apologizing profusely, a gold crown from my bridge came loose and fell into Mario's soup. Mario looked at me with cold interest and asked:

"And with your ears, Romain, you do nothing?"

"You have given the dog away?" Kruschen Salts asks.

"Yes. You see, as nobody claimed it. . . . And it so happened that one of our friends took a great liking for the dog."

"Do you have his address?"

I shuffle my feet.

"Look," I plead. "I want you to think it over. Your dog and my friend seemed to have some kind of instinctive affinity for each other, something almost animal. . . . You see, my friend is an African. Yes, a *Negro*."

Kruschen Salts freezes. His Adam's apple bobs up and down and he swallows hard, his lower jaw sagging below and beyond the call of gravity, and his gaping mouth displays a fine brand-new set of dentures as he stares at me with that blank expression of people who see their quiet world blown to pieces.

There are moments in the life of a couple when their long years together show their mark in an unexpected way: one of the two suddenly begins to speak the language of the other. The words that blossom on my wife's lovely lips come straight from the Foreign Legion and from the red light district of Morocco, where I picked them up in the days of my adventurous youth:

"*Hé ben, mon cochon!*" Seberg says, a somewhat rude but respectful soldier's expression of admiration for a truly mean son-of-a-bitch.

Thus encouraged, I spread my wings:

"My friend is an African student who spent a year studying sociology here. When he met your dog, it was . . . well, like a happy reunion of old friends. Those two just seemed to be made for each other. You won't believe me if I tell you there was simply no way of keeping them apart."

Mr. Kruschen is slowly coming up for air. I don't know to what depth he had sunk, but he was one of those born fighters who refuses to stay down. Pioneer stuff.

"Are you trying to tell me your colored friend has taken the dog with him to Africa?"

"That's right. I even paid for the dog's trip. I didn't want to separate them. There're certain things you just can't do."

The little girl begins to rub her eyes.

"I want my Fido back!" she yells and sobs.

Heartbreaking. I feel about as moved as Genghis Khan reading *Little Women.*

"Poor little thing," Seberg says and, believe it or not, there is a sincere note of pity in her voice.

Let's get this straight. I love all kids, ever since I had one myself. But if I remained untouched by this display of blond sorrow, the reason is, precisely, my love of kids. A cop, by the name of Loder, the adopted son of Hedy Lamarr, shot and killed a fourteen-year-old black girl in some ghetto the other day. And why is it that the average age of kids shot in the ghetto by the police is somewhere between seventeen and nineteen? Why?

"Yeah, give her a popsickle," I say.

Upon reading these pages, the representative in Paris of a very clean-living American magazine told a friend of mine, "Why doesn't Gary go and smell up his own ass?" The reason is simple: everybody is allowed to take a breather. You can't keep smelling roses all the time. You've got to break away from daily routine, occasionally. "And what the hell does he know about America, anyway?" the man added.

I wish some Americans, black and white, would get over once and for all the idea that they possess a kind of privileged, secret, esoteric and exclusive knowledge of themselves. This is particularly comical, coming from a country which has been entrusting the exploration of its deeper secrets and the probing of its subconscious for two generations to Austrian and German psychoanalysts. Besides, with all due respect for the mysterious West, I have to remind them that the greatest revolution of the twentieth century is *visibility.* The whole world walks the streets naked and all the remarks of the kind, "you are not a Negro, you can't understand, you are not an American, you can't understand, etc.," are nothing but racism. There are no places out of bounds for the eye and the mind any longer.

The kids' whimperings subside and a great silence falls, a great white silence.

The sheriff is getting my message. He is getting it loud and clear.

"You had no right to dispose of that dog," he says, his voice shaking a bit.

I nod.

"Sure. Listen, I'm going to write to Africa. Mind you, I'm sure your dog is treated like a king. Anyway, he won't lack anything, out there. There are two hundred million blacks in Africa. That ought to keep him happy."

His face hardens. It's that "law and order" look, with a touch of self-righteous anger. His old rugged hands come down protectively on the two blond heads. The son-of-a-bitch is an excellent grandfather.

But again, the most heartbreaking thing is that this man is *not* a son-of-a-bitch. He is as nice as God can make them.

If evil things were done only by evil men, the world would be an admirable place.

"I'm going to see a lawyer," he says.

"Do that. It always helps."

Jean shows them to the door. Then she comes back, puts her arms around me, and presses her cheek against my head. We must have stayed like that for a long time without speaking, with silence becoming one of those blessed moments when everything is shared. And then I made the mistake of giving her one of my little lessons of maturity, that is, of a weariness which tries to pass for wisdom.

"Jeannie, give it up. You can't reach the *real* ones, the millions and millions of those who are the only ones who can give any authenticity to those who are working for them. You can't start from the top. All the *true* ones, the real leaders, came up from the lower depths, from the hard truth, and they keep their roots down there. But you, at best you deal with the top, with the elite, and that's simply not good enough. It's a *de luxe* situation, it's more being *social* than social work. It's like knowing about lepers only from talking to Dr. Schweitzer. Giving your money away isn't good enough either. You can give your money to them, sure, but unless you get down to the roots and work there, no matter how sincere you are—I know, I know—it is still a *de luxe* situation, a cop-out, like buying peace of mind and a good conscience. And this crowd that hangs around you all day long, they're the fakes, the pseudos, the talkers. Professional Negroes, and you know what I mean by that: people who make a living for *themselves* by being black and nothing else, gaming whitey not out of hatred, revenge or honest-to-God necessity, but just because they're con men, traditional American crooks, hiding conveniently behind their black skins. You've got to face the fact that the black predicament and white guilt offer an ideal situation to the black status-seeker. His status among the white liberals and true democrats is entirely made up out of the lack of any status whatsoever of the black masses. All he has to do is to be a black among the well-intentioned whites: twenty million black Americans do the rest, *they work for him*. And there is another barrier you will never be able to break through: that of your profession. No matter how sincere and well-meaning and determined a movie star is, whenever she involves herself in a real social problem, she just looks more like a movie star than before, flash bulbs, publicity, front pages, irony and winks behind her back. Whenever a film star touches tragic social realities, the realities get second billing, and the blacks, Indians or Mexicans become extras, or, at best, a supporting cast. See what I mean? No matter what suffering you're actually trying to alleviate, you'll always look as if you're standing there on location for stills and saying, 'Cheese.' Or else you have to chuck movies and work at the roots, at the bottom of the ladder. When a movie star uses the publicity that surrounds her name to publicize social injustices she deeply cares about, all she really gets is publicity for herself. And there will always be the suspicion that the movie star is using the blacks not for the blacks' sake, and not for her own publicity either, but as a means of breaking away from the label of emptiness and artificiality that is stuck on her. Indeed, that she uses the 'cause,' Vietnam, the blacks, for her own purpose, to show how 'human' she is, to reach a human being's status. Back to her ego again. Whenever a movie star moves in on a 'cause,' she always gives the impression that she acted in too many movies with a 'social message' and continues to play the heroine in real life, that it's all part of a 'pretending' which seeks to validate itself, a kind of Actor's Studio technique of 'truly immersing yourself in the character you're playing.' In other words, no matter how sincerely you try, you only seem to be trying to achieve that actor's 'sincerity,' and whatever you do for *them* always looks like something you're doing for *yourself*, working on your own image and working on your own problems."

When Seberg gets hurt or angry her voice takes on a curiously earthy, proletarian, peasant, I don't know how to describe it, quality. It sounds as if it were coming from some long-gone mid-nineteenth-century wagon train on its way to the frontier through Indian country.

"I know all that, and I don't give a damn. And I'll tell you why: because what you're saying is *audience thinking*. I don't give a damn how it looks from outside. I won't be dictated to by public opinion. That's *image* thinking, press agent's thinking. I just want to do my bit, period. Who cares if it makes me look like a clown in *their* eyes? What you're really trying to tell me is to care about my image. Are you kidding?"

"All I'm saying is that you do more harm than good, because a movie star who moves in on a tragic reality always gives it an unreal touch, that Hollywood something."

"Listen, Romain, that's a too-goddamn-sophisticated point of view. There's a school with thirty kids in it and let me tell you that their black reality is of a kind that even Hollywood can't make unreal. It's not Hollywood that will give it a touch of unreality, it's the other way round. I mean, it's strong enough to give even Hollywood a touch of reality. Thirty ghetto kids, that's *reality* all right. I got a five-thousand-dollar check for them from Bill Fisher, and that's reality again. It's worth it. I mean, it's worth looking laughable, it's worth all the irony and the columnists' ha-ha-ha and it's worth all the bullshit, period."

I feel her tears on my neck and I know they are black tears gone white. Jesus, you just don't have the right to analyze tears, and I find myself wishing I could achieve that blessed, holy American "naïveté" or "primitivism," the moral and psychological equivalent of Grandma Moses, and get rid of Voltaire, La Rochefoucauld, and the kind of French intellectual cleverness that has done so much for literature and so little for people. There is no substitute whatsoever for a certain basic naïveté, or even a certain squareness, if you are not to be paralyzed by too much worldly awareness and made unable to act by sophisticated over-consciousness.

"A 'school without hate,' you know what that means? If those black kids are really brought up without hate in the only school 'without hate' in this country, they'll be severely handicapped for life. Unable to stand up to the others. It's like throwing the first Christians to the lions. . . ."

My contrived dialectics brought instantly to my mind the coldly interested look on Mario David's face, and I could almost hear his words again: "And with your ears, Romain, you do nothing?" Listen, you old French bastard, I tell myself, why don't you admit you care more about your young wife than about black Americans? I shut up and kiss her arm.

"I know there's that ghastly 'film star,' movie touch about everything I try to do. I'll just stop making movies."

I hear myself saying—why, why did I feel compelled to come up with that?—I hear myself saying: .

"If you stop being a film star, you won't need to find excuses for being Jean Seberg, the film star, and you'll probably feel no need to help them."

"Because that's my only motivation?"

Jesus, please be a good Jew and climb off that cross, for chrissake. I give up.

"Okay, I'm a cynic. But I've had it. I'm clearing out. I can't take it. Twenty million black Americans in my house, night and day, that's too much, even for a professional writer. All that's going to come out of it is another fucking book. I'm going to *do* them, that's all I've ever done for people. Literature. That's what it always comes down to with a professional writer. Another best-seller, more recognition, another literary prize, nobility of feelings for all to see. 'Let me shake your hand, Sir'; then one day maybe you get the Nobel Prize for Literature and you truly know what you've done with the world's anguish, suffering, and blood. You made a success story out of it. Literature, yep. I've already made that out of the war, out of my mother, out of Auschwitz, out of the bomb, out of African freedom, but I absolutely refuse to make literature out of American blacks. Let the blacks themselves get some good literature out of it, that's their gold. You know me, Jeannie: whenever I'm confronted with a situation that drives me nuts and that I'm unable to do anything about, absolutely helpless and condemned to just sit there and stare at it, I get rid of it in a book. A physiological process of elimination. I defecate it. I write it out of my system. Wonderful release. After that, I eat, sleep, and feel better. A new man. But it's high time to stop this self-therapy on the backs of other people's tragedy, so I'm not going to play cannibal on American blacks and feed a new book on their flesh. I'm clearing out. I won't write a thing about the blacks. I absolutely refuse. I——"

"Honey, you'll do that book anyway."

"Jeannie, let's get away *from* it. Let's both go away. You've lived ten years in France. You're French by marriage."

"I'll feel, live, love, and stink American until I drop dead. I can't be anything but an American, you know that, you've just got to scratch the surface. . . ."

"They don't give a damn about you here. . . ."

Bribe her, man. Try bribery. It may work. I grab a bunch of French reviews of her latest European movie from the table.

"Listen to what they think of you in France. François Mauriac: *'The marvelous Jean Seberg is in herself enough to make me love this picture. . . .' 'A talent blessed with beauty. . . .' 'The most sensitive, trembling, touching performance. . . .'* And what do those American provincial types write about you in the New York backwoods?"

She yells at me now:

"Who gives a damn about that, Jesus Christ!"

"*He* sure doesn't."

"I'm staying right here until that school is out of trouble. . . ."

"Okay, and *I* refuse to live with America on my back."

The doorbell rings. I get up to answer it. *Them.* Who else? It's that kind of place. Headquarters: American Idealism and Good Will, ring the bell.

Five ladies and gentlemen in tribal dress. I roar in French: *"Merde, merde! J'en ai assez!"*—"I've had enough!"—and slam the door in their grinning we-know-how-you-feel-buddy faces. I turn toward *my* wife. I think I hollered at her, I always holler when I feel helpless.

"They're there. They're there, with compliments from America. They keep insisting, the heartless bastards. All right, since they insist, I'm going to do it. You know perfectly well I can't resist it. I'm going to write a fucking book about them. That's how I'm going to get rid of them. Genocide, that's what it is, genocide. Books, they help you get rid of everything. Mass murder, and it cleanses your conscience too. You feel great, after you've done it. Another book, you know, and it changes the world and rightens everything with one stroke of your magic ink-wand. It's going to put an end to all the blacks' problems, the way *War and Peace*, *All Quiet on the Western Front*, and a million other books against war put an end to wars once and for all. Books that have changed the world, you know, and if you name me one that's accomplished something except being a book, I'll kiss your feet. So either you come back with me and *to* me or clear the house of the problem for me, or I'll be the one to clear out. . . . I'll stuff your twenty million black Americans in a book and they'll never be heard from again. Self-defense."

She goes to the door, opens it a bit, and smiles ironically.

"Just a second," she says. "My husband is undressing."

I yell, "Jesus Christ, Our Lord and Savior, I'm going."

"Okay, go."

I rush to the garage and jump behind the wheel. Panic. Sheer animal panic. In that famous Proust questionnaire all French writers are sooner or later submitted to, I answered the question "What is the military deed you most admire?" with the word "Flight."

I have fought all my generation's battles, since I was seventeen. I have done my bit. I want no more of that, thanks.

All I ask from life now is to be permitted to smoke a few more cigars.

Except that there's not a word of truth in it. Not a trace of truth. And there's nothing more torturing than being unable to give up hope once and for all.

And so, old man, run away, and fast.

I follow Sunset toward the ocean, but make a sharp U-turn, collect a ticket, and drive back and through Coldwater and across Ventura to "Noah" Jack Carruthers' crummy ark. Through the grounds and into the kennel section and then to that cage. Batka stands up on his hind legs and licks my face lovingly through the netting. I kiss him on his cold, wet truffle of a nose.

"Goodbye Batka-Batiouchka. . . ."

I talk to him in Russian, so as to make sure no one will understand us:

"Please listen to me, brother mine. I'm not asking you not to bite blacks. I'm asking you not to bite *only* blacks."

I think he understands me. He wags his tail. Dogs never fail to recognize their own.

I buy myself a toothbrush and get on the first plane to Honolulu. Then Manila, Hong Kong, Calcutta . . . I make a stop here and there, a few days, just long enough to feel disorientated and to lose sight of myself under the soothing impact of "local color," "exoticism," of all that is supposed to be "foreign," "strange," "picturesque," and "different" from all you are and all you know. A stop here, a stop there, a quick, kaleidoscopic change, never time enough to be truly exposed to reality, gliding over the surface of things, oh, those soothing delights of superficiality. . . . Skip over the surface, old man, travel light and fast, that's how to attain and enjoy a blessed illusion of estrangement, alienation, and indifference. Don't peek behind the painted veil of appearance, don't lift it, or else you'll realize that it merely serves to hide our essential identity of anxiety, fear, and questioning ignorance, the primeval unchanging curse of the "status of limitations" within our genes, brain, and heart, and you'll come once more face to face with yourself, old man, old man forever condemned to infancy and forever dreaming of manhood.

V

My DC-6 was droning through the night above the Khmer temples, towns and rice paddies of Cambodia when back in Los Angeles, Sandy pricked up his ears, rose from his favorite place at Jean's feet, and walked over to the door. He put his truffle to the ground, sniffed, then began to wag his tail, signaling the approach of a welcome visitor.

It was Batka. He had run away from the kennel, finding his way across Ventura, the San Fernando Valley and Beverly Hills to come back home to his family.

Jean was to tell me later there was more love than she could bear in the old dog's eyes. There could be no question of keeping an animal around the house whose presence in our midst, with all our black friends coming and going, was like offering hospitality to both the swastika and the yellow star of David. "I had a lousy night trying to reconcile the irreconcilable. A dilemma which in itself smacked of *poule de luxe* dilettantism, moral sybaritism. There shouldn't have been a dilemma at all, no exquisite scruples, no hesitation. The dog had to go."

The next morning, she called Carruthers.

"So he found his way back home? Great. I'm glad to have that one off my back."

There was something more in Carruthers' voice than mere satisfaction: a true delight.

"You're not what I would call a man who wants to change the world, Jack."

"That's what comes from living with a writer, Jean. You take a dog and you make a world out of it. . . . You know what happened the other day? First of all, one of the blacks who works for me, the youngest of them, tried to poison your copper. Put enough strychnine in his food to knock him off twenty-two times. The dog didn't touch it. Not because he smelled the poison, either. But food served up by black hands, imagine that . . ."

"Jack, it isn't possible."

"Of course it's not possible. Half the things that happen aren't possible. I knew nothing about this little incident. I'm the boss, so nobody tells me anything. But the next day, this kid Terry—he's eighteen, you know, the clean, idealistic age—went to find Fred Tatum who feeds the cur, because he's so white that he apparently smells good miles away, and the dog loves him. It seems, Jean, that you and I have a little odor of our own, something truly special. I can prove it to you dog-in-hand. Anyway, the kid went to Fred and asked him point-blank to poison your racist. Tatum told him he was seventy and didn't have it in him no more. He no longer had what it takes to go and poison a dog just like that. His moral fiber was no longer strong enough. He was too old, senile, in fact, count him out, he didn't want to take part in human affairs any more, call him no-guts-Tatum and leave it at that. I found out what was going on behind my back only because there was a helluva row between Terry and Keys. Keys gave the kid a real thrashing. You've guessed why, of course."

"Of course. It's absurd to take it out on an innocent animal. Keys is intelligent enough to know that."

"No, Jean, you're wrong. Keys is much, much more intelligent than that. So much more that I often feel he isn't thinking: he's scheming. He's not the kind of guy who meditates: he's the kind who premeditates. Anyway, he really gave it to the kid. And then, the day before yesterday, they outdid themselves. I heard them hollering in the locker room and it sounded pretty bad so I went to have a look. I found Terry stark naked and Keys holding a gun in his hand. It was my gun. Terry had stolen it from my office and hidden it in his underpants. Apparently he meant to kill your hound. Shoot him through the head, the way Black Panthers talk—yeah, *talk*. That's what we're coming to in this country. Do you realize what this kind of lunacy implies, I mean, the deep down under accumulation of pus it reveals? It ain't no longer a wound, no Ma'am. A wound, that's frank, open, clean, bleeding, it's kind of healthy—it's no wound and all pus now. Because, it's not a racial problem any longer: it's about how to deal with insanity, mental hygiene, that's what it's about. How you go about curing mental sickness, where do you begin? So, Jean, you can imagine how sorry I was when I heard your pooch got away, just heartbroken."

"Didn't you help him a bit, Jack, you fiend?"

"Nope. Not me. Maybe it was Tatum, or some other white guy, out of the kindness of his heart."

Had I been in Paris then, I would have no doubt received a cable asking me to meet our four-legged white American

E

at Orly Airport. But I was in Hong Kong at that time.

The problem was solved for Jean in a curious way. I don't blame her for falling into the trap. There are worse traps than trusting people.

It was dark, eight or nine in the evening. Jean was getting ready for some night shooting at the studio. Batka and Sandy had just treated themselves to a good dinner in the kitchen and had gone to stretch out in the living room. The sound of a car stopping in front of the house came in from the street and Batka was instantly on his feet, growling, pointing his bared fangs at the door and then letting go with one of those howls that seem to come from the depths of time.

There were footsteps outside and the bell hadn't rung yet when an extraordinary change came over the dog.

He stuck his tail between his legs and began to back away from the door.

He kept on howling, but now there was a whining, self-pitying sound of fear and helplessness in his voice. It would come out as a threatening howl and then change almost instantly into those plaintive little yelps and whines which are a dog's equivalent to crying, between two new feeble attempts at threatening barks that ended up in a sort of brokenhearted nasal whine of self-pity, as if the dog were driven to despair by his awareness of the total lack of credibility in his attempts at fearsome warnings. And still, his body stiff and his head raised high in that time-honored attitude of a dog moaning at the moon, stars, and eternity in darkness, he kept backing away from the door.

Jean opened the door slightly while keeping it on the chain: Keys. A pleasant smile, a quiet cigarette between his fingers, the burning side toward the palm of his hand, the relaxed air of a day's work done and gone, the lean, young body, the evening's soothing coolness and peace. . . . And that smile. . . . I can see it now, full of sharp glittering whiteness, with the night and the man grinning at you with all the brightness of light in darkness.

"Hi there "

"Hi. Wait a minute, I'll lock the animal in the garage."

More smile and more teeth.

"You don't have to do that. Don't bother. Those days are over. He won't try no funny stuff any more."

"Well . . ."

"I know about dogs, Miss Seberg. I really do. That's one thing I know about . . . dogs and snakes, yeah, that's my line. Things have changed, though I can't say we're buddies yet, for now. But things have changed all the same. There's been some progress. You can let me in. I'll be all right."

Jean took the chain off hesitantly.

"You sure?"

Keys pushed the door wide open and walked in.

Batka's growls deepened and grew angrier, more threatening, and for a few seconds it looked as if White Dog were coming back into his own again.

But for Jean, who had seen him leap instantly at the "enemy" with the resolute lunge forward of a good soldier answering the call of duty, the change was fantastic.

Keys moved into the center of the room, cigarette in hand, smiling at the beast, and White Dog, his tail between his legs, his head twisted sideways in a half-screw turn, kept backing away from the black American with howls that were almost pathetic in their helpless fury, small hysterical barks ending again and again in that what-is-the-matter-with-me-why-can't-I-do-it self-pitying whine. Again and again, he would gather himself for the leap but couldn't bring it off, as if unable to break through a mental barrier that was new, frightening, and incomprehensible to him. In Seberg's words: "You could see it went against the grain, against years of training, conditioning, and an inbred sense of what he was all about, against the very meaning of his dog devotion and loyalty toward his people. I could tell by those self-pitying whines and half-hearted attempts at menacing barks that the animal *no longer believed in himself*."

White Dog felt he was betraying everything he had been taught. Jean was standing near the open door full of night and stars, while man and beast faced each other.

"You see, Miss Seberg, there's been some change," Keys said. "Now, *they* are scared."

No, I'm not making it up, I'm not capable of that. I lack what it takes, I lack those three centuries of no name for it. Jean was sure she heard that sentence. "Now, *they* are scared." If these few words, almost Homeric in their sweeping generalization, fail to enlighten you as to what centuries have piled up and up and up in the black man's soul, then you may as well admit that it is not only of the black man that you "have had enough," it is of the soul itself and that you are ready for a more useful gadget.

Police dogs like Batka, I am told, almost all have generations of specially trained animals behind them. Both training and their inbred atavistic capital of push-button hatred are "improved," that is, facilitated by environment, with its automatic way of conditioning. Untrained dogs in black sections of the South will bark at whites just as in white neighborhoods they bark at blacks. Conditioning, training, and environment snowballed through generations until this ugliness becomes second nature.

White Dog was on the defensive. The hatred and the savagery were still there, but fear had built up a new mental barrier between the animal and the black man, and the dog could not bring himself to break through. He would inch forward in half-leaps that followed the rhythm of his barking, then back away again, as if pulled by an invisible leash. His hair bristled, he flattened his ears back, his tail coiled down between his legs, torn between his aggressive, dangerous, fear-inspiring old nature and his new cringing, jackal-like cowardice, an agony of split personality with the two parts clashing with each other, the new and the old, with the bewildered uncomprehending look in the dog's eyes, becoming a dumb, anguished, "Why?"

Keys lit a new cigarette, glanced at the dog, and laughed.

Jean was to tell me later that "there was something sickening about the whole thing. First of all Keys's laugh: it was . . . well, it was a *victorious* laugh and God, there've got to be other and more valid triumphs. This one of man over beast wasn't any more pleasant to see than *any* victory achieved through fear, force, and terror. Because, you see, the first question that came to my mind was: *How did he do it*? Yes, this change, this triumph, how had it been achieved? By what means? Beating? Torture? Attacking those who were out of reach and winning a symbolic victory, with the dog paying the price. The most revolting thing was the sight of that maddened, totally disorientated dog, disobeying his own reflexes, terrorized, lost, trapped, caught up in something that had nothing to do with dogs, entangled in human sickness, hate, fear and prejudice, a dog who was becoming *human* through a typically human *dehumanizing* process, this *historical* dog. . . . It was hideous and humiliating. I almost hated Keys at that ignoble moment of his victory, but in a totally impersonal way, the way you hate it all, the whole damn sick mess. You can't always go on piously blaming everything on society, there are times when you're a louse on your own. The excuse, the pretext, I mean the whole idea of helping an animal with his 'problem,' of making him 'recover,' of 'curing him of his sickness,' all of that, and the dog himself had very little to do with it. . . . It was all about men."

She told him, rather sharply:

"I can see you left him quite a souvenir."

"Self-defense, Ma'am," Keys said quietly. "Yes, self-defense. . . . It's always legitimate. You bet. But I really beat him up—what I call a real beating—only once, when I'd lost my head a little, I grant you that. He's used to me now and that's all the trick there is. After two hours a day of seeing me there inside his cage, with my padded clothes on, week after week, he just started to adjust, period. He figured that he's got to live with it—me, I mean—that it's there to stay, that I'm here to stay, yeah, right here and there's nothing he can do about it, not a thing. He can't scare me away no longer. Neither of us can get rid of the other. . . . I'm real happy to take care of the dog. I'll see him through."

Later, much later, in the light of all that was to follow, I asked some of our friends, who were a bit too quick in taxing us with impudence or naïveté: What would you have done in our place? Word had gotten around and people, often strangers, would phone Jean and tell her they would be happy to give the dog a home. Those offers were either cynically blunt about their reasons or too transparent in their whiteness. Most of our friends answered that in our place they would have taken Carruthers' advice and had the dog destroyed, for, as some of them put it, "You have to draw a line somewhere, after all, even with sensitivity." I don't agree. It seems to me that there are too many lines drawn as it is. For the last forty years, the escalation in the denunciation of "sentimentalism" coming from liberals, Communists, and Nazis alike has not been particularly conspicuous in leading to a "spring of reason": it has ended in Auschwitz, terrorism, and Prague. The world is more conspicuous for its brutish callousness than for its "sentimentalism," and that so many liberal intellectuals choose this time to make of "sentiment, sentimentalism" a kind of moral and intellectual sin is very curious indeed. There is no reason why we should be made to choose between Queen Victoria and Hitler or Stalin, but let us at least admit that "oversensitivity" and "sentimentality" are not exactly what threaten our civilization right now. And so I refuse to lower my sights where our dignity is concerned. I refuse to devaluate, to give in to inflation, to accept the notion that a hundred dollars' worth of suffering is worth no more than one dollar on today's market, in other words, that in terms of "sensitivity," a hundred dead are required today when one would have been enough yesterday, before inflation set in and devaluation came.

Jean was hesitating. I understand only too well this strange trait of character in people blessed or cursed with a generous nature: they're always eager to trust you and to prove it to you by giving you tokens of their trust. I cannot boast of a generous nature myself, since I never forgive anything, and forget even less. Yet it happened that a crook was once successful in robbing me for one reason only: he looked every inch a crook. I felt the need to be forgiven for my unreasoned, purely physical, and almost racist antipathy, and I signed a contract with him.

"Now, of course," Keys was saying, "if you want to sell the mutt, you can get about four hundred dollars for him. He's not just an ordinary watch dog. He's a real son-of-a-gun. An attack dog. The best I've ever come across. . . . Yes, Ma'am, he's the real thing. What with that crime rate, you know, all the white folks in L.A. are looking for one."

"Aw, come off it, Keys, don't give me *that*. I'm in this thing up to my neck, you know."

He assumed a look of deep regard, even of respect. Jean was watching him rather beadily, but there was not a trace of irony there, nothing but *too much respect*.

"Oh, I know that. People like yourself, and so many others, have helped us a lot. People like Burt Lancaster, Paul Newman, Marlon Brando, Shirley MacLaine . . . the *real* American people."

He was probably dying laughing behind that impassive

façade. But it didn't show. The man behaved as if he had swallowed the whole world long, long ago, and not a ripple was left on the surface.

Resentment and hatred have a dynamic power of their own; they can move mountains. That's how many a beautiful country has been built. Solid stuff. Foundations.

Jean had made up her mind. Once more, as so often before, as always and forever, she showed herself true to her nature, which meant above all trusting human nature. Seberg is that kind of a Midwestern American and there is just nothing you can do about it, no matter how long you've lived in France with her.

"Okay, you can take the dog back, if Jack is willing to have him."

"That's no problem. He can't handle the snakes without me. You always get bitten when milking them and it takes years to get really immune. A hornet can bite me, my arm won't even swell. Yes, Ma'am, there're only two other guys in the whole State of California who can say they're truly immune to venom. Butch Perkins, in Santa Barbara, and Jeff Kalinsky, in San Diego. All the other so-called 'snakers,' they'll just pass out if you throw a coral in their lap.

"Why is this dog so important to you?"

He shook his head and laughed.

"There you've got me. I've always liked animals, since I was a kid. That's why I chose this kind of work. I wanted to be a vet, but I dropped out of school in the eighth grade. Had to work. Well, I'll soon be in business for myself. There's not one real good kennel in the whole black community here. I feel they could do with more dogs, a lot more. And I'm a real pro with dogs. The best. Yes, Ma'am, the best. If I can make it with your friend here, that'll prove it. Those things get around."

All this must have been happening in a wonderful smell of roses. Whenever I leave Jean alone, I am immediately replaced by bouquets of roses. Dozens of them come to fill the void, all with visiting cards, and I have estimated at various times that my flower value is about a dozen roses per pound. It is flattering and very satisfying to know that as soon as you leave your gorgeous wife alone, an impressive number of people rush to the florist's in the admirable hope of replacing with roses your sweet-smelling self.

"And Keys, I know one of your helpers tried to kill the dog. What if he tries again?"

"Terry? That's over. He got the point. Smart kid. He's outside, in the car, I'm giving him a lift home. Why don't you talk to him?"

The kid was leaning against the car, counting the light-years up there in the sky.

"You don't have to worry, Miss Seberg. That was a crazy thing I did. It won't happen again, I promise you. Your dog is in good hands."

And that was it. The next day, Jean took Batka back to the ranch. I would have done the same thing had I been there. During all the years I have lived in daily contact with Jean Seberg, I have regained from her some of that brave candor you need to win by losing. By which I mean that what matters above all, win or lose, is to keep your trust in people intact, for it is less important to be again and again disappointed, deceived, betrayed, and mocked at by them than to keep your faith and trust in them unshaken. It is less important to let, for many more centuries to come, all the beasts of prejudice, hate, and deceit quench their thirst at your expense than to let this sacred source dry up within you. It is less important to be a loser than to lose yourself.

I was then somewhere between Phnom Penh and Angkor Wat.

Part Two

PART TWO

POST CARD

VI

Forty-eight hours after my return to Paris, a *France-Soir* reporter called to tell me that Jean's brother David had been killed in a car accident. Eighteen years old. . . . I catch the Chicago plane that same day to be with the Sebergs in Marshalltown, Iowa, in the heart of that Middle West which is probably to America what a 1924 bottled Chateau-Laffite is to French wine, when properly preserved in stable conditions in a good quiet cellar. It is difficult to imagine more pleasant, friendly, and "un-psychological" people—by which I mean people who are sufficiently well-balanced, straight-forward and self-assured to spare you the kind of special "handling" required in dealing with the average neurotic personality of our time. But then, but then. . . among the "nice" folks who come to express their sympathy to the stricken family, I begin to hear references to "the other tragedy" which is grieving the town: a lovely, well-brought-up girl from a much-respected family has married a Negro. The father died of shock, the mother is not much better off, "and yet they are such nice, such wonderful people. . . ." Never a more decent family has been stricken by a more indecent blow. Fate, that goddamn foreigner—a Greek, really—is great at hitting below the belt, a notoriously dirty fighter.

The fact that a mixed marriage between a white girl and a black man could be viewed as a "tragedy" of the same order as a young boy's tragic death instantly unleashes the sneering, teeth-baring animal in me, all the intolerance of intolerance that is the curse of tolerance. I try to hold myself in check, but I am too old a dog now to be able to learn new tricks. So I let go, lash out, ashamed of myself, which makes me even more aggressive. I inform my audience that no one better than I can understand this racial "tragedy," as I myself married an African Negress back in 1941, in the Ubangi. Yeah, a black girl, walking around naked, bare-breasted and bare-assed, the greatest, the loveliest little ass that ever graced this earth, take it from a Frenchman. A dismayed silence falls upon my audience, a silence so thick you could cut it with a knife and take it home with you as a trophy. And I am almost telling the truth, except that if my "black" marriage did indeed take place, on the bank of the Shari, during the war, it had been celebrated under tribal customs and not under French law, and the father of Louison had given me his daughter in exchange for a hunting knife, fifty yards of silk, and five jars of Dijon mustard. They listen to me and I can almost feel their sympathy flowing toward my in-laws: they thought Jean Seberg had married a decent man. And so I sink in deeper and deeper: the son I had with my Negress is now a member of the French Communist Party. When some of my audience tries to flee, I utter the magic word "de Gaulle" to hold their interest. I am about to tell them that de Gaulle, as is well known, had a Negro great-grandfather on his Jewish grandmother's side, but a sudden feeling of hopelessness and gratuity and vanity overcomes me: you just can't play Groucho Marx with these people, they are too nice, this kind of backlash aggressive humor, to be understood, needs a common ground of common suffering, or your nasty humor comes out merely as nastiness.

I get a hold on the clown in me, while the youngest of the folks around me says, with a tolerant smile:

"I'm afraid you can't really understand this. You don't have twenty million Negroes in France."

True enough: but *we* have fifty million Frenchmen in France and that ain't all fun either.

I walk out ashamed of myself, feeling cut-off once more from people by that terroristic sense of humor so totally un-French but that used to be so American: W. C. Fields, Chaplin stealing from kiddies, Mark Twain, O. Henry, and their last survivors, from Will Rogers to the *Hungry i* . . . America no longer laughs at itself. It's getting smaller.

That night I held in my arms my young wife shaking with uncontrollable sobs, and her despair and sorrow were for me that personal reproach and accusation known to all men whose virility is first of all a need to protect, to defend, and to remedy. Never before, in all the frustrations I have known, has everything that makes me a man challenged with more savage and vain anger that thing we call destiny, for lack of a more ignoble word: that battle we are always losing without even being permitted to fight it.

The fields around Marshalltown, caught between winter and spring, lay low and sultry. Nothing rises above the horizon, nothing stands out, there is an air of acceptance over the land. "To sleep, perchance to dream. . . ." That kind of a place. It reminds me of Russia. Nothing there to fit a mood of rebellion, of protest, of brandished fists. It must not be easy to be a writer here. For it is quite obvious that when a writer talks of rebellion, he talks of literature. . . . What else?

There are almost no blacks here and hardly any Jews, so the little town knows no *direct* fear and it is nice to be able to drive around and go everywhere without a leash. No need to keep a constant grip on yourself, nice people, hospitality, no hate, no fear, quiet certitudes and faith, you could almost call it a happy place, if happiness can have twenty thousand inhabitants and be content with that.

"We have almost no Negroes here so the sexual malaise is nonexistent," a doctor tells me, and adds, "Sexual fear, you know. . . ."

Yes, I do, but I don't believe it. I am aware that psychiatric studies almost all point to sexual fear as an important factor in the white-black relationship, or lack of the same. The "dimensional" myth and the awed envy or hostility it breeds no doubt play a part in the white outlook. This noble legend, the solidly established dimensional superiority of the black, is one of the funniest things I have ever heard in my life, though in a country as size-conscious in everything as America, with its natural penchant for scope, records, greatness, measurements and, generally speaking, a taste for the bigger-than-life in all things, this suspicious, sneaky, downright curiosity and worry concerning the proportions of the average black instrument makes sense, both psychologically and socially. It is normal that for a nation that has built skyscrapers, size should be almost a status symbol, and if we remember that no other nation in the world is so virility-conscious, with two phallic generations of writers, from Hemingway to Philip Roth, talking about erections in awed, proud, almost epic terms, as if of some kind of fantastic achievement, no wonder that this subversive, dangerously competitive, overwhelming, strikingly magnificent, record-breaking "they-never-quit" reputation of the black man's magical wand is something to be reckoned with.

As French Consul General in Los Angeles from 1956 to 1960, I had to write several reports on the racial situation in California for our embassy. Told repeatedly that this "dimensional" element played an important part in whites' prejudices, I asked a local public opinion institute to conduct a survey on the matter and the institute polled some hundred and twenty Los Angeles call-girls for me, white as well as black.

The results were as astonishing as they were inconclusive. The majority of the white professionals answered affirmatively, when asked: "In your experience, have you noticed that your black partner was 'bigger' than your white partner?" But the majority of the black girls had noticed nothing special in blacks, as opposed to whites: according to them, "the thing" varied with the individual. Our ambassador in Washington at that time was Monsieur Couve de Murville, and he is a man who likes clear, precise reports, but I was unable to provide him with anything very definite on this subject. The most heart-warming answer was given by a young woman I later asked to meet. Her answer to the down-to-earth question was: "It isn't the quantity, it's the quality that counts. And there's such a thing as *feelings*." Underlined. The first part of the answer could be put down to the professional pride of the craftsman who likes to do a good job, but the phrase "and there's such a thing as feelings" enchanted me. I wondered if I had at last met the woman of my life. Although the Poll Service tried to wriggle out of it, I got her name and invited her to dinner at Romanoff's. She was a pretty girl, about twenty-three. She spent her free time studying literature at U.C.L.A. Since there is nothing more satisfying for an intellectual than to meet a whore who is studying at the Sorbonne, or its Californian equivalent, I truly felt the wind of grace over my brow. We were only at the hors d'oeuvres when we began to talk poetry, and when dessert came the word "existentialism" was uttered. American whores are twenty years behind: in France, they would have been talking Structuralism and Michel Foucault. I did not ask the girl why she followed this "profession": as a writer, I couldn't afford to sound so bourgeois. I did cool off a bit when I learned that she was married and the mother of a little girl of five; her husband (he has since become a television producer in New York)—and this is the God's truth—drove her around in his taxi from customer to customer. I remember that a deep depression came over me: it wasn't the moral question that was getting me down, but the feeling that I was getting old and no longer up to it. I was definitely knocked out when I discovered that this girl, who "did" about ten customers a day, neither smoked nor drank coffee. She was a Mormon and wasn't allowed coffee or tobacco. Holy Moses! I have since asked a friend, Professor Goldburg, why, in his opinion, about eighty-nine per cent of the white girls had asserted that blacks were "bigger," and why their black sisters had answered in about the same proportion that there were no real dimensional differences between the two races. According to this eminent psychoanalyst, the black girls had wanted to reassure the white man about his "bigness" out of fear, while the white girls had tried to make "their" man feel small out of bitterness. I doubt it. But the fact remains that I have been unable to clear this point for Monsieur Couve de Murville who, I hasten to add, had never asked me for this bit of information.

This "dimensional" obsession in America, especially in writers, is a constant source of amazement to me. From Mailer to James Jones, from Faulkner to Hemingway and to Philip Roth this preoccupation of the American intellectual primate with his banana is so persistent, vocal, and repetitious that in the end it amounts to a gigantic, general, ever-threatening castration. The most pathetic example can be found in the story Hemingway tells about Scott Fitzgerald. It seems that Fitzgerald was tortured by the idea that he was "small." Hemingway conducted an expertise and assured his insecure friend that he was perfectly all right. To prove this beyond any doubt, he dragged Fitzgerald to the Louvre to show him the phallic dimensions of the Greek statues. How could two adults, two of the most famous writers of their time, arrive at such nonsense? What deep anguish does this American phallic fallacy hide? I have never come across this "dimensional obsession" in any other country. And, as the Reverend Father Charrel has pointed out so properly, did Hemingway himself ignore the elementary fact that the measurements "at ease" don't mean a thing? In Father Charrel's words: "The only thing that counts in this field is the noble heights to which inspiration can carry you."

Or should we consider this *idée fixe* as one more example of American perfectionism where gadgets are concerned, their keen interest in the latest and most powerful model?

I fear, however, that the reason goes much deeper. Almost every citizen of this most advanced technological society feels trapped in the complexities of a universe which as an individual he can no longer control. He has become a kind of "insert one coin" manipulated by a push-button distributing machine, the button receding farther and farther away from his reach, while the automatic, implacable and anonymous gears of bureaucracy became more and more authoritarian, irresistible, final, and crushing. This human "insert one" token is channeled through the prefabricated circuits of an artificial existence. No wonder he so desperately endeavors to emphasize whatever trace of life-force is left in him. Devirilized, powerless to assert himself, a mere "thing" transmitted through channels, used and then eliminated at the other end into retirement and the cemetery, the man of crosswalk signs and of the bureaucracy of living sees no other way of asserting his "power" except by erection, and he sticks his "virility" under your nose as a proof of his "he-existence." This "phallic proclamation" is really what the American Declaration of Independence is coming to. Pornography, so prevalent on stage and screen, with testicles brandished like defiant fists, has become the last stand of nature, a nostalgia for a more natural life and a more natural environment, a dream of wilderness. It is the wretched self-defense of a man who, in all senses of the term, whether ideological, philosophical, or moral, is fighting the threat of castration. The "phallic declaration" is a sign of confusion, anxiety, a dream of nature. When nothing else is certain any more, with all the values crumbling, orgasm becomes the only thing "they can't take away from us." One thing is certain, anyhow: The American dream is in danger of becoming a prick.

In a psychological contest such as this the "black giant" of the track, football, and baseball fields, the "African" only one century removed from the jungle, the "tiger," the "panther," becomes a symbol of virility to be envied, and therefore, fear and hatred.

The "phallic declaration" is yet another clue to what is probably our most persistent, oldest myth: the myth of "the return to the source," with its eternal echo of paradise lost. As the signs of our intellect's failure to cope, solve, transcend, and prevail become more and more evident and distressing, orgasm becomes a kind of ersatz solution, the instant coffee of self-fulfillment, the only satisfying answer, something that truly "makes sense" in a senseless world. You have only to study present-day American literature to conclude that it reads as if all the Philip Roths, Norman Mailers, and so many other talented writers were constantly amazed at still being able to achieve an erection, whispering in the dark: "Look, Ma, no hands!"

VII

Jean is to continue her work on *Pendulum* on location in Washington, D.C. and we leave Marshalltown three days after the funeral. But her dead brother's presence will keep us company for a long, long time to come and the now eternally young David Seberg will show himself time and again in those sudden, unexpected tears that appear out of nowhere in my wife's eyes—unleashing in me a savage, helpless, almost growling hostility and belligerence, aiming its futile threat at Fate almost as if Fate had a throat in which I could plant my fangs. But it all ends in clenched and empty fists, our way of coming to grips with destiny, or rather, of coming to terms with it. The Sword of Justice, the childish Knight of Righteousness in me, is condemned once more to a state of inner raging, ending in self-hatred at my frustration and impotence, a mini-ocean churned back into mere literature at each attempt to transcend and to overcome, reduced again to murmuring the words of man's first defeat, that never-missing link between ape and Einstein: "Well, there's nothing we can do about it." I take Jean's hand—a sublime consolation—and ask her about our menagerie. I learn that our son, Diego, only six but already, like his father, given to introspection, and also, no doubt, having taken literally Socrates' advice: "Know yourself," swallowed a tape measure in a scientific effort to fathom his inner depths. The cats were fine.

"And Batka?"

A shadow falls over Jean's face. She has kept a spontaneity of expression, an abandon and directness in the outward manifestations of her feelings and thoughts that is something like a last trace of childhood on those lovely features, the sweet refusal of a worldly mask.

"I don't want to talk about it."

"Keys has killed him?"

"No."

She withdraws her hand and looks out of the plane at the Mississippi River twisting below us.

"Come on, Jean . . ."

"He began by starving him. . . . Well, not deliberately, but then, you know, the dog refuses to touch food when it's brought to him by . . . by black hands. There was a terrible row with Carruthers, simply because Jack went and fed the dog once himself. 'He'll take his food out of my hand, or he won't get any.' That was Keys's stand. Carruthers called me up. He was hollering on the phone and I could hear his fists pounding the desk. . . . Yes, 'Noah' Jack Carruthers . . . the man they say's been through hell and high water and never loses his cool. You bet! He was bellowing like an old moose and taking it out on the table, bang, bang, bang . . . you could feel that his fists just longed to get at *our* faces. . . . You know what I mean. "Take this goddamn dog off my hands or I'll do away with him myself. . . . This whole business has got nothing to do with a dog any more, and my place is for *animals*, d'you hear me, Jean, for real flesh-and-blood animals, not for your own stinking problems, white, black, or green, screw them all. . . . Take *your* problems off my hands. . . . Why don't ya' give the dog to some nice Berkeley students, that's where he belongs. . . . Get rid of it, I'm telling you. . . .' "

Some *it*. I can hardly see them deporting twenty million blacks to Africa.

"What did you say?"

"I said okay, of course. Grabbed my car and went to the kennel. Except, you see, *Keys wouldn't let me take the dog. He refused to part with him*."

"I don't believe it."

"He *won't* give up the dog. I found him in Jack's office and I thought they'd both gone nuts. They are . . . well, they're not that kind of people, normally, I mean, you wouldn't think they're the sort of men who could lose their heads over something that was no longer a dog at all . . . I don't mean to sound patronizing, but . . . well, you hardly expect them to lose their heads over something that, after all, had a tail, four legs, and a cold nose. Can you imagine Jack Carruthers, that rock, that block of ice, on the verge of hysterics? No? Well, I saw it with my own eyes. And Keys wasn't much better. Jack was screaming his head off and that half-paralyzed face of his had a nervous twist running across it, like lightning. Keys had lost his voice, every time he opened his mouth nothing would come out, and when he did manage to speak, it sounded as if he'd glued together broken bits of voice.

" 'No one has the right to make this animal starve,' Carruthers was yelling. 'Not at my place. Not here. I don't approve of that sort of training method.'

" 'And what . . . training . . . methods . . . do you approve of?' Keys screamed. He was almost choking with words coming out between gulps. 'The methods they used on him in the South?'

"I really thought Jack was going to have a heart attack. His patched-up face was so taut it looked as if it might crack open. His whole head was like a clenched fist. He was holding his voice back, you know, the way you do when you're making a tremendous effort to control yourself, and when he spoke, it sounded as if his voice was coming from six feet under ground.

" 'That's right, Keys. Tell me I'm a racist, you'll have a point. Because that's what I am: a racist.'

"Keys just stood there, his mouth gaping in astonishment. He was really thrown this time.

" 'Yes, I *am* a racist. Only not the way you all are, black or white. I'm a racist because I've had so much of your fucking human race that it's coming out my ass, whether you're yellow, green, blue, or chocolate. I chose animals thirty years ago, *real* animals, not the fake ones, who pretend to be something else and better.'

"They had both calmed down a little.

" 'You can't put that dog back into circulation,' said Keys. 'You have to straighten him up first.'

" 'That dog is too far gone for what you call straightening up, and you know it,' Jack growled. 'You can't make him any different. They've done too good a job on him. You can't change it now.'

" 'Well, let me try,' Keys kept insisting.

" 'Not by keeping him short of food and water. That's sadism. You're taking it out on the dog. You're making him pay for what his masters are!'

"Keys went gray with rage.

" 'I don't go looking for a dog when I want to get even with his masters. . . . I go looking for *them,* with my gun.'

"I tried to interrupt, but you can imagine. . . ." Jean went on, "Jack was shaking his finger at me.

" 'I want her to take the animal away. The dog's going to starve to death and it'll get around. They'll say Jack Carruthers trains animals by torture. I'll have the SPCA on my back. Their lousy inspectors have been asking questions already. I had to lie. I said the dog was sick and was refusing food. A thing like that can ruin my reputation.'

"This professional argument of 'It's bad for business' was something Keys apparently understood, because he nodded agreement.

" 'Sure. I know. Look, Jack, all I'm asking is that you let me try for another two weeks or so. The dog won't die. He's pretty solid.'

"And then Keys said something that truly shook me. . . . It was so totally unexpected, what with all that hate around. He said: 'He's a fine dog.'

"It was spoken with such sincerity, so . . . almost lovingly, that Jack could find nothing to say, he simply looked for a while as if he was going to burst another blood vessel, out of sheer despair.

" 'Okay,' he finally managed to growl, and that was it.

"Keys went out, and Jack turned toward me.

" 'Can you figure out that son-of-a-bitch? That dog really means something to him. Why? Why should *he* care, of all people? Why should he want to change things? Keys is a Black Muslim. They say that they get a paid trip to Mecca every time they bring in five pairs of pink ears. It's pure, straight hate with them, right? So what does he want to prove with that dog? That hate can be cured because it's only the result of training and can be treated? Fine, great, but then why doesn't he give himself the treatment too? He's so full of hate you feel like looking for a first-aid kit, the moment he comes along. Can you make that out, Jean?'

"I told him, I think, that the word 'hate' was misapplied, that the sickness itself was a deep neurosis which was contagious and . . . well, you know, I really didn't know what to say. But Jack wasn't listening anyway."

" 'That mutt's driving everybody nuts,' he said."

I felt completely on Keys's side.

"There's no question that this thing can be cured and Keys is right to try. He told me that the very first day: 'You can't give up on a dog.' Jack is biased. The fact that Keys happens to be a Black Muslim doesn't make him *only* a Black Muslim. There's still plenty of room left."

I don't think I ever before in my life misjudged a man so badly. I saw in Keys my own little idealistic ferments, a cheap-trash hallelujah of universal love and brotherhood, deep sunk deposits of a humanitarian creed, a kind of Red-Cross-meets-Boy-Scout in liberal praise of Montaigne, Rousseau, and Léon Blum–Salvation Army, to which, mock myself till I burst, I shall belong as long as there is a breath of life left in me. No matter how savagely I keep tearing at myself and at all my unshakable belief in *you*, how desperately I try to weigh myself down with cynicism, in the vain hope of sinking to the muddy bottom where lie in dreamless peace so many of our ships, the tearful tremolos of a comical "let's-love-each-other" aria ring on in my blood, the only anthem I have ever been able to learn. An eternal "Ave Maria" of sensitivity, "humanism," "liberalism," "sentimentalism," the idealistic bleating of sacrificial sheep always ready to lay their heads once more on that sacrificial stone of dumb mulish faith in man's essential Rousseauesque "goodness." Please, somebody, put him away. You can't change the son-of-a-bitch, he's a true believer. And when I realize that everything I am writing here will see the light in print, the intellectual eunuch and effete snob in me can almost hear the testicles of real men sounding the charge in the name of hardboiled "virility."

Hard types, the hardest you can get. No wonder they keep on talking in terms of eunuchs, effeteness, and phallic splendor. They are truly the men who have built this world, we owe *that* to them, and let us never forget that the world we live in has been built by these strong, virile men, which is enough to make you crave for femininity, enough to make you believe that only femininity can save the world.

VIII

We land in Chicago, just as two department stores go up in flames on the edge of the black district. Arson. In the airport waiting room, a few black and white passengers are watching the smoke on the TV screen. The young hostess behind the counter has tears in her eyes.

"How is it all going to end? All our culture is collapsing. . . ."

I try to see only the positive side of this cry from the heart: a little American girl from the Middle West behind the counter of a shabby airline talks "culture" to me and is perfectly aware of what is at stake.

We look at the burning store on the screen. It's the latest news, and I like it. I like it because I love America. I'm happy to see her squirm, to see her hoist and turn and feel the hurt, while out there in the Communist East all the pus and wounds and sadness are about as visible as life at the morgue. America is feeling its pain, as all living things do. Vietnam is the worst thing that could have happened to Vietnam, but perhaps the best thing that could have happened to America: the end of the big sleep, of overconfidence, the saving grace of doubt, soul-searching, self-questioning, an impossibility of "more of the same," a summons to metamorphosis. No one can say what the new America will be, but I know that Vietnam and the black challenge will save her from rotting slowly, imperceptibly on her feet in an immobility of structures, sclerosis, and invisible hollowness. This is not a country that can accept unhappiness as part of being American, it goes against the grain.

A black redcap next to the young hostess nods.

"*They've* done it again."

They. He's old, *they're* young. I often feel a gap here between old and young that is much stronger than any color line . . . and this is a hopeful sign again. The girl dries her tears. She looks at me with that instant trust people here, who feel lost in small towns and backwoods, offer spontaneously to those custodians of centuries-old wisdom, the Europeans. I feel like taking off my Frenchman's crown and rubbing it for a bit of extra shine.

"Do you think it will blow over?" she asks me.

I have a deep mistrust of things that "blow over" because they often blow you to pieces.

"Look," I tell her. "You don't need to worry: it won't blow over. A black minority is trying to help the whites get rid of the past and they're bound to succeed, because there's no future for the past, no matter how beautiful it is. You either get rid of the past or it gets rid of you, which is another way of getting rid of it. There are two possibilities:

either blacks will succeed, and America will change, or they will fail, and America will change even more, though more painfully. You can't lose."

I feel ashamed as soon as I finish speaking: next time, I ought to try healing the sick by the laying on of hands.

There are half-a-dozen blacks and about fifteen whites in the waiting room, and they all watch the stores burn without a word passing between them. There is one thing the newspapers don't say: in America, you *never* see what one calls in France, in journalese, *une discussion qui dégénère en bataille rangée,* a discussion which degenerates into a pitched battle. At the origin of all the outbreaks of violence, there is either an incident clumsily or brutally mismanaged by the police, or some false report, or a provocation of some kind. Never a *discussion.*

"I'd so love to go to Europe," says the girl.

Jean writes down our address in Paris and gives it to her. I shudder. Seberg spends her time giving our address to all the young Americans here who believe in Atlantis. That's how one day I found six beatniks sleeping on the floor of our apartment. One of them had been carrying her address around religiously for four years, and he had shared it with friends. There are some simple souls who will never understand symbolic gestures.

We reach Washington in the afternoon, welcomed by the cherry trees in bloom. My last trip here was in 1960, when I was Consul General in Los Angeles. Couve de Murville was my first ambassador here, and I am probably the only man in the world whom blossoming cherry trees make think of Couve de Murville. A brief moment of nostalgia. I cannot say I miss him—Couve de Murville is not the kind of man you can say you miss—but I liked his well-dressed coldness and that icy appearance which probably hid secret torments and an overly controlled inner tumult which showed only in quickly passing ripples of irritation.

That evening, in the taxi taking us to dinner, we hear on the radio the news of the assassination of Martin Luther King. The driver is a black. Jean turns so pale that the driver seems even blacker by contrast. He speeds ahead and then asks me to repeat the address of the restaurant. I repeat the address for him. He goes on driving straight ahead, then, again, in a muffled tone: "What was that address again?"

I wait until he gets some kind of grip on himself. We go round and round the cherry trees. They are bathed in floodlights, an unreal phosphorescence that gives them the look of a frozen, petrified ballet.

"What was that address again?"

I hear Jean's scared voice:

"Is it a white man who killed him?"

No answer.

Jean looks at me almost imploringly. Yes, I know. The sickening, ghastly thought that Martin Luther King may have been killed by a black as was Malcolm X when his triumphant, growing, inspiring personality began to be viewed as a threat by the hoods around Elijah Muhammed —that latter-day version of Father Divine-plus-guns—is not the product of a white man's fancy or sick wishful thinking. To deny that this thought, this horror, had crossed many a black militant's mind is to belittle the scope of the American Tragedy.

"Is it a white?" Jean repeats.

Almost hopefully so. . . . The driver doesn't answer. With those frolicking cherry trees, we are the first white thing around since he has heard the news. His hunched shoulders give an impression of hostility which is nothing but a projection of my own feeling of guilt and shame. For the next few days I will thus read hate on every black face, a hate that more often than not isn't there at all. My own self-hatred. . . . The cherry trees around us, delightfully dressed up in their floodlights, now have the absurd air of people who come in evening dress for a party that took place last year. The driver drops us at the Hilton. I resist the cowardly temptation to overtip him just because he is black and Martin Luther King has been murdered.

"*Ça va sauter,*" Jean says. "All hell will break loose."

IX

It does, the next morning. By two in the afternoon, almost seven hundred fires are reported in the capital, and several of them are only a few blocks from the White House. As always, the young rioters burn mainly their own houses, which means that for every store kept by a white, five black families will be homeless. A Jewish antique dealer with a long white Babylonian beard down to his waist appears on the TV screen. His store has just been looted.

"I don't hold it against them. You have to understand them. . . ."

The Jews are favorite targets, first because some of the stores belong to them, and then because the blacks need Jews just like everyone else. The fashionable lie in Stokely

Carmichael's circle is that Jews are the principal "slum-lords" in the ghetto, whereas the truth is that fifty-two per cent of the all-black buildings and twenty per cent of the buildings that are mostly black are owned by blacks. But then the Carmichaels of this world can only subsist financially and psychologically by lapping up all the hate-nourishing pus of history.

Another nondescript white, who could be Greek, Italian, Armenian, or all three, is filmed against the background of his wrecked apparel store: a pair of long johns in the smashed window is all that is left of his merchandise. The long john shows its behind to us. "Why didn't the police shoot? It's a shame. The police stayed in their cars while those hoods looted my shop under their very noses." He would have preferred to see kids killed for a few pairs of long johns. They were probably of a superior quality.

The Mayor of Washington, whose name is Washington and who is black, has given orders to the police not to shoot, except where human lives are in danger. I learn that my friend Selv Dressler got himself knifed in a telephone booth while taking pictures. Some idea, that, holing up in a telephone booth, where you're cornered like a rat! The TV shows scenes of looting filmed by black reporters. In a few hours a kind of Congolization of the city begins to be felt.

The Sheraton-Hilton is like a luxury ship abandoned by its crew and set adrift; the personnel is black, but their absence is not a strike of protest: none of them dare go through his own black neighborhood to come to work. Isn't it comical that I should experience a kind of relief, a satisfaction, when blacks and whites share something, if only fear? With the extreme fragility of big American cities—of all modern cities—restaurants close from lack of food, garbage piles up higher and higher even as you watch—these mountains of garbage, always the first sign of civilization breaking down. The smoke from the fires drifts over districts that are perfectly safe from "danger," but the rumor spreads round that "they're coming out." Traffic is a monstrous stream of metal: everyone with a car is trying to get out of the city. Whites make up a bare forty-seven per cent of the population of the city, which is entirely surrounded by the so-called "black belt," not unlike the Communist "red belt" of Paris. The crime rate is the highest in the U.S.A. A distinguished fifty-five-year-old lady, a famous "hostess" of society functions, was raped by blacks while walking her three dachshunds in broad daylight, right in the middle of the city, in a public square, and then patiently queued up at the police station to report the affair. A pride of matriarchy, that rocklike lady. She later confided to our ambassador that she had been very afraid for her dogs: the hoodlums kept threatening to kill them.

In the hotel lobby, the Cherry Festival tourists prowl nervously around their luggage, waiting for the buses to take them to the airport. Air services have been tripled and quadrupled. Their faces are worried and their reactions out of all proportion with the perfectly nonexistent danger. The least one can say is that perhaps America has found her new Redskins, but certainly not her new pioneers. . . . Fortunately, as I am taking a walk around the abandoned cherry trees, I come upon a couple of true Americans after my heart, the kind I dote on. Their added ages must be something like a hundred and fifty years. The old lady is taking a picture of a particularly gorgeous cherry tree, and I swear the tree is posing. Her husband looks like a very old tree himself, a dry, graying one with wrinkled bark that will never know bloom or spring again. His impish blue eyes give me a conspiratorial wink.

"With all this mess around, we have it all to ourselves." I tell them: "I love you," and leave those staunch Americans to their cherry blossoms.

In the evening, the "situation deteriorates," whatever

that may mean, and twelve thousand federal soldiers are brought to the capital. Curfew is declared. A few minutes before the time limit, as I walk by the White House, I have the privilege of witnessing a historical sight. No one who saw it is likely to forget it: a machine gun on the steps of the United States President's residence, pointed toward the street; it was to disappear an hour later, on Johnson's personal order, but I did see it and it was beautiful. Nothing gives a better impression of powerlessness than a lone machine gun at the entrance to the vital center of the biggest and most powerful democracy the world has ever known. America has at last become a country where something new can happen.

There isn't a single car in the street now. On the sidewalk, I notice a particularly depressing phenomenon: a few blacks and whites hurrying home avoid each other's eyes, and all of them look sad. They don't seem to be aware of the privilege they have: that of living a historic moment, a moment when you could hear, albeit barely, the whimper of a new world being born. If I were Russian or Chinese, I would wish with all my heart that America would pull successfully through its forthcoming mutation. I would remind all those, Russian or Chinese, yellow, white or black, who talk of "burying" America, that this country is an immense continent, and to bury that kind of corpse, you need a lot of room, the whole earth, as a matter of fact. All those who are digging America's grave are making their own funeral arrangements.

Back in the hotel, as I walk along empty corridors, my eye catches, through an open door, a scene almost perfect in its ugliness. A fat woman is sitting on the bed in her panties and bra with tears running down her face. She is hollering at someone I can't see, but whose invisible presence seems to be that of the perfect American husband of the Rotary-plus-Daley type.

"I want to go home. I want to get out of here."

"Sure, honey, sure. We'll be all right, we're getting out tomorrow. We'll be all right."

The idea of any danger whatsoever is asinine, yet the rumor in the lobby is that "they" are going to come down and set fire to the Hilton. Hear, hear: "They'll come on us from all sides, close off all exits and smoke us all out like rats." It's an interesting idea, because it's typically a rat's idea. This panic comes from within, from deep within, and it bears no relation to the existence of any *exterior* threat. What is showing itself there is guilt, mother of all anxiety and terror. And also, perhaps more than anything else, it is the phenomenon of the familiar suddenly becoming completely alien and new to you. America has lived safe in the smiling knowledge of "her" Negroes and, suddenly, she no longer recognizes them, and the natural consequence is fear. Do you know the story of the sailor Dybienko? He was the faithful guard of the young Tsarevitch, the hemophiliac child who was to inherit the throne of Russia. The sailor had watched over the royal child for years with a touching devotion. He had the complete trust of the Tsarina. When the revolution brought the world down on their heads, a member of the royal suite unexpectedly entered the Tsarevitch's room in the castle where the imperial family had been first interned. He saw the sailor lolling back in an armchair, having his boots taken off by the terrified, kneeling royal child whom he was cursing profanely.

Which just goes to show that you can never really count on your servants.

X

Ever since the riots had begun, I had been trying to reach by phone a man whom I shall refer to here by the name of his last-born and eleventh child, Red. I first met him in Paris a couple of years after the Liberation, when he was "supported" financially by Pigalle whores and studying at the Sorbonne at the same time.

The girls of Pigalle hadn't waited for Black Power to discover that "black is beautiful." The physical glow of this child of California was a value that the society which rejected him so totally prohibited him from *not* exploiting: it ordered him to get all he could from his striking good looks, the way black boxers and athletes of my generation fell back on their muscular gifts to try to make it in the only way left open to them. You have to be a stinking hypocrite, a forger of fake "moral" values to accuse Malcolm X of having been a "pimp," or my friend Red of having been a *maquereau* in Paris in the early fifties. If you look at the present state of opportunities open to Africans in Paris, for example, those who accuse so many of them of "procuring" are actually damning the countless whites in colonial Africa who spent a good century saying to their "boy": "Bring me a girl tonight." The marginal sexual aspects of colonialism gave birth, among other consequences, to the infamous institution of "sucking boys," a willful murder of the child's soul. The whole business was the result of an absolute rejection of the black race outside the human family, to the point that the wretched men who indulged in these "facilities" often didn't even have the "excuse" of homosexuality. In America, you have only to read the autobiographies of Claude Brown, Cleaver, and so many others to realize that the psychological, moral, and economic conditions in which the young ghetto black lives, struggles, develops or dies take away any trace of significance or "moral" meaning from the fact that such and such a black who is today a lawyer, a political leader, or a writer was, "when starting out," a man who lived on prostitutes' earnings, a criminal, a drug-pusher, or an addict. Rare are the blacks who haven't had a whore among their maternal ancestors, and the real whore there was the white society. Blacks whose female ascendants haven't been used to give their first kicks to white male virgins are few. There isn't a Negro today who would feel any hesitation in admitting that his mother or grandmother was a whore. The shame is not on him. To be a pimp in those circumstances is meaningless in terms of "blame." The Negro has been forced into prostitution, sport, or crime, just as the Jews had to fall back on usury. They were given the corner on that particular market.

I had helped Red in Paris, when he had a bout with

tuberculosis. I had taken a liking to that American ten years younger than I. I recognized in him the oceanic tumult of my own adolescence as a *heimatloss*, penniless refugee. We had been through similar trials. I, too, had had to survive, one way or another. He had learned French very fast and spoke a perfect *argot* with a rather funny American accent. I remember your prophetic phrase, Red, in 1951, when you were stuffed with penicillin, a result of the kind of risk you run in *that* profession. You were thundering at the Picasso exhibition: "Sooner or later, young people will begin to treat society the way Picasso treats reality: they'll smash it to pieces. . . ." His two eldest sons are twins, and one of them lives, or rather hides, in my place in a maid's room, rue du Bac. He was one of the very few people I have ever dared to consider as a true friend—call it misanthropy or overexigence and leave it at that.

I get through to Red at four o'clock, via a call to Los Angeles to get his phone number. The curfew has been announced for four-thirty, by the mayor.

I recognize the warmth in that voice, despite all the years that have gone by. . . .

"You can't come here alone, Romain. You look white."

"I have to see you, and that's all."

"Right now?"

"Yes, right now. I don't have anything special to say to you, so you can see it's really important."

"All right, I'll send some brothers to get you." The American accent is stronger, but Pigalle is still there, and his French is effortless.

I expected to see two fear-inspiring heavies, but the "bodyguards" turned out to be two frail teenagers in a beat-up Chevy. Fifteen, sixteen? But they were apparently exactly what it took, because as we drove along, the young cats who came up to the car with bottles of gasoline walked away again as soon as they heard the magic words which today echo from one end of America to the other: "Soul Brothers." Fascinating, this intrusion of the word "soul" into the language of American blacks, if you recall that the word "soul" until 1860, the date of their liberation, meant "serfs" in Russia. The "soul" was a unit to be bought and sold. The price of a soul at the time of Gogol's *Dead Souls* was, depending on the condition of the merchandise, in the neighborhood of two hundred and fifty rubles, about the equivalent of fifty-five dollars. Soul Brother, Soul Brother. . . . The kids fall back.

A house is burning, but no one is taking notice. Yet only fifty yards farther on a crowd is watching houses burn on a television screen in a store window. The real thing is there, a stone's throw away, but they prefer to watch it on the little screen: it has been specially chosen for them to see, so it's got to be a better show than that house burning near them. "Media" culture at its apogee.

In Red's apartment, there are about ten people: half of the women wear African dress and natural hair. In all my previous years in this country, I had never seen a black American woman without a wig. I had loved black women without knowing that those beautiful, soft tresses were imported from Asia, via Hong Kong. I love women enough to find this modish bushy wilderness on their heads a plus: there seems to be more of the woman, with that growth, and there is never enough of her as far as I am concerned.

They accept me with a trace of irony. There is pride in the air. That slightly condescending and sardonic welcome a civilian is given in a front line H.Q.

Red comes in ten minutes after me. He is now a man of forty-six, but only his face shows the marks of twenty years of political struggle. The strength and power of a body that always brought to my mind centuries of carrying loads, and of *manpower*, in the literal sense of the word, haven't changed since the days of our youth. One of those men whose width

—broad shoulders and massive chest—makes them appear smaller than they are. The features have lost some of their finesse, but not due to fat: they have merely taken on a different kind of hardness, which is no longer the chance result of bone structure and muscles, but comes now from the expression and the will and spirit behind it. He is worried: his wife is about to give birth. He's afraid the clinic may be set on fire. . . .

"You can see what a clever piece of work that would be: have the clinic sent up in smoke by the heat, and then they'll say it's the rioters themselves who burned it."

His French isn't a bit rusty.

"Come on, they won't do that, what the hell."

"No. They probably won't. But it's an idea, *non?*"

For an idea, it is an idea. I settle down on a threadbare armchair. But I'm capable of having ideas, too:

"What if you set fire to the clinic yourselves, so that you could say afterward that it was police provocation?"

"To do that, we'd have to pick a white clinic."

He holds out his pack of cigarettes to me. *Gauloises.* We both laugh.

"When's the baby due?"

"Any time. . . . This is my second wife, and my twelfth kid. I intend to keep at it . . ."

He gives me a light.

"You know, for blacks, the first thing is to screw like mad. That's what it all boils down to: numbers. That means no pill and no diaphragm, no contraception and no abortion. The more we screw, the more we screw them. We've studied the statistics: by screwing all we can, we çan hit the fifty-million mark within ten years . . . almost a quarter of the population. If we forbid even whores to use the pill or a diaphragm . . . within ten years . . ."

I say:

"*C'est du désespoir.* It's sheer despair."

He looks at me with surprise:

"A nigger who isn't desperate is a nigger who's finished."

It is true that in English "desperate" is nearer to "anger" than to "despair," which is wonderfully reassuring.

"You can go all round the problem, you won't find any other solution: genocide or love."

"Red, you know damn well that rich societies never go for genocide. It would be an offense to luxury."

"The only solution to the black problem is between the legs of our women."

"Why not between the legs of white *and* black women?"

"There's no one here, in this room, who doesn't have white blood in him. There's no antibiotic to cure that. But right now, interbreeding is bullshit. Sex has never been less capable of breaking through the barriers."

It's true.

It's an odd paradox, but the more liberal you are, black or white, man or woman, the more committed you are to the civil rights struggle, then the more you avoid interracial sexual relations, so as not to give any substance to the racist arguments. I mean the kind of argument that explains white women's participation in the black struggle by sexual compulsion. Anyhow, with the pill and the diaphragm, all that business of miscegenation is absolutely devoid of a genetic future.

I have often noted a particularly pathetic and painful phenomenon: when you talk with blacks about the white blood in them, they will rarely tell you: "I had a white grandfather," but almost always: "I had a white grandmother or a white great-grandmother." Why? How sad you can be, Truth, and how stupid you often are, Psychology! Not one of the young blacks wants to admit that his mother was screwed by a white. But they seem to derive a satisfaction from the fact that a *white* woman got laid by their black grandfather. . . . A frightening posthumous revenge directed against your own blood.

Red puts his hand on my shoulder.

"Hey, do you realize we've been arguing for three-quarters of an hour and we haven't even talked to each other?"

He shrugs.

"Goddamn awful."

"You can say that again."

It's come to the point when any black and any white who meet here, even if they're the best of friends, always end up talking color. Ralph Ellison, in his powerful book, described the black American as "the invisible man." But what about now that he has become visible? This sudden, new visibility, which, as it increases, tends to make him more and more visible as a black, and less and less visible as an individual. A strange return to the beginning. The black American was reduced to the color of his skin because he had no existence, and here he is again, reduced to his skin once more, because he's beginning to exist more and more as a black.

I tell Red that Maï is sick. I phone her every day in Beverly Hills since my arrival in Washington.

"I think she's going to die. She miaows so sadly on the phone. . . ."

He laughs.

"Ever heard of a cat that miaows cheerfully?"

I feel relieved that in the middle of the violence, scarcely hours after Martin Luther King's death, Red hasn't told me:

"Go ahead. Break my heart. Talk about your sick Siamese cat. It's the right time."

There's an explosion behind my back: one of the men in the room has thrown a bottle into the television set. It hisses, flickers, smokes, and dies a kind of viperine, dragonlike death.

"The bastards."

He is right. Since the assassination, on all the channels, there's an uninterrupted flow of eulogies, praise and noble words for Martin Luther King. Six weeks earlier, Stokely

Carmichael himself, then at the peak of his antiwhite popularity, had called him a "coon." The nonviolence movement was considered finished and its apostle a failure. He only had to die to come to life. The boob-tube is particularly sickening: a nonstop procession of black and white faces singing the praises of the man who, with Malcolm X, had been the most significant and influential leader in decades, with an unerring gift for touching that Jeffersonian something, still so vivid in America's psychological makeup. The cryptlike tone of the announcers, the rose water flowing everywhere, radio, TV, press: the oldest way of making up at the least expense. In all my life, I have never seen anything like that posthumous discovery of a man nobody gave a damn about forty-eight hours earlier. I much preferred the frank stinking cynicism of the white bitch we heard in the lobby of the hotel, after the assassination; it threw Jean into the only physical fight of her life.

"Well, I call that a good job well done."

Red looks out at the kids milling in the street with gasoline cans and bottles in their hands.

"What are your tactics now?"

He shakes his head.

"There're no tactics. Everything is spontaneous. Our people live in a state of constant provocation: that of the wealth of white America pushed in the faces of over twenty million blacks with almost no buying power and stripped of their rights. Do you think we're the ones who got the Watts revolt going, with its thirty-two dead? The real organizers were the white storekeepers who sell their stuff to an underprivileged population, *in poor neighborhoods,* at a cost almost thirty per cent higher than in rich districts. There's no public transportation, so a black brother who doesn't have a car can't get to work, even if he could find work. . . ."

"What about you?"

"I'm recruiting for Vietnam."

I sit there, blinking. This time, although the most profound characteristic of the black situation is its absurdity, I lose all contact with reality. Or with absurdity. Same thing.

"And what the hell does *that* mean?"

"I'm recruiting our kids for Vietnam. . . . Not easy."

He must have caught the frightened look on my face, because he nods in agreement.

"Yes."

There is nothing I find to say, nothing. I sit there in sheer stupidity, then I say feebly:

"What about the Vietnamese? What about them, in all this?"

"Yeah, sure, well, I'll tell you something: right now, I don't give a damn. The only brothers I know as long as the struggle lasts are black. *Black.* I don't give a shit about the others, not one of them, just now, no matter who they are. The only thing that counts is that, thanks to Vietnam, we'll have seventy-five thousand blacks back home, all with the best, the very best training in guerrilla warfare. It sure isn't their intention, but the Pentagon helps us. I mean, the real know-how they give you, fighting in the streets and in the jungle, infiltration and all that, is like building up a professional black army. . . . The best. I reckon that makes us about sixty to seventy-five thousand potential instructors, and each one can set up a combat group here. And that's why I consider any black who wants to prevent our kids from going to fight over there a traitor. If the Vietnam war finished today, it'd be a disaster for us. We need at least three or four years of fighting over there to set ourselves up in a big way. Real big."

"Where will that lead you ultimately?"

" 'Ultimately,' that's just metaphysics, as far as we're concerned."

He hesitates—a flicker of disbelief, of doubt, of "knowing better than that," of American horse sense showing through the fabric of a wild dream:

"But I'll tell you something, *mon vieux* . . ."

He jumps from *argot* to English, and back into French again.

". . . What we're after and what we'll get *ultimately*—that's the word you've come up with, *non?*—is an independent black nation made possible and kept going by white money for at least one generation."

That an old friend like Red, the man who knows me better than all the books I have written know their author, should come up to me with a hymn to the Republic of New Africa shows more than all your studies put together how far that championship contest as to who talks bigger raises the stakes higher and proves himself more demanding and a "hundred per cent black," has gone within the ranks and leadership of Black Power. The greater the frustration, the greater the dream. That is how, behind ghetto walls, Jews became lovers of abstraction, cabalists and Einsteins. An unbearable reality, combined with the impossibility to change it, tends to lead to abstractions for abstraction's sake, and unreality becomes more realistic than reality itself, more true, more convincing, simply because it looks at you with the eyes of justice.

The temptation is to say nothing. This is not logic speaking, it is hurt, and you can't argue with that. But this man is a close friend, and masking your thoughts for tactful reasons of compassion isn't good enough.

"Come on, Red. Not *you* or not *that*. This talk about the Republic of New Africa is really seeking refuge and solace in myths. . . . Messianic talk."

"Look at the Jews. Israel. . . ."

"Listen, maybe someday you will have an all-black 'independent' state in the South. But that can only happen when all 'colossus-nations'—U.S.A., Russia, China, India—

reach that far-far-off stage of our civilization: the end of nationalism and the emergence of local semi-independent communities, a triumph of the human scale over the inhuman monster-states. It is possible, it may happen, but in that context 'black' or 'white' won't mean a thing anyway. It will become totally irrelevant. What I am saying is that a 'black Israel' within America postulates such a change of attitude, tradition and outlook that if and when it takes place, the scope of the mutation it presupposes will make it obsolete, a throwback solution to a no longer existing problem. Right now, all this kind of talk means is putting the screws on white society. Tactics. Nursing a dream at the expense of today's reality. It's harmless. Do I need to point out that Ron Karenga's getting less trouble, to say the least, from the F.B.I. than the Black Panthers who don't talk about carving a 'black state for the blacks' out of America? Ron Karenga's attitude is as *safe* and nonsubversive as Carmichael's when he calls for the destruction of 'all that is white.' That isn't subversion. That's big mouth. No danger there. White smiles all around."

What hurts me is that mask of blankness, that guarded mask on the face of a man who has always trusted me before. . . .

"*Tu vois autre chose, vieux*? Do you see another way out?"

"Yes."

. . . I had left them back there in Paris, 108 rue du Bac, fifth floor, living in those *sous les toits* former servants quarters where all that is young and struggling—the future of France—lives, thinks, and gets ready to take over from us. He is young, black, and American: one of Red's two twin sons, Ballard, aged twenty-two. She is twenty-three, French, white, very white and pretty in that unpretentious, unshowy and moving way a girl's face sometimes achieves, a victory of inner beauty over mere perfection of features.

Ballard is a deserter from the U.S. Army in Germany. The desertion had nothing to do with "protest" or "dissent," with Vietnam or "rejection of American imperialism," as with so many draftees who seek asylum in Sweden or elsewhere. Ballard went A.W.O.L. and became a deserter out of love for a French girl. He had met her in Wiesbaden, where she was *au pair* with a German family. She had been sick, a bout with pneumonia, was told to take a long rest and went back to Paris. Two months after the separation, Ballard *a fait le mur*, as we say in French, "went over the fence" and love took up once again its traditional *La Bohème* quarters under the roofs of Paris, which is the best thing that has ever happened to a roof.

I think of Ballard, sitting on the bed, a hippie medal on his bare chest, and I can almost hear his voice filling with its truth the uneasy, *empty* silence that has fallen between Red and me.

"Fuck 'em all."

He repeats it again and again, scornfully, spitefully, with that angry resentment against all the vicious laws, limitations, and tyrannies man imposes upon his own kind, as if those of nature were not cruel enough.

"Fuck 'em dead. To begin with, I don't want to go kill some yellow son-of-a-bitch as training for killing some white son-of-a-bitch later. I don't dig that. Fuck 'em all good and proper, man, and take 'em away in strait jackets. What I mean is: screw them. Absolutely, I mean, and excuse me if I vomit. You know, there's a limit to everything and when you reach it, there's no more limit. No more limit, it gets so big on you, you just don't give a damn about any of it any longer, because the way shit keeps piling up around you it's not shit no more, it's world government."

He throws his cigarette butt out the window.

"Anyway, I got her pregnant."

Madeleine is washing dishes in the sink by the window.

Her pale soft skin has the kind of smooth matteness that is both light and shadow, evocative of cool fountains, Spanish patios, and Moorish veils. Delicate, fragile bones and that black, flowing hothouse hair of the French girls in Algeria Albert Camus loved so much. . . . Her parents had arrived a few days earlier from Toulouse, where they run a restaurant. They are *Pieds-Noirs*, "black-feet" as the Algerian-born French call themselves, a mixing of some distant Spanish Sanchez with our old Auvergne, that province which has often done for France what a prudent sense of measure can do for true greatness. No one had "warned" them that Ballard was black. They came to see me; we talked about things, then I said, now, this is how it is, he's a Negro.

"Oh well," the father said, and the mother, whose shyness had a nervous smile with a gold tooth in it, didn't show any surprise, shock, or whatever.

And then Madeleine's father said something that frees a man completely from the color of his skin.

"We would like to meet him."

As a rule, in France no less than in America, the words, "a Negro" always seem enough to describe a man in his totality. These French folks from Algeria knew better.

They saw him.

The only thing that upset them was the desertion.

"A man can't do a thing like that to his country," said Mr. Sanchez, whose name, by the way, is not Sanchez.

Ballard looked unhappy.

I said:

"There'll be an amnesty, sooner or later. Vietnam can't go on much longer. . . ."

"And what will happen in the meantime?"

"They can live here. I'll take care of permits. No problem."

. . . I feel this silence between Red and me is driving us apart, it carries us away into exile from each other, it's conning us of twenty years of friendship. But I am wrong: the silence is nothing but a question he won't ask, though it's there all right, behind his sullen, stern expression. The silence is all about Ballard. He can't forgive him his determined pursuit of a *personal* chance, his desertion, both from the Army and from his blackness. He is deeply hurt that his own son should refuse to go and get his "training" as a future Black Power fighter out there in the U.S. "guerrilla school" in the jungles of Vietnam. This grudge or shame is not much different from what a die-hard American flag-waver feels when his son refuses to fight for his country.

"Any news from Philip?"

His face lights up. A smile at first, and then he quickly hides his fatherly pride in a laugh.

"He's doing fine. Learning the ropes. Just grabs as much of it as he can. Two years in the Marines, and now he's got a transfer to a topnotch unit, you know, the best, as good as the Green Berets. *Un vrai mec, celui-là.* He's the real thing."

My mind goes blank. This is one of those situations where I am losing contact not only with reality, but with the human brain itself. The perfect logic of this absurdity, the paradox, the unreality of this overly realistic logic which makes a father smile contentedly because his son is an American hero, a member of a crack unit, out there, in Vietnam, and thus getting "topnotch" training which he will then put to good use fighting white America, raises a question that is no longer merely one of ideology, dialectics, tactics, or fanaticism, but the question of our brain itself.

It becomes more and more obvious to me that all ideologies raise the question of the nature of our brain every time they raise the question of the nature of our society. With the weight of available information and evidence, it is difficult to deny the flagrantly apparent fact—from Auschwitz to Prague, and from Vietnam to racism—that our intelligence is the victim of a persistent, hereditary, genetic flaw in our brain, of which our intelligence itself is unaware at the very moment it carries out the orders it receives from that original *defect*. In Red's case, in the face of such absurd, delirious and yet at the same time perfectly practical, sensible logic, it is really the human brain crying out for help. The pride, the satisfaction, the fatherly smile, all this because his son has become a hero killing "Charley" as "training" for the future black-against-white battles in the streets of American cities. . . . A world of phantasies, a groping for a fourth dimension by a mind and a soul caught within a three-dimensional ghetto, and seeking an emergency exit through the realistic planning of unreality.

What made all this so difficult for me to bear was not merely the quality of despair so perceptible in this groping for a transcendental, almost mythological way out. It was the very presence of Red, his earthy, massive, solid physical aura of a born fighter, the kind you can see in Diego Rivera frescoes of Mexican workers and peasants. If only Red had the hate-filled, tight-lipped, sharp-featured, white-burning physique of a fanatic, of one of our French ideological abstraction addicts, the whole thing would have been much more *normal* in its abnormality, more acceptable and easier to bear. But my friend had the strong, self-assured presence of a man whose feet are firmly on the ground and whose head is far removed from the clouds of bloody phantasies and messianic idealism.

I look at the black men and women around me, almost asking for help. But we're speaking French and they are out of it. African dress, African hair, earrings, one wonders at the absence of tribal scars. And under this disguise, the presence of what is most typically and authentically American: its black people. A strength of belief, an idealism untouched by sophisticated worldliness, and the total absence in their vocabulary of the one word that is the a-b-c of

France: skepticism. The quality of sacred naïveté that has carried mankind victoriously through defeat ever since it first crawled out of the primeval sea and which, once upon a time was the hallmark of the American Dream.

I am fighting desperately to control my urge to tell him the truth, the blunt, hard, sobering truth about his son, his *American* son.

He is a hero all right.

I saw in Paris a few of Philip's letters to his brother. I have one right under my eyes, as I write this. The letter is dated September, 1967. At that time, Ballard was still with the Army in Germany.

Here it is:

> I keep hearing all kinds of talk about "deserters." Sweden they say, is full of them. Well, we don't have any of that here. We never had one in my outfit. That just don't happen. But fellows keep hearing about it in the news they get from home, so maybe it's true. There are guys who are just born civilians, they have no guts, they have no business being in the Army. We have nothing but real fighting men here. The best. Volunteers, no draftees, no snot-nosed kids. The real thing.

And hear this: Philip plans to *stay* in the Army. He wants to make the Army his career. He repeats that over and over again in all his letters to Ballard. I know nothing of what his original intentions were when he volunteered, but this I do know: a black man has found his true place as a man, as an American, by taking the oldest road to man's "virile brotherhood": which is killing a "common enemy." You give people a "common enemy" and you give them equality, virile comradeship, and brotherhood. That's how it's always been and that's how it still is. You get yourself a common enemy and brotherhood sets in. Nothing surprising there: brotherhood isn't made for dogs.

Any son-of-a-bitch like myself who has been bombing and killing right and left for many years will tell you that if it's brotherhood you want, you will find it in combat units. There were no French, Arabs, Jews, or blacks in the Foreign Legion shock troops or in my "Lorraine" squadron. There were only brothers who killed and got killed. I am not quite sure that's what General Eisenhower had in mind when he said: "There are no atheists in fox-holes."

I don't remember having ever experienced such a surge of compassion, warmth, and of love comparable in its close-to-tears intensity to what I felt as I stood there listening to Red rave on at me in blind, mad ignorance of the all too human truth about that son of his out there in Asia "learning the job." It was so clear, so unbearably clear that, in his imagination, Philip was to become one day something like Black Power's Che Guevara. And that crazy hope, born out of centuries of subhuman, inhuman, devirilization, was burning in the eyes of one of the most hard-headed, practical, realistic men I have ever known, a man who had in him the makings of a great American statesman.

"That skunk hardly writes me any more. *Too busy,* I *guess. . . ."*

Translation: Too busy killing Charley, too busy learning the job. . . .

". . . But then, they've got military censorship out there, so he can't write what he really feels. They've taken him out of combat right now. You know, Phil reminds me of your Ben Bella. An N.C.O. in the French Army, fifteen years of service, all the French medals you can think of, all this to learn patiently, cunningly, how to kick you out of Algeria. . . ."

Then, suddenly, quietly:

"How's Ballard?"

"He's going to marry the girl."

"Won't work. Never does. He'll end up the way I started over there. Kept by whores."

"I don't think so."

He shrugs me off.

"He'll end up kept by that girl who'll be turning tricks in Pigalle. They haven't got a chance."

"His in-laws'll look after them if he can't find work."

He stares at me with disbelief.

"You mean they approve of the marriage?"

"Yes. They think Phil's all right."

He mulls it over, obviously confused. France is not a monolithic country. There aren't only bastards there. The one credit you have to give that old country is that it is a thousand things and not all of them stink, which is about the closest you can get to civilization.

"Phil's thinking about officer's rank. *Il va passer officier. Il est malin, ce salaud-là. . . .* He's a smart one."

The smile tries to be cynical, but the pride isn't. I think of a good American father, star-spangled banner and don't ask what your country can do for you, ask what you can do for your country. . . .

Flaring up again:

"Blacks who holler against the war in Vietnam are playing white America's game. This war is the best thing that ever happened to us. Every time they talk peace, I get scared. . . . Jesus, we're being given our best chance ever and we've got to grab it with both hands. Best training in the world for our revolution, that's what Vietnam is. . . ."

Madeleine had lent me a few of the letters Philip had written to his twin, and they are here in front of me. The letters are full of *we*. "We do what we can to help these people here, but they have to help themselves, *we* can't keep doing their work for them. . . . *We* try to fight corruption, but *it just seems to be part of their nature.* . . ." A black man writing about a different race with unmistakable superiority. . . . "*We* can't stay here forever, so they've got to learn democracy. . . . *We.* . . ."

I begin to panic in the little living room, stuffy and hot,

with that eternal box of the air conditioner against the window and why is it that manufacturers can't design something less repulsive in its ugliness? A wild beating of the heart, a choking feeling: my old mysterious claustrophobia is at my throat again. Something in me is there as if by mistake, trapped, locked up and trapped within a human shape and skin. Something in me has blundered into a man's makeup. Call it "soul," for lack of a more scientific word, and leave it at that.

"I'll drive you to your hotel."

We leave. As we walk downstairs—everything that has four or five stories in America speaks of the nineteenth century—he suddenly asks, with a trace of irony:

"How's your white dog coming along?"

I stop and blink at him.

"Now how the devil . . . ?"

"Jean told me about it a month ago, in L.A. Heartbreaking, eh? *Ca crève le coeur.*"

I don't like that mean smile.

"Yes, Red, we are what is known in France as 'bleeding liberals.' . . . Come to think of it, I prefer bleeding to blood baths."

He pats me on the shoulder.

"Come on. You won't hear a word from me against liberals. Sure, they're ineffectual. Inefficient. But they're the buffer *tiers parti,* third estate between reaction and us, they've always been that. Reactionaries always had to cut through liberals to get at the activists and it drives them nuts, because it tears the mask off their faces and reveals them as reactionaries. . . . I know how you feel about that pooch."

"The dog is being re-educated."

"Fine, great. What about re-educating the environment?"

"I've got a dog on my hands, not a historical task."

"How's Jeannie?"

"Great. Lovely. . . . All I want is a little peace and quiet."

"Yeah, I hear there's a hormonal slow-down after fifty."

"*Va te faire foutre.* Screw you."

He shakes his hand and goes "tsk-tsk" with an expression of wonder.

"I must say, that idea of dousing a dog with gasoline and setting it on fire. . . . Poor Jean, she was shaken. . . ."

I don't know what the hell he's talking about, but this is not exactly the time to ask questions about what I take to be a metaphor.

It's not every day that it is given to you to see a civilization blow sky-high just when it is at the peak of its wealth, world influence, and power.

XI

At every street corner cops are chatting, looking bored or laughing in their half-tracks, watching absent-mindedly or with amusement as store windows are smashed with bricks or iron bars. The most unusual audience this new kind of "living theater" ever had.

What is immediately apparent when a race riot reaches its maximum intensity is the "every man for himself" aspect. Looters of all ages—I saw a crippled, arthritic Methuselah helping himself to some psychedelic neckties—crash into each other, elbow each other out, ignore each other, or quarrel violently over goods in an "I saw it first" argument. Housewives look as if they were merely out shopping in the chaos of overturned shelves and merchandise. Businesslike ladies with families back home go about it reasonably, discriminatingly, not just grabbing whatever there is in a panic of greed, but carefully choosing the best and the most practical, what they really need, after thinking things over a good while. There are those who lose their heads and who aren't even aware of what they are grabbing, and those who seem to be shopping peacefully, looking at labels, prices, and trying things on.

This is not a rebellion: this is response. The rage of looting is the natural response of countless consumers that our baiting society of provocation incites in every possible way to buy without giving them the means to do so.

I call "society of provocation" an affluent society given to constant exhibitionism of its wealth, summoning one and all to acquisitions, possessions, and materialistic enjoyment through high-pitched never-easing-off advertising and tempting, teasing displays of goods and a continuous show of riches in the streets, while at the same time refusing all possibility of keeping up with this challenge, in terms of satisfaction, to a considerable segment of the population. Millions of underprivileged, frustrated people are both incited to possess and denied possession, teased and refused satisfaction, which means perfect psychological and social conditions for either neurosis or revolt, or both. Advertising and the exhibition of wealth becomes a summons to progress or to a revolution, a call to social justice or the overthrow of society.

Who can pretend to be surprised when a kid from a black ghetto surrounded by a materialistic carnival of luxury stores, restaurants, supermarkets, super-cars, a whole merchandising universe in which everything has been professionally designed to whet your appetite and make you "go for it," actually does so, with the only means available to him in the situation of neglect, frustration and rejection, breaking through the economic barrier by smashing windows and looting? The entire "civilization" around him is totally bent on convincing him that he cannot do without this or that, the latest "must" from General Motors, Westinghouse, a grocery store, when the TV and radio and all the imaginable means of advertising and conditioning to "buy" bait him and goad him and, in fact, order him to "go get it, get it, get it."

And bear in mind that America as a whole, with its glut of prosperity, has the same effect on the masses of the under-developed, starving "third world" as a Fifth Avenue luxury store on the psyche of a Harlem kid.

This continuous provocation is an entirely new phenomenon in our civilization, if only because of the proportions it has taken. It's the equivalent of a call to rape.

In the smoking streets through which we are driving, the big grab is on and no one really cares what he grabs as long as it is possessions. Can you tell me what that long-necked boy with a purposeful, businesslike expression on his intellectual-looking face plans to do with the naked store dummy he is carrying under his arm? Somebody has already ripped the clothes off it and all the poor thing's got to offer is a kind of trophy of wax ass and wax tits. And what about that happily, proudly parading fellow with a cigar in his mouth and nine or ten wastepaper baskets piled up in his arms? Possession, period. Get it, man, get it. I can understand far better the other fellow over there, walking away with a load of toilet-paper rolls: there's no telling what the future will be made of. Small kids, their faces smeared with jam, are breaking bottles of gefiltefish and gobbling up the fish on the spot, while a fat, bespectacled lady lifts a tiny pair of black lace panties to her bulging middle and her neighbor meditates over a handful of drugstore costume jewelry with all the concentration of Hamlet looking at that no less trashy skull. And here is another thoughtful "client" who, after feeling a melon, shaking it, and listening to it, puts it aside and picks out another . . . while the kids on the rampage smash another shop window.

Who says they're looting? They are *obeying*. They are answering in the only way they can the "come and get it" call raised around them night and day, through months and years, by all the mass media; they are carrying out the orders of our merchandising hell. Looting is a triumph of subliminal persuasion.

Red is driving the Chevy at a snail's pace. He nods toward some youths throwing melons against the window of an office-supplies store.

"Do you realize they don't even know half of the time what started this?"

He steps down hard on the brakes, stops the car.

"You don't believe me, *pas vrai?* Right, let's ask 'em."

He leans out and gestures to the kids. Fifteen, sixteen? These are alley cats, shaved heads, watchful, suspicious eyes. . . .

"Tell me, sonny, you know who Martin Luther King was?"

"No Sir."

"And you?"

"No Sir."

A third boy comes by, his face still tight with excitement at the "come and get it."

"He's just been killed."

"You know who he was?"

A moment of hesitation. Then it comes, spontaneous, entirely devoid of any personal knowledge, thinking or caring, the kid merely comes up with what he must have heard so often:

"He was an Uncle Tom."

While I choke, Red shuts the door and steps on the gas.

"He was an Uncle Tom. . . ." Coretta King's face passes in front of me, perhaps the most beautiful woman's face that I have seen in my lifetime in its sorrow and quiet anguish. It evokes for me the essence of mythological femininity from Ruth to all the Queens of Judea and Egypt, a face that an immortal picture taken during her husband's funeral, revealed to the world. An expression of dignity in suffering that all our wretched Michelangelos and Bellinis and all our professional *Pietàs* have striven in vain to create.

I am overwhelmed by sheer, blind fury. It is aimed at nothing and all things, it has no target or visible enemy, it is the hate of a dog looking for a throat. It is the hatred which gets hold of me whenever I am once again confronted with a manifestation of our greatest spiritual force, which is Stupidity.

"Red, there was a lot of black fiendishness directed against King. You don't think that the murderer——"

"Could be. A nigger, yes, could be. But niggers are all the white man's work. We're *blacks*. You've turned some of us into niggers——"

"Hey——"

"What is it?"

"Only, that's the first time you included me in 'them.'"

"Come on, that's just a way of talking."

A group of teenagers come out of a drugstore they're looting, their arms full of boxes of Kotex and Tampax. I double up with laughter. Red shrugs.

"Nothing funny there. Sanitary napkins are great for making Molotov cocktails. They hold the gasoline better."

We drive now through a quiet, empty street, turn left and then . . . Red stops the car.

What follows may or may not be what I am tempted to call "the truth about Stokely Carmichael." I am inclined to think I give him too much credit.

I don't believe the man has got a black future.

Let me make myself clear. Carmichael is the kind of "enemy" a white-superiority establishment should cherish and strive to protect. His total rejection of, in his own terms,

"everything that is white," including the "Marxist" and therefore "white doctrine" orientation of the Black Panthers, is an
extremely comfortable cop-out: the sort of "ideological"
stand so totally devoid of any danger for white society
or of any constructive hope for the blacks that it is difficult
to imagine a safer, more hypocritically calculating position
for a black "militant" in America. It is a *de luxe* ivory tower
attitude that has the great advantage of looking like an avant-
garde fighting position. It is white smoke in black people's
eyes. During the last two years, after a pioneering period in
the thick of the battle—is it because things became too hot
and dangerous for a man having made such a loving investment in himself?—he suddenly rose above the mêlée, the
blood and the jails to the perfectly harmless and safe heights
of the "all that is white is unacceptable" position. Getting
fat somewhere out there in Africa, at the patrician Nkrumah's
court, the same Nkrumah whose chief doctor and personal
physician was the infamous assistant to Dr. Mendele in the
Nazi "medical" extermination camps, and whose pilot was the
favorite lady pilot of Hitler. Carmichael's facile and no doubt
fruitful anti-Semitism is a pathetic "You-show-me-yours-I'll
show-you-mine" kindergarten stuff. Admittedly, there are
some tragic Jews and Negroes who feel they will never
achieve true psychological "equality" unless they can be
Nazis too. "I'm so free, folks, so equal, that behold! I too can
be a Nazi." "Everything that is white should be destroyed" is
an ideological platform that is "gaming niggers" and, as far as
purpose, help, hard work, fighting or you name it, is concerned, amounts to sybaritical collaboration with white
elite society. It smacks of scorn for the black intelligence
and common sense and sinks to conning. When you read
Eldridge Cleaver's letters and writings from exile, there is
one thing, at least one, that you know: here is a man saying
to America: "This is also my land, I built it with my black
hands and I want it back." It is an infinitely more difficult,

courageous, exigent, and danger-wrought position than playing court jester to Nkrumah.

I saw Carmichael with my own eyes, standing in front of a department store with a group of some fifty to seventy youngsters. He was screaming. I have no right to put together the words I was able to catch only now and then, and I have to fall back on the reports of a black journalist present for such words as were published in the press.

The scenario may be summarized as follows: appearance of Carmichael in the street among the young rioters. He goes into a department store and orders the staff to leave and close shop. He walks back into the street and—here again, I am quoting the *black* reporter—he starts waving a small-caliber gun, shouting: "What are you doing here empty-handed? Go back home and get your 'pieces!' "

At that moment, one of the kids pulls a gun from his pocket and shows it. A police car is fifty yards away. Stokely's reaction, according to the press:

"No! I don't want to see one drop of black blood lost here!"

I have no way of knowing—unfortunately, for it would be to Carmichael's great credit—if this account is correct. But if the press can be trusted, the episode is of capital importance to all those who wish to understand the extraordinary verbal violence of the black militants and its remarkable achievements. I have heard them yell at me time and time again in my own apartment in Paris that America is in for rape, murder, and all-out "kill and get killed."

The psychological result of this is evident to all those who take the trouble to meet young black people. That result is a total break with the past, white-inbred feelings of inferiority and of "you-are-a-nigger" guilt. The Jewish people have been through it. If you repeat over centuries to a human being "you are subhuman," it is hard for the person concerned not to be *persuaded*, not to feel subhuman and even to behave as a subhuman creature. Innumerable Jews have been, throughout the ages, thus "persuaded" by Christian anti-Semites, to the point that many gave in to self-hatred and some began to conform to the anti-Semitic persuasive caricature of the lowly Jew: they became Shylocks and Fagins. Their sense of dignity had been destroyed and they became distorted and lowly.

This has also been the black man's lot. But it is over, very much over, and this is the achievement of the "murderous" all-defying appeals to violence of people like Rap Brown, the early Stokely Carmichael and, above all, the Black Panthers. *The verbal violence, so infuriating to whites, not merely reduced the need for physical violence*—how many whites have black radicals actually killed over the years, including the police, in politically motivated aggressions?—*but it succeeded in giving the young blacks a feeling of total psychological equality with the whites.* This is the black revolution that has *actually taken place.* The rest may be even more difficult to achieve, but at least the civil rights battle won't be fought by losers.

Far from provoking "massacres"—where are they?—the incendiary verbal violence of the ghetto leaders removes the need for physical violence.

What is called "ghetto rhetoric" stems from the psychological need to *dare.*

It is not simply "letting off steam." It is taking your testicles out of hock.

Carmichael's attitude in the street was typical of this "reconquest of your soul." He hurries into that store, gets the whites out, orders the doors closed. Back among the youthful crowd, he sends them home "to get your weapons," —("pieces") while, nine times out of ten, none of them have any, which amounts to clearing the street. When one of the youngster shows suddenly a mean-looking pistol Carmichael yells, "No, not a drop of black blood is going to be lost here,"

I

which, while unquestionably saving the kid's life, saves white lives as well. And yet, the purpose has been achieved and a major psychological battle won: there are very few young "niggers" left in America today. And fewer young "Toms."

And there is also that unbelievable verbal inflation of our time, the swelling of words beyond all reality of meaning, which seems to portend some total exhaustion of vocabulary to be followed, hopefully, by some at least approximate authenticity that has almost completely gone out of the relationship between word and truth. The extravagant claims of both commercial advertising and political propaganda have broken any link of authenticity between the product pushed by the big sell, deodorant or ideology or President, and its true nature. The toothpaste, the ideology, or the leader that will "save" teeth or humanity run neck to neck in the race away from truth and reality, and even Pope Paul VI himself, alas, doesn't lag far behind. Did he not announce the other day that the revolt of the Dutch clergy against the rule of celibacy is a "crucifixion" of the Church?

Who can top that?

Or must one really remind the Pope what the crucifixion was?

It is in the context of this mountainous swelling of words which have become tinsel wrappings over any kind of merchandise put on the commercial or political market, in this perspective of constant escalation in search of superlatives, with the price of words, in terms of true meaning, getting cheaper and cheaper, that the so-called incitations to murder or violence of the black extremists should be viewed, for, after all, there has been so far no irreparable passage from word to deed. Let's say that there is about as much "deed" in the Black Panther's bloody words as there is actual "deed" in our words like democracy, freedom, dignity, brotherhood, peace . . . you name it, we've got it.

Red lets me off at the Hilton. I get out and am about to

tell him *"Mon vieux*, be careful," but the comical enormity of this kind of advice to a man in his position reminds me of the advice my mother gave me during the war. I was returning from leave, heading back into the thick of anti-aircraft shells, low-level bombing and German fighter attacks, and my mother told me: "Don't forget to put your scarf on when you go flying, you've always had a delicate throat."

"Red, what is the truth? Even if you get twenty-five thousand black Vietnam 'pros' in your ranks, there'll still be a hundred thousand Vietnam 'pros' facing them. . . ."

The face is all closed up. I had never seen him sad before; all the black sadness went into the blues or was swallowed long ago. Have you met any "sad" black kids recently? Whatever you may have read in their expression, it wasn't sadness, I bet. Sadness, that was niggers.

"Well, if we fail . . ."

There's a moment of hesitation, as he stares at me. I believe that for one brief second he is seeing me as a white man. But it's a twenty-year-old friendship, and there is no black and white in *that*.

"I don't think it matters much if we *fail* now. . . . We've achieved something like a total victory: there are no more niggers among our youngsters. Okay, so we'll fail. *We* . . . the ones they call the 'extremists,' the 'radicals.' So what? It means that we've done for the moderates everything they would never have been able to do without us. *Sans nous* . . . without us, they wouldn't have a chance. *Grâce à nous, ils vont pouvoir jouer.* . . . Thanks to us, they may be able to make it. In the case of the black revolution, extremists do the dirty work for the moderates."

"Salut."

"Salut."

The Chevy drives away.

XII

Back in my suite and ten minutes later, I find myself pulling hard on my leash, trying to hold back an itching right foot as it pleads to kick in the ass one of those big Hollywood stars, all wrapped up in their egos, princes of nothing enthroned in that alcohol-swollen, stinking "Kingdom of I." There they dwell in the constant fear that for a few seconds the world may be caught thinking of something else besides them. He is to play the male lead in a picture with Jean which I have written and am supposed to direct, and he has flown in from Hollywood for discussions about his and Jean's parts and the relationship between the two characters. For the last two days he has been hanging around talking "psychological background" while the riot-torn city echoes with fear, rage, and anguish around us. One of those incredible sub-products of the Actor's Studio technique, which plays "psychological reality" with its students, mixing psycho-drama and group analysis in an attempt to hit upon that "inner truth" and "authenticity" which amount to a pains-takingly nurtured neurosis; a search for "reality" and "identity," the results of which can be observed in a genera-tion of actors who have broken with both, and whose never ending "what the hell am I all about" results in a total preoccupation with themselves.

Ever since his arrival here, the guy has been rapping about a love scene in the script that he hadn't "cracked" yet, and that he wanted to rehearse with Jean, to "live" it. Here he was once more, waiting for me in my suite, soaking in bourbon.

On the TV screen, the open coffin, the face of Martin Luther King and the slow march of people filing past it, black faces of all ages, with, often, that total blankness, that lack of expression, which is to a human face what silence is to the lack of adequate words. But the whiskey-guzzling King of I has other fish to fry. His eyes have that oily pale-ness, both transfixed and translucent in their coagulated blue, of the confirmed alcoholic. He prattles on and on. All he wants is to rehearse the love scene with my wife in his bedroom, that's why he flew here. He is bitter, shocked in his depths of artistic integrity, because Jean Seberg re-fuses to come to his bedroom and perform. She'll do it, she says, but only if the director is present. Now, he doesn't want any goddamn director bothering him; there's got to be a real feeling of intimacy there, a truly genuine approach, see? It's essential that the two actors get to know each other. I mean, get real close, find out how they really react to each other, small things, you know, how each of them goes about it, the gestures, the movements, we've got to feel each other, to live the situation, so that later, when filming, there's a point of reference, a bond of experience, something to fall back on. . . . Couldn't I, as a creative person myself, convince Jean to go down to his suite for a bit of rehearsing?

In short, this little son-of-a-bitch whore is asking me to persuade my wife to get laid by him.

On the TV screen, the dead face of Martin Luther King.

The King of I doesn't give a damn. Not one glance. Glass in hand and glassy-eyed, he raps on, working himself up to a kind of verbal climax. You can feel the fear of the sex act and the need for verbal self-reassurance.

My hands are almost pulling away from me, little animals tugging on their leash, they're after that bottle, grab it, hit the idiot over the head, come on. . . .

The whole business would have been farcical, but for the dead face of the apostle of nonviolence on the TV screen.

Nonviolence, nonviolence . . . Dr. King, did you really know what brute animal force within us you were trying to exorcise?

"We can't reach any kind of authenticity, of artistic integrity, unless we have a point of reference in reality. Jean doesn't seem to get that, I'm a bit disappointed in her *as an actress. . . .*"

Jesus Christ, holy Moses, and all the saints, help me. . . . I rivet my eyes on the biblical face of Coretta King. . . . Nonviolence, help me please!

I make a compromise.

A kick in the ass isn't really *violence*. It's good-natured, sort of. And it's refreshing to have an ice bucket emptied on your face, while you're trying to pick yourself up from the floor.

I even help him back on his feet.

My movie fell through right there and then. It was never to be made. The most expensive kick in the ass in the history of butt, since the movie was budgeted for three million dollars.

I switch off the TV. I feel that those dead eyes saw me do it. How do you get rid of the world, good God? Peace. All I want is a little peace and quiet.

It was that night, as I was undressing, that Red's mysterious little phrase flashed through my mind.

"Jean, what's that about pouring gasoline over a dog and setting it on fire? You spoke to Red about it."

When Jean looks guilty, you'd think she was eight years old.

"I didn't tell you about it because you would've thrown one of your fits."

"Well, what is it?"

Most of our friends knew about our "problem" dog and so did some of our neighbors on Arden. I was somewhere between India and Thailand when a group of young white radicals knocked at Jean's door. There were four or five of them and the most articulate member of the group was the son of a wealthy businessman whose magnificent estate on Crestwell Drive reigns in tropical splendor among its exotica of plants, trees, rock gardens, pools, high above the green lovely lanes of Cherokee and Beaumont. This is one of those corners of the world where beauty dwells, and I would often drive up into the hills and sit there in my car soothing my inner turmoils with all that loveliness.

Jean had asked the youngsters in. The cautious, if not downright hostile, French way of talking to strangers through a barely open door goes down badly with Americans. They are very hospitable people, which explains all the murders.

"Miss Seberg, we're from the S.D.S., Students for a Democratic Society, I'm sure you know. We know you try to help the movement. Right now, we're building a common front with all those who are against the war in Vietnam, for a nationwide protest. . . ."

Jean told me the boy was a strikingly handsome fellow

and this may sound irrelevant, but it isn't as far as Seberg is concerned. She suffers from a bad case of "sympathy at first sight" and has in her that streak of romanticism which tends to confuse physical beauty with that of the inner treasures of the human soul. I say this without a trace of irony for her idealism, but with a deep resentment for all those who are not like her. Idealism, liberalism, and the general mixing up of humanitarian emotions with ideas is considered today as a "dogoodnik's" opiate by all honest-to-God shit-eating realists. I happen to believe firmly that man, in terms of culture, liberty, and dignity, is incompatible with realism and that it is almost totally irrelevant to argue if such a man exists; it is enough to build a civilization around this nonexistence. If God has failed, it is not because He does not exist: it is because humanity has never been able to behave as if God did exist. A good Christian is not a man whose purpose in life is to prove the existence of God.

"We're trying to reach people, Miss Seberg. Their sensitivity, I mean. Hit that nerve, you know. If you could spare us a few minutes. . . . As an action, you'll immediately understand how dramatic and effective our demonstration can be . . ."

"Sit down."

They did. No doubt Sandy went round shaking hands. Would you like a drink? The bastards . . .

Batka was back at Noah's Ark. Anyway, those white kids would have run no risks. They smelled real good.

"I believe you have a vicious dog and you want to get rid of it."

The guy was stroking Sandy. Sandy offered him his paw. That dog loves everybody, which I consider a lack of loyalty.

"I don't see what my dog has to do with Vietnam," Jean said.

"You see, for years we've been burning the people over there with napalm. Whole villages. People read this in the paper over breakfast, watch it on TV, and don't give a damn. It just doesn't get through to them, it's become part of the daily routine; in fact, they look at it and it's become so familiar they can't see it, really, any longer. It's a thing that has lost its reality. Now, all these people who no longer react to burning people with napalm would raise a terrible howl if the same thing was done to a dog. *That* would be cruelty, man, real cruelty! They'll suddenly get an idea of what's going on in Vietnam. So we're going to get a few dogs, douse them with gasoline, set them alight, and send them running in front of TV cameras so that this whole nation will see it. . . . We know you're for peace, Miss Seberg, so we thought you might like to participate by giving us your dog."

. . . The year was 1968, if you count only Jesus Christ.

"Get the hell out of here," Seberg told them.

"That's an instinctive, irrational reaction, Miss Seberg. Why don't you give it some thought? These tactics call for a correct critical analysis, and you can't deny that if the war in Vietnam is shortened if only by a day, the sacrifice of a few dogs. . . ."

"I never said I was a Marxist-Leninist," she told them.

"We know that. We are merely appealing to your *humanitarian* feelings."

Jean was up in arms and I wish I had been there. Though I must say her sweet face is not made for hate.

"Your little stunt is the same kind that leads to lies in the name of truth, Stalin, the hanging of Slansky in Prague in the 'higher interest of the party.' You've come to the wrong person. I'm just not political enough for shit."

They got up. One of them even came up with an admirable statement:

"Vietnam is not even a matter of politics any longer. It's a matter of human decency."

You may think the whole incident was nothing but a

student's prank, or even a "woolly-headed liberal's" provocation by some staunchly patriotic kids on a film star who dares to take herself seriously. I must dispel your illusions on that score. This was a true, die-hard, sincere "antiwar," "anti-man's-inhumanity" manifestation. It has since been carried out elsewhere, and only recently in Berlin, and the papers reported these *facts* in November, 1969.

I was away and these young "left-of-the-left" Nazis were able to leave the house without a memorable handshake.

We flew back to L.A. the next day and after leaving Jean at Arden, I drove directly to the kennel.

XIII

I confess that the White Dog was assuming symbolic proportions in my mind and you may well shrug them off and show the usual patronizing impatience of a die-hard, feet-on-the-ground realist for those whom you see as more inclined toward "poetic justice" than to everyday humble struggles and truth. I am not apologizing for myself, as I am certainly more impatient with myself than those who, after all, don't have to live with me the way I have to. I am sorry to be the kind of democrat who believes that the aim of democracy is to make not only Man, but also man, to make all men aristocrats. I cannot see democracy as anything other than an ultimate nobility. And, of course, America is the only nation in history to have *started* out as a democracy. What happens here is the world.

Besides, my nerves, which are supposed to be of steel, had begun to give way. I have never had a crack-up here, but this is a country famous for its "know-how."

There were nights when I would wake up in nameless terror, a terror that was animal in its refusal to obey rational, lucid thinking. Why should I deny that I was identifying myself with that dog in his cage, unable to formulate the question that was torturing him, and without a master capable of answering the "Why?" that is the only question worth asking on this earth? There were moments in Washington when I felt certain that they—either Jack or Keys—had put White Dog to sleep out of sheer mercy, because he has been ruined forever, and nothing but death could be a solution. I remembered the nice, young German whom I had heard talking in a train compartment, on my way back from Sweden, in 1937. "Now, sure, this is not the Jews' fault. You can't really blame them. They've been made the way they are by other people. They've been spit upon and told they were *drek* for a thousand years, and they've become just that, *drek*, through sheer persuasion. *Ja,* they've been persuaded, convinced, or whatever you may call it. But the point is they fit the image. They're too far gone, you can't undo that. You can't change them. I really think all you can do is to kill them off painlessly, out of sheer mercy." I had attacked the guy with a beer bottle and spent five days in jail in Düsseldorf.

I had kept calling Carruthers on the phone from wherever I happened to be during those months and he kept answering patiently: "Get off my back. Keys is the one who handles the dog now. He's in charge."

Keys. I had never met a man who had that kind of . . . of symmetry with me. That is the best way I can put it.

It is Sunday and there is no one at the ranch.

The caretaker, Fred Tatum, is an old trapeze artist from Ringling Bros. times. He must be over seventy. Yes, Keys is taking good care of the dog. The old man falls silent, chews his tobacco, and looks as if he wants to say more, but thinks better of it, mumbles some appropriate remarks about the smog that bitches up the spring and hands me the key.

Batka's warm welcome is up to my expectations, an affectionate nudging, smelling, licking, with his paws on my shoulder. I notice that he looks in great shape, well-fed, contented, his coat shining with good health. Then he runs to his leash and looks at me meaningfully. A few barks inviting me for a nice walk. I take him for a run in Griffith Park and he frisks about happily for an hour reveling in the good outdoor smells. On the way back, I stop at Hugh's Market for some groceries, leaving the dog in the car.

I must have spent a quarter of an hour shopping. When I come back to the parking lot, I see that Batka has escaped from the car, after pushing the window down, probably with his muzzle. I had left it a bit open to give the dog some air.

There is a baby carriage parked against the wall, no doubt by one of those young mothers in bright pants wandering around the market, and Batka is up on his hind legs, his front paws against the carriage, peering inside with keen interest. I smile and start walking toward the carriage, and then . . .

I don't think I have ever felt so scared in my life and yet, God knows . . .

I am paralyzed with fear, holding my shopping bags under my arms, my whole body turned into ice . . .

It's a black baby.

Batka's nose is barely a few inches from the little face and comes closer . . .

And then . . .

White Dog glances at me, bright-eyed, as if amused, as if inviting me to share in a good joke.

Then he turns his mug back toward the baby, wags his tail, and proceeds to lick the little black face.

My relief and gratitude are such that I feel my face going to pieces.

I walk to the dog and take him gently by the collar.

His ears are pricked up and he has that bright, expectant look of a dog who has found a playmate. The baby kicks his feet and laughs. Batka sniffs him and tries to lick his face again.

I drag him away to the car, get inside, shut the door and sit there for a long while, drained of all strength.

I snap out of it and drive slowly toward the valley. I keep a loving hand on the dog's head for company. I give a full account of the miracle to Tatum, but the old boy doesn't seem too happy. A kind of mute disapproval. He keeps looking oddly at Batka.

"Animals," he says vaguely. "Yeah, I know animals, known 'em all my life. You can make 'em do anything."

Cold bastard.

I waited impatiently for Jean to come home to give her the exciting news. White Dog was on the way to complete recovery. Now admittedly, it wasn't a real full-size black, it was only a baby, but you have to begin somewhere. . . . She didn't appear overenthusiastic. She listened with a tired air, took off her shoes, and said with a trace of irritation:

"Big deal. At this rate it's going to take seventy-five years. Who wants to wait?"

To my surprise, "Noah" Jack Carruthers came up with almost the same reaction, the next morning.

"Yeah, well, if we're to begin at the cradle, there'll be lots of fun."

Jackie-boy had greeted me with one of his sour here-comes-my-toothache-again expressions. I seemed to have a nauseating effect on him, like drinking a glass of vinegar slowly. True, he was in good company. There was a whole population of baby chihuahuas at the infirmary. He was feeding them with a dropper. At the back of the room, the vet and Terry were attending Miss Bo, the distinguished lady chimpanzee whom you may have seen on TV in an ad urging you to brush your teeth with the newest "hundred per cent better" toothpaste, with enzymes of course. Miss Bo had swallowed a whole tube of the stuff, including the tube, and was in the middle of a stomach-pumping session.

"I'll tell you one thing, Gary."

Americans have a way of changing my perfectly Russian name—*gari,* meaning burn, in Russian, as in "burn, baby, burn"—into a typically American "Gary" by shifting the accent from the second to the first syllable. My ego thus feels the humiliation of being reduced to the lowest common denominator of American first names.

"I'll tell you, Gary, you have no use for animals."

"Ask my friends if that's true."

"I don't care. That dog's become an abstraction for you. Some kind of crappy symbol. I knew from the start that was what was going to happen. The same goes for Keys. You intellectuals, you're catching."

"Oh, come off that 'intellectuals' talk, Jack. If you can't stand intellectuals get yourself elected mayor of Los Angeles."

"You've got to overbid everything, that's what's with your brainy group. You've got to make everything up into a bigger issue, you've got to generalize. And it's contagious. Keys was an honest-to-God, white-hating Black Muslim, but you've gotten on his brain with your abstractions."

"Rubbish."

He pauses a while, then shakes his head and says with almost grudging admiration:

"The son-of-a-bitch. Never saw a more determined guy. He scared the shit out of me. Listen to this . . ."

One balmy day Carruthers had driven up to the ranch along Magnolia, and although most of the zoo is hidden by thick, tall, pink and white laurel bushes, you can see the kennel from the boulevard, with Batka's cage in the foreground. You can also see Waltzing Mathilda, the giraffe—nothing seems more lovely than a giraffe, when it's there all by itself with that long watchtower neck rising above the horizon—and the entrance to the snake pit adorned with a huge warning sign in red: WE ARE A BUNCH OF DEADLY SNAKES AND WE DON'T LIKE YOU EITHER. KEEP OUT. The chimpanzee's villa is a little farther away, to the right. It is more luxurious than the rest of this little residential zone, as some of the chimps under contract to studios are at the top of their profession among the stars of the big and small screen and Jack feels he has to give them a certain social edge over the others.

Jack had crossed Vale and was about to make a turn toward the entrance, when he almost crashed into a fire hydrant. He had caught sight of Batka and there was a black baby sitting alone with the dog in the middle of the cage. He stopped the car, grabbed the burning cigar that had fallen into his lap, and shot through the ranch entrance. A minute later he was in the cage. It was then that he realized that the child had not gotten into the cage by accident, but had been deliberately left there: Batka was held back by a chain and the child by a belt tied to the bars. There was no danger at all.

Jack didn't know Keys's family, and he didn't know at that time that the child was his precious snake-and-venom specialist's son. He let go with a terrible roar, out of a sheer feeling of relief, no doubt. When Jack swears, it's something, and I am not only talking folklore; it's more like a whole culture complete with world outlook, solid religion and literary background, with mothers playing a very strong part in that unquestionable gift for strong imagery. All of those within reach of his voice ran up immediately, and Keys was first on the spot. He had raced up so fast that he still held a snake wrapped up round his forearm, with the head sticking out of the man's fist. He had been busy extracting the venom and hadn't had time to put the reptile back in the pit. He was standing there in front of Jack with the snake opening and closing its mouth above the clenched fist. A pleasant confrontation altogether, and while they yelled at each other, Jack learned that Keys had been putting his son in White Dog's cage every day God has made for more than a week.

I must confess that while he was telling me all this, the first explanation of Keys's motives, or rather, the first suspicion that came to me, was the same that had crossed Carruthers' mind, and it wasn't much to the credit of either of us.

The suspicion was that Keys was deliberately *training* his son, and that the purpose was to accustom him to the showing of hate. Batka in one of his fits of white rage was a frightening sight, and in that perversion of logic which always occurs when psychology parades in reason's disguise, both of us concluded that Keys was thinking of his son, and not of the dog, and that he had put the kid inside the cage to expose him to the sight of hate and to train him to feel used to it and impervious to it. It would be only too easy to accuse me here of being a writer given to flights of dark imagination: the same suspicion had crossed Carruthers' mind and explained his fit of rage. Both of us were wrong, but it tells quite a bit about the depth of what America is up against. The truth of the matter was the simple fact that Keys knew dogs well. A dog, particularly a big, strong animal sure of himself, always feels protective toward all small living things, particularly mammals. He either shows them indifference and condescension, or an ironic paternal superiority. The child ran no risk at all, but even so, his father had taken the precaution of tying up both dog and kid to keep them apart.

"At first, I put the kid outside the cage," he explained. "The dog was real friendly from the start. I kept at it for a few days, then, as Chuck wanted to play with the doggy...."

"What's the idea?" Jack asked.

Keys studied him for a while, then smiled. Jack was to tell me: "No, you can't say he was staring at me. He was aiming between the eyes."

Keys said:

"I want the dog to get used to *our* smell."

Jack told me: "I had this sudden urge to hit him. He was deliberately giving it to me, taking it out on me, that's it. Just spitting in my white face, and I don't care if it's white, I care that it's a human face. But what the hell was I to answer, when you knew the part that bit about smell has played and still plays in segregation, in buses, in cafeterias, in the whole goddamn racial bullshit. . . . He had me there. There was nothing I could say. I had to swallow it."

"Now we've made it," Keys said. "You can go into that cage and untie them. The dog will be happy and the kid too. There's no risk. I know about the insurance, sure I do. . . . I take full responsibility. Go ahead."

"If you're nutty enough, go and do it yourself."

Keys held out his hand.

"Here, take it."

Jack grabbed the snake lightning-quick. "In such a situation, my friend," he explained to me, "you have to act real fast and get hold of them in the right place, and I'm sure if I'd shown a trace of hesitation, that fiend would've just thrown the snake into my arms. I was too busy watching the twister to think of stopping this devil I'm paying two hundred dollars a week. None of us knew that Keys had already managed to become real buddies with your mutt, except perhaps that kid Terry, who looked as if he was going to die laughing. Some joke. I've never really learned to like snakes, you know, so I guess I didn't look my best right then, with that black twisting piece of hate in my fist. Well, Keys went inside the cage, untied the dog and the kid, and you would've thought they were one big happy family. Friendly as hell. I wish you'd been there. You would've loved the sight, Gary. This big reconciliation, universal love, your line, exactly. I can't say I felt overjoyed. I'd been proved wrong, though I have a lifetime of experience with animals. I never would've believed you could change an old, well-trained police dog like that. Never saw it done before. Well, I was proved wrong. Yep, let's put it this way: there's a new generation of dog-handlers on their way up. I guess Keys has a great future ahead of him in the field. Anyway, you'll be happy to know there are idyllic scenes between man and beast going on in that cage out there. . . . A regular garden of Eden. . . . The snakes are the only ones left who won't play ball. They just aren't very trusting. Neither am I. . . . Why don't you go out there and warm your heart a bit?"

I must have looked as moved as if beauty and love descended upon the earth holding hands to the sound of a heavenly choir.

"Your Keys is quite a guy."

Admittedly, no one can claim to be able to read a man's thoughts in the look he gives you. But Jack's expression was so eloquent and explicit that it clearly said: "Here's one of the biggest suckers that has ever lived."

At the other end of the room, Miss Bo let out the groan of a Victorian lady in childbirth.

You really have to have preserved deep down inside you some blessed trace of the eight-year-old kid you once were to be able to experience the delight I felt when I saw the black man sitting on the ground, busily looking for ticks on Batka's belly. The dog was lolling on his back in a trance of voluptuousness, his mouth open in something like a smile of sheer bliss. Keys raised his eyes, gave me a "Hi there," and turned back to his love affair.

Scene of peace and friendship. Eucalyptus trees, little birds singing. Idyllic sweetness of air and light. Peace and quiet at last.

There were some hens clucking around the cage. *White* hens. You can get really nutty in this country.

Batka remained on his back, but turned his head a bit toward me, opened an eye and gave me a polite wag of the tail. That dog was smiling. I have known two or three dogs in my life who actually smiled, and Batka is one of them. It consists in half baring the teeth, while the lower part of the muzzle twitches: *skalitsa* is the Russian word for it, in case you wish to know the exact word.

"Well, you've done it," I say.

Keys goes on rubbing the dog's belly.

"Not quite yet."

"You can't do better than that."

"Oh yes I can," he says.

His eyes go over the dog, who looks like a full-bosomed beauty falling asleep after a good rubdown.

"He's a fine animal. Real bright."

I can still see him, here, before my eyes even now, in my home in Mallorca, where I am writing this, and though a year has gone by and so many things have happened, his presence, far from fading away, looms larger and larger until it takes on almost mythological proportions.

I doubt I shall ever forget him.

One of those narrow-hipped, lanky Americans who grow taller than the rest of us through some secret virtue of American soil. A narrow moustache above very thin lips, with their hint of some far-off, Spanish blood, and the kind of blank look that doesn't expect anything from you and has nothing to offer in the way of trust, sympathy, or rancor. It's a look which keeps everything under wraps and doesn't come out to meet you. The structure of the face has that hacked-out-of-stone quality which makes up for the almost feminine delicacy of the features, and gives it a brooding, sullen tenseness, and the studied, deliberate absence of expression emphasizes the granite immobility, bordering on ruthlessness, which is described as "savage" in references to African warriors, and as "noble" with Crusaders or Napoleon's marshals.

On his hands, gray scars from snake bites. Tatum told me that this strange man had an almost magical immunity, that he was completely immune to the venom of all American snakes. "Maybe he's got some kind of secret, you know," the old man had added, with a wrinkled grin, "from father to son, special herbs, that kind of thing." But it was only an acquired immunity, which involved the interaction of serums with progressive resistance resulting from snake bites. I have seen him stand in the pit in a mass of writhing snakes, extracting a reptile's venom, while it twisted and lashed its tail in his fist. Pity it's so much more difficult with people. . . .

He stood over the pit and the snakes with an air of indifference, as if merely performing a chore, and yet it was difficult for me not to feel that he was rising *victoriously,* that here was a black American who had become invulnerable.

He leans over the dog and scratches his belly. Batka closes his eyes in happiness.

I watch the scene with a smile wet with emotion, a smile that seems to have inherited all the humidity of Victorian handkerchiefs.

"The dog's got a long way to go yet," Keys observes. "Sure, he accepts me. I'm the one who feeds him. I take him out for runs. I look after him; I scratch his belly. I take good care of him. He can afford to be nice with me. . . . *I'm his house nigger.*"

My smile breaks up and there's no picking up the bits. There is nothing you can do with that son-of-a-bitch. He is beyond help. You can't even say he's got a chip on his shoulder: it is more like some sort of total historic recall.

Do you remember exactly what a house nigger was? He was a black servant who was a part of the household, served his masters devotedly, and took care of their children. In exchange, his masters were nice to him, often considered him almost as one of the family and assured him of a privileged situation among the other slaves, the "field niggers."

I've often heard militants use this expression in talking about blacks who have succeeded in white society, and secured a high position for themselves within the establishment.

"I'm his house nigger."

Keys comes out of the cage. He lights a cigarette, inhales the smoke dreamily, and throws away the match. Then suddenly, without looking at me:

"How about giving me the dog? For keeps, I mean. You'll be better off having him off your hands and I'd like to have him."

"Why's it so important to you?"

He keeps on staring.

"Well, I put a lot of myself into this business, you know. Took lots of time and patience."

I say cautiously:

"I can't promise anything. I'll talk it over with Jean."

I drive slowly back over the hills and down the Canyon, passing from eucalyptus to palm trees, looking down on what is left of the once magnificent wilderness, with its wide and bleeding ochre wounds left by bulldozers. To hell with Keys. No point in brooding over a hostility so haunting that it seems to be following me.

I pull up in front of the house of Stas, my poor builder of ideal cities with a do-it-yourself kit. They tell me his days are numbered and that he hangs on to life by a sheer miracle of tenacity. I am convinced it is his determination to complete the building of his City of Light that keeps him alive.

XIV

A young black opens the door of the little house on stilts buried deep within the thick green vegetation of Laurel Canyon.

I find Stas in his shed, sitting in front of the City of Light. It has grown impressively since my last visit: the Palace of Culture, the workers' homes, the museums, the universities, the recreation centers, the trade union headquarters, the parks and a building called the "Permanence of Liberty," the writers' and artists' quarter, the stadiums and the theaters look splendid. Only the Universal Church still seems to be hesitating between different architectural styles. With its minarets, domes, spires, and symbols uniting the cross, the hammer and sickle, and other more or less obscure emblems, it looks as if it were ready to take on almost anything, while actually producing a depressing effect of emptiness.

Stas has gotten terribly thin. Dressed in a gay psychedelic bathrobe which seems to mock the ghostly pallor of his face, he stares thoughtfully at his work. He appears glad to see me and watches rather anxiously for a sign of appreciation, as I inspect his personal Brasilia.

"Great," I say. "There aren't quite enough prisons, though, and your stadium should be surrounded by a wire fence. Right now, in France anyway, most football games degenerate into murderous scrimmages. You really ought to protect the ball."

I learn from him that the young black man who keeps him company is wanted by the police.

He walks in at that very moment with a thermos full of tea. Stas drinks tea almost continuously, driven by a terrible thirst which is characteristic of his sickness. Alec, as he is introduced to me, holds the *Examiner* in his hand, and begins to talk with a high-pressure volubility that is more liberating for him, no doubt, than informative for me.

The object of his wrath is two lines in the paper, informing the public that a liquor store has been held up by "two men." Both were wounded and arrested. Their names are given and Stas's young protégé knows them. He is indignant, because the newspaper passes over in silence the fact that the two aggressors are blacks. . . .

"The press keeps the wraps on, no reference is made to color, because the publicity might help us. The idea is to make our revolutionary action look like jive gangsterism, without reference to color, so as not to give our people pride. We're going to demand that every time a 'crime' is committed by the brothers, the papers say it's blacks who struck out. We'll blow up their offices, if necessary. They're fucking careful not to mention color. They say 'John Smith' and that's that. Why? To keep our strength hidden from the black masses, that's why. . . . They might feel encouraged, you see, and they might even want to help us. . . ."

He sneers, his face covered with sweat. He is sitting on a packing case drinking one cup of tea after another. I catch myself thinking that I've never seen a black drink so much tea, just like a Russian. He's got the shivers, and I know that tense, feverish expression, the aggressiveness, the drops of sweat: it is the face of fear.

"Seventy-five per cent of what they call 'crimes' are carried out by our brothers. We want this to be known. But the pig press deliberately avoids any mention of color, because they know damn well every single one of these 'crimes' is guerrilla action, and they don't want to drive the fact home, because they don't want us to get the benefit of publicity. . . ."

I catch my breath. Good God, the tacit code of the American press for at least forty years has been never to mention the ethnic origin of a criminal. Whenever the code was broken by some reactionary sheet, the liberals denounced this as racism.

Now the Che Guevara syndrome is inverting the process. The truly lunatic fringe of the extremists is trying to cash in politically on every black rapist, thief or murderer, and make revolutionary capital of their actions. Anything that is simply the work of hoods is christened rebellion and terrorism. Nice idea, in theory, clever stratagem in the self-deluding paranoia of the state of siege, but it has one major inconvenience: it works the other way around. By turning all common criminals into fighters and heroes, all the true fighters and heroes are made to look like common criminals.

I say to Stas in Polish:

"Zwarjowal. All-out nut."

My poor friend, the Knight of Our Radiant Tomorrows, mumbles into his limply drooping blond moustache that looks like Sandy's yellow tail:

"He's in serious trouble, just now. Very bad. Please, try to show some sympathy for once."

I look at this raving cat without listening to him, which helps me to see him better. He is sweating like hell, and contrary to what I thought, it is not the effect of the hot tea he keeps swallowing. His eyes are wide and frozen, in contrast to the constantly moving lips.

"He's going through a bad time," Stas mumbles. "Close to a nervous breakdown."

"Anything interesting?"

Stas disapproves of my hostility, which is nothing but the effect of the other fellow's open hatred for me. It's catching.

Stas lowers his eyes and feeds his soul on the sight of the Palace of Culture at the heart of his future paradise on earth. He doesn't answer.

"I feel loved and trusted here," I mumble.

One thing is clear: the black cat is in a state of absolute panic, engulfed in a tidal wave of terror.

"You can't keep him in this condition, Stas. You ought to call a doctor and give him tranquilizers."

"Don't talk nonsense."

He is right. A white man offering tranquilizers to a black activist, that would be an insult. Like not taking him seriously. I mean, telling him he is not Che Guevara, but a nervous wreck.

The trouble with hysteria is that it's contagious. This kind of high-pitched, all-out aggressive hostility bounces back and forth like a ping-pong ball. *I feel my anger rising for no reason at all, no other reason than the atmosphere of hostility in which I feel immersed.* I emphasize this sentence because it helps to understand how unbalance in others throws you off balance yourself, how emotional frenzy spreads, snowballs, grows beyond all reason without any link between cause and effect, until it becomes sheer beastliness. My breathing gets faster and faster. My mouth is

dry. I have to make an effort to control myself, and there is no reason for this rising tension, which is already looking for release, a pretext for a liberating blow-up.

The kook must read something mean and nasty in my narrowed eyes, because he throws me the classic bullshit of all racists, xenophobes, chauvinists, and other condescending guardians of a privileged, exclusive, out-of-bounds-for-foreigners, rare and profound knowledge:

"You can't understand this anyway, you aren't an American."

"So you yourself feel a hundred per cent American, after all?"

"How can you lack compassion to that degree?" Stas mumbles, in Polish.

"I'm supposed to turn the other cheek?"

"You talking about me?"

He watches us suspiciously.

I am choking.

"Sure. I've had enough of treating every raving black with the solicitude due a pregnant woman."

"Why don't you go take a nice walk in the garden?" Stas suggests tactfully.

I get a grip on myself. Well, I make a good try, anyway. But the guy keeps aiming his nervous tics at me, sneers of sheer hate, and I'm telling you, it's catching: I begin to feel those insectlike zig-zags running over my own face as if ripples of hate were jumping from him to me. We sit there a while, our minds filled with fist-fights and kicks in the ass, our nervous twitches bouncing back and forth from one to the other.

"Che Che cha-cha-cha," I growl.

"What was that?"

My voice is high-pitched, not like my voice at all.

"First of all, if you hate liberals, as all you real fighters do, what the hell're you doing sitting here under the roof of a notorious liberal pants-wetting sucker?"

He throws me a real super-tic and I send one right back, a beaut.

He looks for his voice somewhere deep in his knotted throat and comes up hoarsely with that emergency-exit formula, known to all trapped smart-ass dialecticians:

"That's *his* problem."

"*Merde*," say I.

He swallows his Adam's apple and I swallow a pint of saliva.

"If he wants to help us, that's his business. He knows we're using him."

"Right," Stas says, as masochistic as a chamber pot.

"You liberals get a kick from helping us. It makes you feel good. Getting rid of guilt. By helping us, you really help yourself. We don't owe you shit."

"Your creep is so full of crap it's like Little Red Riding Hood reading the Little Red Book. . . ."

My voice sounds as if a strangler were at my throat. My body is rigid with anger, and a desperate, almost paranoid resentment, amounting to self-pity, directed against myself to boot, and that means the "I" of all human situations and predicaments—the "I" that cannot be accepted much longer in its subhuman, prehistoric, barbaric, humiliating indignity—gets hold of me and ends up in a Nazilike urge to punish the whole blind herd for the unbearable fact that I am part of it. An almost physical craving for total alienation and transcendence, an idiotic aspiration to break with all that is human, so as to realize the impossible: to become a man at last. And as is usually the case with me, when my mind lashes out in search of a short-cut to some total self-expression, it jumps elliptically over the hurdles of coherent thinking. It all comes out in one sentence flashing through my brain: *they have no right to do this to a dog.* Self-pity, yes, and it reminds me of Sandy's nasal whine.

"This young man is in very great danger," Stas murmurs. "Please remember that."

"Police?"

"No."

I shall never know if Stas—may peace be with him in that true City of Light he now inhabits, no doubt, still busily planning a better and more openly democratic paradise, with its green pastures more equitably shared—I shall never know if Stas was himself fully aware of the nightmare which entrapped the young man he was sheltering.

"Wanted by the police" was actually a police-spread rumor, for the purpose of establishing the "reputation" of an informer. I have no right to claim this as a certitude, as the whole "game" of guessing who's who in the F.B.I.– Black Power struggle is by its very nature based on false-hood, slander, and paranoia. I may be completely wrong. I only heard the poor guy's name once. I am almost sure it was Rackley, it may have been Rigley, or something like that. I am only certain of the first name: it was Alec or Alex. And the body of an Alex Rackley, twenty-three, with marks of torture on it—cigarette burns, boiling-water burns, multiple deep cuts—was found in Connecticut in the spring of 1969. In August of the same year, Bobby Seale, chairman of the Black Panthers, was arrested and accused of having ordered the murder.

Alex Rackley was an F.B.I. informer—or so the police claimed—and Bobby Seale, according to the police again, had taken part in the "interrogation" of the young man, conducted along the line of our own methods of *la question,* practiced both by the French Army in Algeria and by the *fellahin.* Rackley had been a member of the Black Panthers for only eight months: the dates coincide, and if it was indeed the same young man, both his neurotic condition and the fanatical militant "over-bidding" of his talk, appear in quite a different light: he had just made the no-return plunge to treason.

But his actual identity, the importance of the fact that

this was or was not the Alex Rackley of the case, is only relative. From whatever angle you look at the Black Panthers' situation, you will find nothing but provocation, infiltration, informing, a "kill 'em all" state of siege, repression, and suffering. The black organization most hated by the police is by far the least numerous. At a minimal cost in *white* lives—once more, I am asking here a question, How many whites have they killed? Ten, fifteen?—this strident, ridiculously small group of men and women has achieved more in the all-important task of giving young blacks a feeling of *psychological equality* and of breaking completely the process of psychological castration than any movement you can think of in America. That fact is apparent to anyone who is in contact with the young. Those who wish to kill off the Black Panthers to a man will never be able to deprive them of this victory. It has already been achieved, and from the dry, cold point of view of history, what can happen now to the Black Panthers is not important. Never before has a smaller group of men achieved more, and at a smaller cost in terms of actual bloodshed.

The poisonous, sickening atmosphere in which the militants live goes beyond the Rackley case, typical as it may be. For what is even more typical is that there was another stoolpigeon involved, a certain George Sams, Jr., twenty-three, who testified against Bobby Seale. And that raises even more fascinating questions and possibilities. . . . . How to get the Panthers' leaders' hides? How to get them clean and proper, without always shooting through a door at a sleeping man? All it takes is a bit of smart thinking. You put an informer to work, and then you use another informer to tell on the first one. From then on, everything takes care of itself. Old routine, centuries-tested mechanics—tradition, in fact: nothing like it. Was Rackley deliberately sacrificed by those who employed him?

I wish to make once more absolutely clear—you have

been warned—that I am not, repeat *not*, dealing with facts here. No Panther ever talked to me of this matter, and I have no more access to their files on the police than to Mr. Hoover's files on black radicals. I am *not* formulating accusations. My purpose is to convey at least a small impression of the poisoned, sick, treacherous atmosphere of suspicion, provocation, uncertainty and continuous state of siege in which the Black Panthers live and work—yes, work, and it is probably the most successful group therapy undertaken in the long struggle against deliberate psychological crippling, maiming, and snickering "friendly persuasion."

I came out of the house sickened, exasperated and guilty. I should have kept a firmer grip on my leash. But passion is contagious, whatever its cause, and what the young call "bad vibrations" are catching. Besides, my nerves were shot, and you have to be in a perfectly balanced nervous condition not to be thrown off balance by unbalanced types.

What I had really gone through was an experience of psychological backlash. . . .

I was beginning to feel like the kind of white who "has had enough of the black problem" which gave me a teeny-weeny hint of how the blacks themselves must feel. If I were black, the very mention of the "black problem" would drive me amok. And yet I believe the Problem has no future in America, simply because I believe America has a future.

Back home, with Jean at the studio, I was seized once more by a craving for some magnificent, total separation from myself, from that "I" I cannot abide, tolerate, or help. A craving for solitude wholly unprecedented in the history of loneliness. Is it some sort of aristocratic egomania? Does my "I" feel debased and humiliated by its all too human nature? Montaigne's famous words—but are they Montaigne's?—"Nothing that is human is foreign to me," words

I used to consider noble and inspiring, take on a nasty, insulting, cynical meaning. . . .

To satisfy such a longing for another and a better planet, you have to create a whole new world. Which I proceed to do in my usual comical way: I spend the whole afternoon writing.

XV

Every time I now pay a visit to Batka, I am made to feel an intruder, an outsider and a pain in the neck, the sort of man who sits next to a couple of lovers in a park. A beautiful friendship is in the making. As soon as Keys goes into the cage, the dog sits up on his hind legs and tries to lick his black face, then rubs himself against his legs with affectionate grunts. I watch with a tender, approving smile, smug and snug in my now confirmed belief that nothing is ever lost, that all it takes is good will, hard work, and patience. I am proud of myself. I have accomplished something. I stay there feeling I am receiving my reward, a prize for virtue.

Batka's behavior when all three of us come together there is tactful. He rushes up to me, baring his teeth in a pleasant grin, and wriggling his behind. He then indulges in his favorite joke, which is to nibble at my beard as if he were looking for the fleas it must be full of. Then back to Keys, so as not to hurt anyone's feelings, back to me again, going through this demonstration a couple of times. A person with a writer's bent toward fiction would say he is inviting us to fraternize and to seal a pact of friendship.

"Well," I say in the end to Keys, during one of these visits, "I think the dog is ready to go back into the world and take his place in society. He has recovered."

"I wouldn't bet on that. He's accepted me all right, but when Terry or another·brother comes near the cage, he's at it again."

He laughs and suddenly his teeth seem to be the only thing in sight.

"There are good niggers and bad niggers for him now."

"You can't keep a dog from making a distinction between people he knows and strangers. That's normal."

"Sure, that's normal. But you know what isn't normal? It's that a white man's smell doesn't get him, but a black man's smell. . . ."

"Aw, come off it, Keys."

He is squatting on his heels. He gives the dog a last friendly tap and gets up.

"I'm just making a technical remark. The most important thing, in that kind of training, with police dogs, is smell. That's how the dog learns to recognize his *own* people."

There is no trace of arrogance in his attitude. Very quiet, very matter of fact. There exists a whole literature about the "excitable" emotionalism of blacks. The ones I know rarely lose their cool. Some of them act as if they had been killed long ago.

"Are you trying to tell me something?"

"Yeah. I think maybe you shouldn't come here too often. The dog gets confused, he doesn't quite know where and to whom he belongs, you see that in the way he keeps running from you to me. What are your plans, exactly? You thinking of taking him back to Europe? I'm going to lay it on the line. This dog's taken a helluva lot of my time. Gave me lots of trouble."

"I am aware of that."

"Now, if I've been through all this business only so that you can take the dog away, goodbye and thanks . . . that ain't fair."

Batka is sitting between the two of us, his tail sweeping the sand. His eyes keep going from Keys to me as if he knows that his fate is being discussed.

I hesitate.

I feel like a man in charge of souls. I can't possibly take the dog with me on all my hops around the world, and yet I'd feel like a traitor if I told Keys: "Okay, keep him."

"I'm asking you a straight question. Are you going to give me the dog?"

I keep mum. This sudden direct challenge, yes or no, hits upon a secret flaw, some oriental trait in my character, and I often think it comes from my Tartar ancestry. I cannot bear finality, the last decisive word, the irreversible. . . . And add to that dislike of points of no return, the strange mentality of a chief of a clan or of a tribe, again perhaps inherited from some *khan* leading his "golden horde": all those who are "mine" can never be left behind, and this even includes objects. An odd atavism, which has come a long ways since the days when my ancestors were buried in the *Kurhans* with their most prized possessions, their falcon, their horse, and often their favorite wife.

"Well, what about it?"

"The dog will be staying in America, anyhow. If you really care."

"Sure I do."

"There's plenty of time. We'll talk more about it."

XVI

Back home, I hasten to bury myself in an entirely imaginary world: I am writing a love story. I am brought back to reality by a lovely girl I shall call Clara. She shows up with her boyfriend.

I had managed to avoid her since my arrival in Hollywood. I like her very much, but she makes me feel too miserable. She's the kind of person you badly wish you could help, but cannot, and so you keep away from her.

Clara had almost been a star in the movies, and actually made it in a tremendously successful TV series. She is known among black extremists as a nigger lover. This stinking term, coined by whites, is now used at least as often by blacks. I sincerely believe that for some black militants—

and particularly for their wives—there is no human being more despised than a white woman who goes from one black lover to another. And yet, seven or eight years ago, when Clara was just beginning to take an active part in the civil rights movement, sex had nothing to do with it, and I even remember a meeting when she had made that very clear, and in a truly witty way. The purpose of the meeting was to raise funds, and it took place in her house in . . . never mind. At that time she was at the peak of both her looks and her professional success. A big, thin, narrow-hipped girl, a real redhead with those freckles that make women look like kids until they are close to forty. After forty, they look apologetic.

There were a few whites there and about twenty blacks, men and women. Almost all of them were in African dress, in that affirmation of "negritude" that actually goes no farther back in time than the cotton cloth manufactured in Manchester. I see no other future for this need for authenticity than rings in the nose, plates in the lips, and facial mutilations.

Clara clapped her hands for silence and attention. Her speech was brief and effective.

"Before carrying on with the serious business at hand, let me make a remark for the benefit of some of the guys present. Every time I say 'No' to one of them, they come up with a nice bit of analysis. Apparently, deep down there in my subconscious, I'm still bearing the scars of my childhood in a racist environment, in my sweet home state of Georgia, and that's why I can't bring myself to go to bed with a Negro. Okay, so let's have this little matter out once and for all. If one of you fellows can prove here and now that by my screwing with him I can contribute something to the civil rights struggle, well, great, let's go upstairs, my bedroom is on the second floor. Raise your hands please and I'll lie down happily and produce right now. Okay?"

There was a general outburst of laughter, though its main purpose was to cover up a considerable amount of embarrassment.

After that, serious business was discussed. If I remember the figure correctly, Clara herself signed a check for forty thousand dollars that evening. To earn that sum, after taxes, an actress has to earn some two hundred thousand a year. All those who can identify the girl I am talking about know that the greater part of what she was earning went to various organizations.

But you can't live and work shoulder to shoulder with men you admire for their tenacity and courage and disregard them as men, blocking off any normal relationship between man and woman. Clara finally took a black lover, then another. The fact that they were black was totally irrelevant; I don't think she even noticed at that point that they were. Living and working with people, you lose all awareness of the color of their skin. If you live in France, you don't come back home saying: "I've met a Frenchman." But there was a period, in the years following the murder of Malcolm X, when fanaticism in a political vacuum began to border on paranoia and imbecility, like all fanaticism. That was, historically, when white liberals were first under attack from the militants, and in certain quarters word went out to use the white sympathizers, but never to forget they were enemies. That was the beginning of "gaming whitey," and it is now as dead strategically as Carmichael. Rejecting white liberals and cutting off your nose to spite your face is a form of scorpionesque self-hate that smacks of a neurotic love of tragedy for tragedy's sake, and with Le Roi Jones' talent, you may get something out of it in terms of poetry, but I do not believe the black masses are after poetry right now.

It is difficult, for those who haven't come close to it, to imagine how much hatred, vengeance, and despair a neurotic black fanatic—and let no man make me say more than I am saying here: *a neurotic black fanatic* bears no relation to perfectly normal black-white couples—can put into the act of laying a white woman. Cleaver has told it all admirably, with reference to the rapes he himself committed. Sex is an outlet by its very nature, but there are those who have more to let out than others. Anyway, Clara was both used and abused, screwed and despised. She became a "sex joke." By that I mean that dirty smirk on a man's face, behind a woman's back.

With a Protestant conscience, and the fundamental, though diffused, unformulated guilt that often leads to self-punishment, that is, to masochism, Clara's mental makeup gradually became twisted. She began to see herself as a kind of expiatory victim redeeming the white race and its sexual exploitation of black women. She was becoming exactly the kind of woman you find in a pathological couple, when two symmetrically similar neurotics come to grips, and sex becomes pathology, expiation, vengeance, sadism, all kinds of delights. She was rushing frantically toward self-destruction. Being a writer sometimes inspires certain confessions, and Clara's quotes from her "love dialogues" had the obscene flatness of an all-out, no-holds-barred, sado-masochistic relationship. The ideal conditions of the "here, take that, you white bitch," and "yes, darling, yes, give it to me" were realized to perfection.

I am glad to see her, in a rather apprehensive way: she drinks too much and drunks are anathema to me. She kisses me. Her thinness has become bony; there is that feverish euphoria in her enthusiastic words and quick movements that show all too clearly the effect of pep pills. She is still very attractive, but it is the kind of beauty that already announces the coming of a parched dryness of the skin, and an eye accustomed to the passage of seasons can already detect, ten years in advance, the mask of a fifty-year-old woman whose age is not the working of years but of self-hatred.

Her escort is a young black man in a blue blazer, very polite, pleasant, and very much at ease in his American skin.

After the traditional fifteen minutes of the latest police brutalities and of what they say about Ron Karenga—and they have a lot to say—there comes the painful moment when the ex-star (one of the most difficult *exes* to bear) begins to talk about her movie offers, the parts she has been turning down, her latest agent. . . . The young man studies his fingernails. We are all more and more embarrassed. Jean is back from work and is listening in stricken silence. The lead in this, the lead opposite. . . . Another drink, and another. We *know*, and Clara knows that we know. Yes, they have just asked her to play the lead in *Paint Your Wagon*, a fifteen-million-dollar musical, Alan J. Lerner, Lee Marvin . . . Josh Logan begs her to accept. . . . Jean looks at me in consternation. She had accepted the part in the movie two weeks earlier, the contract was already signed, Clara will be so hurt. . . . The young man turns angrily toward the girl.

"Why don't you shut up?"

"But, honey——"

He jumps up and takes away her glass.

"You've had enough."

The lovely green eyes fill with tears.

"You're a bastard. You're such bastards, all of you. Now that I don't have any money left. . . ."

He turns toward us. He is a nice guy, and it so happens that he has talent. The real thing, not just polite reviews because he is a black writer. His first play is one of the best I have seen from the new black school of writing which is taking over from the Jewish writers, and there is one remarkable thing about it: it is totally devoid of hate. He is only twenty-six years old, so I guess he will see the new day.

I take him out onto the patio and he tells me that of all the money Clara has given away, almost none went to serious organizations. It went into creating new and better and more clever and sounder, in terms of strategy, and more "fighting" groups, each with a "new" approach, each with a different and "more urgent" purpose and indeed, many of them do have a more urgent purpose, which is the economic survival of their "working committees." They are created not for the relief of blacks, but for the relief of whites. They are nothing more than group therapy for whites. The blacks in those mushrooming set-ups are actually self-appointed therapists who relieve the whites of their money while relieving their conscience. The Catholic Church used to be great at that. Pay for your sins, you'll feel better. The aim of some of these organizations is not to help the people, it's to exist. Black leadership should take a mighty look into all this.

We go back into the house; I am trying not to look at Clara. Anyhow, she isn't really there any more. What remains of her is what amphetamines do to you when they clash head on with liquor.

I knew another girl like her, a girl of extraordinary beauty, Lynn. She was a Texas girl and you may have seen her in *The Arrow and the Flame.* One evening, she had gone to bed after taking those pills, and they found her lovely body three days later, pancaked against the wall in her folding bed, which had closed.

Clara sobs hysterically. She says to Jean:

"I'm telling you, honey, you either work for them or you screw with them. . . . You can't do both."

"Shut up, for chrissake," says Mark.

"Let her talk," Jean begs. "She'll feel better."

". . . Because, if you begin to mix the two, everyone thinks you're pathological. No one believes you're with blacks be-

cause of your ideas, but only because of your hot ass. . . .
Give me another drink."

"No, you won't. There's a meeting tonight."

". . . Because, hon', when your ass gets mixed up in it,
everything gets screwy, distorted, sick. The worst thing you
can do for civil rights is to fuck with them. That's what
all the real mean racists, black and white, want you to do,
that makes you fit the 'white trash' label. . . . You're playing
into their hands. That way, they can say that all that stuff
about justice and equality, it's just an excuse to get your
kicks. . . . And there's another thing, hon'. . . . A black
bastard isn't black any more. He's just a bastard."

"Amen," says Mark. "Do you really want to make that
meeting?"

"Of course I do. Marlon Brando's going to be there. Barbra
Streisand's going to be there. Jack Lemmon. All big-time
Hollywood'll be there. I can't possibly not go. I can't do that
to them. The committee, I mean. They need my name for
prestige. Come on, let's go."

And so we went. . . .

XVII

It was in the home of a producer in Bel Air, and Coretta King and the Reverend Ralph Abernathy were guests of honor at the meeting. And indeed "all big-time Hollywood" was there. And Marlon Brando and all the others.

I came out of it badly shaken. The purpose was to raise funds for the Poor People's March on Washington. The organizers planned to put a hundred thousand people on the road to the federal capital, by bus, horse, or any means that came to hand. The people were destitute blacks, Mexicans, Indians, Puerto Ricans, and they were to build a Poor People's village, a mile from the White House.

The whole idea had been conceived by Abernathy and bore a touching biblical mark, with its echo of the Virgin

Mary on her donkey and the Star of the Good Shepherd. In terms of actual strategy, it also bore the mark of a completely out-of-touch provincialism, and looked like something more concerned with the Bible than with the poor. For if there are still Wise Men around in our time, all they seem to bring in the way of gifts is napalm, tyranny, and bloodshed.

And the very expression "poor people" was the kind of terminology that immediately puts the whole thing out of the field of ideological struggle and dignity, and merely smacks of the wet kiss of charity.

And now imagine a gorgeous residence in Bel Air, everything that Hollywood can bring together in terms of talent, beauty and wealth, a buffet groaning under an almost Russian weight of *zakauskis*, caviar, and champagne, flashlights, mikes and all the stars, some of them so famous and so mythological that before actually identifying them, you wonder at the *resemblance*. Now, hear me out: you can be rich, famous, beautiful and a liberal, and you won't catch me yapping at that. As for the liberals' perennial inability to *materialize* their beliefs—well, liberalism is a light, it has never been a road, and if it shows you a direction, it won't tell you how to get there. So let all those who keep harping at me for "laughing at liberals" remember that a man's sacred right is to laugh at himself. It only proves that he can take it. It also proves he is sure of himself.

Now the gentle-looking Dr. Abernathy gets up and, with a few words and the skill of a conjurer, brings before my eyes a little wooden church, the cotton fields, slaves all dressed in white rushing to hear the preacher. Frankly, lovely as it is, I do not believe it fits the times or the spirit of the young men around him, Reverend Jesse Jackson, or Andrew Young, and so many others. Only Jackson, a black who is among us as if he had come back from the future for a look at the present, dares to let the cat out of the bag:

"Generosity, yes, sure. But we can't solve the problem of twenty million black Americans without a change in American society as a whole." Good Dr. Abernathy proceeds to describe at great length the last moments he spent in the motel room he shared with Martin Luther King at the time of his murder. A pathetically sincere attempt, intolerable in its naïveté, a burning and yet ineffectual desire to confer on those last moments an aura of biblical light and immortality, transforming the murderous savagery of the deed into a second-rate crucifixion, devoid of the narrative genius of the apostles.

Please, Dr. Abernathy, please. . . . There you are telling us about that shaving cream Martin Luther King was holding in his hand a few minutes before he was killed. There you are telling us how he passed that tube to you, because you had forgotten your own, and how he said, if you wished to help yourself to it, you were welcome. Yes, of course, I know, I understand. His tube of shaving cream will become a relic. It will acquire an odor of sanctity. It may start something wonderful, something full of peace and love. Yes, how well I know! But you forget there's no more room left in the Bible. It's booked up, it has been turning people away for a long time. Take it from me, Dr. Abernathy, though you may consider me a cynic. God won't show up at his black rendezvous. He's already missed quite a few others.

Quite frankly, I expect more from men like the Reverend Mr. Jackson than from the Almighty, no blasphemy intended: it is just that the two of them are not walking the same beat.

I won't be too harsh on my neighbor, and I shall not give his name, for the sake of his grandchildren. Taking advantage of a change of speakers, he whispers in my ear: "There's at least thirty million dollars' worth of entertainment in this room. Can you imagine?"

True enough. They are all there, from Belafonte to

Barbra Streisand, and two hundred others, and they are all listening to Dr. Abernathy tell them about the march of the poor people and about that shaving cream that has just acquired an odor of saintliness.

In the first row, Marlon Brando, sitting with his Tahitian wife. A jacket of rawhide leather, a lion's mane, a rolled-up collar underlying the chin. He was one of the first actors to come up with generous all-out help for the civil rights "cause." I am putting the word in quotes out of respect for invalids, the way you help them with their crutches: it has been overworked so much, it's in bad need of help.

He steps up to the mike. A silence—you know, one of those Brando silences—and then he looks sternly at the audience:

"Those who aren't here tonight, they better have a good excuse."

I go "*Jawohl*," get a stab from Jean's elbow—or was it Natalie Wood's?—and shut up.

But the threat made everyone feel uncomfortable. Besides, he was hamming it up. The place was full of professionals: damn it, he ought to be able to do better than that.

But the worst was yet to come. After a few words about the millions of children throughout the world who fall victim to mental degeneration brought on by undernourishment—Brando has helped UNICEF generously and tirelessly—he stresses the importance of the present meeting and the necessity to keep up the work started here tonight. For that purpose, he calls for the formation of a steering committee and asks for volunteers. Out of some three hundred personalities present, thirty raise their hands: obviously more than enough. If there were three hundred people in a steering committee, all it would mean is that there would still be a steering committee to be made up.

And here, in one sentence, Marlon Brando suddenly reveals more about himself and about the deeper nature of the relationship between certain white friends of militants with *themselves*—I do mean with themselves and not with the blacks—than a long psychiatric study. He glares at the audience and at the thirty raised hands. He braces himself, balances his shoulders in that famous half-roll, then the chin goes up. He is acting. Or rather overacting, for the sudden violence in his voice and the tightening of his facial muscles and of the jaws bears no relation whatsoever to the situation, however he may truly feel about it. The reaction is not in any way spontaneous, but calculated, premeditated, and entirely self-centered, in the sense that the man is concentrating on projecting his own image, or rather an image of himself he graciously favors, and if there is any sincerity at all in his voice, it is that of the eternal spoiled brat:

"Those who didn't raise their hands, get the hell out of here!"

Whenever a man behaves like a jerk, I feel as if I have lost face myself.

I am fully aware that Marlon Brando was acting out the "to-the-wall" situation of the Black Panthers. But when you happen to be a millionaire who doesn't even run the risk of a kick in the ass, the effect is not that of a panther, black or white, but of a *de luxe* poodle pissing on the carpet. There was something truly sickening—and sick—in this bullying, this provocation, in that phony air of a down-to-the-last-bullet desperado, in this aping of quite another kind of hostility, an authentic one, which rises from the black blood on the pavement.

The three hundred actors, writers, directors, producers had only moments before stated in writing what help they wished to offer in terms of money, work, or both, and they simply did not feel qualified to sit on a steering committee in charge of the funds.

"Get the hell out of here...."

Let us forget Marlon Brando and his White Panther act that didn't come off.

What is important to say is that there are misfits among white liberals and militants who use black America's tragedy and its authentic feeling of injustice for pathological reasons of their own, a transfer of their personal grudges and feelings of inferiority or unfulfillment out of the psychological field into the social, so that their paranoid tendencies appear on the surface as a perfectly valid feeling of social resentment. In this way those who harbor within them a slightly paranoid sense of persecution use the resentment of truly pathological grudge against the world.

There are personalities who have reached what is known as "the summit of success" and yet frequently harbor a deep sense of frustration and rejection because their ego is constantly racing after their super-ego, a race the ego is condemned to lose. And people who feel "alienated" because of this egomania tend to identify themselves with a human community that is really in a state of both alienation and social "inferiority," so that the King of I finds at last in them a kingdom over which he can reign.

The black radicals know all this only too well and often refer to it jokingly. They are perfectly aware that the "help" offered to them by certain whites is motivated by personal neurotic reasons and that it often amounts to "using" the American racial tragedy for motives that have precious little to do with the black situation per se. One black leader once said to me, grinning, as he watched a famous Hollywood personality stroll away: "We've helped *him* a lot."

Before the meeting was over, we were offered a few fine comic interludes.

The young producer who came up to Jean wagging his tail and tried to talk to her didn't look at all like a frank, open typical bastard; no: he had a clean-cut, crew-cut, all-American ivy league, Brooks Brothers, "my son the officer and gentleman" appearance. A few weeks earlier, he had given Jean a hundred-dollar check, out of the sincerity of his heart and of his much trumpeted liberalism and progres-

M

sive outlook, for that Montessori "school without hate" which was Seberg's contribution to childhood. Then—after all, you've got to get something for your money—he had asked Jean to dinner at Connie's. I said Yes, Jean said Yes, and it all looked nice and friendly until Jean came down with a head-splitting migraine, no doubt induced by this act against nature, and after vainly trying to reach the gentleman on the phone, canceled the outing by telegram. He called back, insisted, persisted and for the next few days became a nuisance and a neurotic bore.

Then . . .

One day my adorable wife—we have been ten years together and I still adore her, mostly for her pioneering disbelief in people's ugliness—came home, sat down, and stared at me.

"Would you believe it? That little creep has instructed his bank to cancel his hundred-dollar check."

Mais oui. We have a word in French for guys like that. We call them *les masturbés.*

I shall never know what it was he still wanted from Jean, but as he tried to speak, Seberg almost turned yellow with dislike and—cross my heart!—emitted a long, loud, viperine hiss the like of which I've never heard before and hope I shall never hear again.

Then there was the magnificent cry from the heart of a young director, husband of a famous blonde actress, who rose and addressed the audience in these terms:

"It's simply not enough to give money. We must go into the black families, have dinner with them once a week, get to know them."

Friends, the year was 1968. Yes, the egg of Christopher Columbus, monstrous in its enormity, suddenly emerged in its triumphant evidence in the midst of the richest and most powerful society in history. *We must go into the black families and get to know them.* Yes, I repeat, in 1968.

And it wasn't Daddy's America which was thus suddenly waking up: the fellow was thirty-seven years old. There're over twenty million black Americans and they have been around for some time. There is Watts, a twenty-minute drive. . . . Christopher Columbus' egg grew bigger right there in front of me, like in a Ionesco play. *Eureka!* The discovery of America by Americans. *Ah, putain!*

Around the platform, Belafonte, the Reverend Mr. Young, the Reverend Mr. Jackson were desperately trying to keep straight faces. *We must invite them to dinner, go into the black families, get to know them.*

I had the impression that Young was shaking like a leaf and was going to burst out laughing, along with Columbus' egg, that white egg full of black laughter, the blackest, richest laughter in the world.

As I mentioned, the contributions each of the personalities present wished to make had been spelled out discreetly on slips of paper and enclosed in envelopes, so as to avoid any possible embarrassing comparisons between the figures.

But someone had forgotten we were in the capital of show business. This kind of anonymity went against the grain. I shall not tell the name of the *sympatico* star who was first to rebel against these veils of tactful discretion, but after licking his envelope and closing it, this popular comedian and one of the nicest guys in the profession, jumped to his feet and roared:

"I donate every goddamn bit of the salary from my next picture!"

The floodgates had opened. From one end of the room to the other, in an instant pitch of excitement and enthusiasm, they all began jumping up, yelling figures, outbidding each other, with the frenzied delight of Wall Street on a good day, bursting into applause at some particularly high and impressive offer, with the totals of the fund rising and hitting the ceiling, and the Dow-Jones average losing its head. Emotion overswept the place, there were tears in the eyes, and even the Reverend Ralph Abernathy, who had quietly dozed off on the dais during the speeches, woke up beaming, while Young and Jackson and Belafonte stood there with that look of total blankness which comes from trying politely to keep your face straight.

And towering over all this the haunting, unforgettable dignity and beauty of Coretta King. You don't often get a chance to repeat yourself with gratitude, because certainties don't come your way often. I shall therefore repeat that in all my life I have never seen a more beautiful and noble woman's face.

XVIII

I don't want to harp about liberalism: I shall only say that whatever obvious ridicule, ineffectual stammering, stuttering lip-service without-actually-doing-anything-about-it, and generally speaking, natural inclination toward velleity you may find in it, liberalism has always been my only guiding light. It is as absurd to turn toward it in search of a practical program, strategy, actual "doing" and solving, as it is absurd to ask the Christian dogma to come up with a technical plan for a five-year economic and social "great leap forward." Its main role in these beastly times is to point out clearly where beastliness lies, which task liberalism does accomplish, and in the present darkness this is no small achievement. It helps you immediately to situate yourself, to choose your allies and recognize your enemies. It reminds you constantly of what civilization should be about. It is an inner drive, not a road map. Soul has no hands.

But it can also be dressing-up, a show-off of surface elegance. A sham is a sham is a sham, and a phony, lip-service type of liberalism, while doing no great harm, is particularly infuriating because it turns a spiritual light into a sort of Elizabeth Arden beauty salon, with the unique purpose of beautifying your little Kingdom of I.

We are driving back from the fund-raising meeting in the company of the agent Lloyd Katzenelenbogen, his brother Saint-Robert, and agent Seymour Blitz—all three in the throes of *mea culpa*. They're beating their breasts, and I feel like offering them the ashes from my cigar so that they can throw them over their guilty heads. The merit-badge of intellectual elite status in America is guilt. A display of social guilt is a must for the moral upper-class establishment, and with the so-called common people you will never come across it: they have a natural reluctance toward exhibitionism. To show your "bad conscience" is proof that you have a good conscience in perfect working condition and, indeed, a conscience at all. It shows your high credentials. I hardly need mention I am not dealing with sincerity here: I'm talking about affectation and window-dressing. A civilization worthy of that name will always feel guilty toward man: it is by that sign that you recognize a civilization.

My three passengers are working hard on their *auto-critique*. Lloyd Katzenelenbogen is the one who reaches the greatest heights of tolerance, self-denigration, and understanding: he is the agent for some of the best fiction writers and playwrights of today.

"*We* are getting exactly what we deserve, harvesting what *we* have sown. When a Le Roi Jones calls for cutting our throats, or Black Muslims say among themselves that all whites should be castrated, sure it's hard to take, but this is nothing but a reflection of the crimes *we* have been committing for centuries, from the very beginning of the slave trade. . . . Behind every black who burns or rapes is *our* crime. . . . *We* are the ones who chained them together like animals in *our* slave ships, in filth and sickness, so that fifty per cent of the 'cargo' died on their way——"

Seymour Blitz breaks in:

"*We* have no more right to forget what *our* ancestors did to the Negro than the Germans have to forget Hitler. . . . *We* have committed a crime against humanity which makes the so-called violence of the blacks today look like baby's play. . . . *We*——"

I double up with laughter. I can't control it, this is one of the funniest things that has ever thrown me into convulsions, and I have been through some convulsions in my life.

"What the hell is the matter with you?" Seymour Blitz barks, biting his cigar furiously.

"I'll tell ya' what . . ."

I wipe the tears of mirth.

"Yeah, I'll tell you. All three of you are Jews from Eastern Europe. Even if you yourselves were born here, your fathers and grandfathers were still rotting in the ghetto between two pogroms and denied every human right, while slavery no longer existed here. But when you blame your own Jewish ass for slavery, when you say '*we*, the slave drivers,' you get a hell of a big bang out of it because it makes you feel one hundred per cent American. You assume the 'American guilt' because it shows how integrated and assimilated you are, even if your 'slave-driving' ancestors were actually being killed off at the rate of a thousand or two in a good year, depending on the mood of the Cossack's *atamans*, or of the Tsar's ministers. You'd rather to think of them as white slave-trading gentlemen than as Jewish niggers. Makes you feel you truly *belong*. I'm not saying you don't give a shit about the blacks——"

"Why, thanks!" yells Saint-Robert, who is Jewish, as his name indicates so clearly.

". . . but it helps you to get rid of that 'I am an insecure minority' feeling. If your gran'dad was a slave-driver, that makes you, if not quite *Mayflower* and wasp, well, the next best thing to it. You make me sick. In 1963 I was at my lawyer's home in New York when the news of John XXIII's death came on TV. . . . There were only Jews there, and you've never heard such sobs, crying their hearts out, you'd have thought they'd just lost their Lord and Savior Jesus. . . ."

"He's high," Saint-Robert declares firmly, and this is true enough, though I never touch liquor or grass or LSD, because I have a nice, Mafioso complicity with myself, and I can't bear to be deprived of such pleasant company through drink or dope. But I do get high; all it takes is indignation: that's how you become a writer.

The atmosphere is decidedly chilly, so we agree to have dinner at the Bistrot to salvage a few bits of our friendship. Our conversation at this Hollywood summit is kept at the highest level and never falls below four hundred thousand dollars against ten per cent of gross. Then Saint-Robert, forgetting that feast of understanding on our way here, begins to fulminate against the recent anti-Semitic demonstrations in Harlem. Since the pseudo-Islamized black fringe began to attack Jews as Jews, and not merely as whites, some of the Jews began to react racially. It's the famous backlash. The stupidity of it all is enough to make you cry, as my mother, who never cried, used to say.

On my last trip out here, I had run into my first anti-Semitic Negro, at none other than Lloyd Katzenelenbogen's home. He was a writer of some sort, Lloyd's client. It was beautiful. Lloyd was so full of understanding it was begining to look as if he didn't give a damn. He kept offering that other cheek with a patience that was the closest thing to total, ruthless disregard for human cheeks I have ever come across. The dialogue—I am quoting from memory, and it's a bit unreliable, as I had to leave the table twice to get myself back on my leash again—went more or less like this:

The Militant
> You Jews, you own the ghetto. Buildings, homes, stores . . .

Me
> Goddamn lie. Fifty per cent's owned by blacks, the rest is multi-national.

The Militant
> You are the pawnshop owners and the money lenders. You sell us your goods twenty per cent higher than they cost in white neighborhoods. One of these days we're going to cut your ears off.

Katzenelenbogen
> Have a little more chicken.

The Militant (helping himself)
> Thank you. You bastards're bleeding us white.

Me (in French)
> If your black shit-eater keeps asking for more, I'll oblige.

Katzenelenbogen (in French)
> You can't understand. You've got to be an American to understand. We have been castrating them for centuries. They have to assert themselves. Shut up.

The Militant
> Of course, there's nothing personal in what I'm saying here. I know where to draw the line. I'm perfectly aware that you're different, Lloyd.

Me
> That's right, Lloyd. Some of his best friends are Jews.

The Militant (it's salad time now)
> Look at the soul stations. . . . Almost all of them belong to Jews.

Me

>Meaning, without the kikes there would be no soul stations in America?

The Militant

>I mean Jews are making all the profit.

Me

>Do I get it correctly: you are anti-Semitic, aren't you?

The Militant

>You're not American. You can't understand.

Me

>Because, after all, your Republic of New Africa is eyewash, and you yourself feel a hundred per cent American?

Katzenelenbogen

>Romain, that's racist talk. Have some cheese.

Me

>Drop dead. Anyway, I find the idea of a black anti-Semite attractive. It goes to prove that blacks need Jews the same as everybody else.

This anti-Semitism is partly due to the mask of Arabism and Islam some blacks are trying on in search of a spiritual elsewhere. Ninety-nine per cent of them ignore the historical fact that Arab conquerors massacred their ancestors, were the first to reduce them to slavery and sold them like cattle on the hoof, turning them into eunuchs, servants, converting them to Islam by the sword of the same name, and destroying the original African religion, which was animist.

It would be inexcusable and downright ignoble to blame the present-day Arabs for these crimes, which were not regarded as crimes at all in that historical period. There is nothing more absurd than hindsight moral judgments passed by the present on the past. But to make the leap from that to seeing in Islam the spiritual home of the African soul and its cultural identity takes a few light-years' travel, and when Malcolm X wrote about his feeling toward whites:

"How could I love the man who has raped my mother, killed my father, and reduced my ancestors to slavery," that was exactly what he was doing when he took up his journey to Mecca. . . .

"What about that dog of yours?" Seymour Blitz asks.

"What about it?"

"Still with the S.S.?"

I concentrate on my food, while the agent tells the story to the others in a compassionate voice, as if he were talking about a member of my family who had been assistant to Eichmann.

Katzenelenbogen says nothing. But he seems interested.

He was.

He phoned me the next day.

"May I see you?"

For quite a while now, he's been trying to become Jean's agent.

"Come along. What have I got to lose?"

He is there twenty minutes later. Accepts a Bloody Mary. Sits there quietly.

He's an immaculate dresser. It all comes from Carroll's, but with that strong personal something that makes you want to buy it from him. Shining buttons, cuff links, watch, and what with that light ginger hair, freckles and amber skin, he looks pure gold.

"I want to talk to you about that dog," he says. "I thought it over last night and I've spoken to my wife. I think we might be able to help you."

"How's that?"

"Well, obviously, the dog can't be kept in a cage the rest of his life and you can't look after him either, with all your travels."

I begin to smell a rat. I can almost feel my hair bristling. I stare at him.

"I think we could give your dog a good home. Our house,

as you know, is in a fairly isolated spot and the dog could run around freely. . . ."

He looks so sincere and natural and he represents so many good writers that without that radar I have, right in the small of my back, which begins to send warning signals up my spine at the approach of an underwater swimmer. . . .

Blacks are supposed to be responsible for most of the crime in big cities, and since Watts, lots of people in L.A. have been taking precautions.

With a dog like Batka, any black coming near a home would hear a howl that would touch him right in his atavistic something—and it explains, aside from economic reasons, why there are mighty few dogs in black families.

Now the gentleman before me is one of the most outspoken liberals: pacifist, marcher, protester, shoulder-to-shoulder with the blacks, you name it, he's got it.

I keep my cool. What the hell, this is show business. Katzy is one of those "progressives" who are all show and no business.

"Sorry, friend. You came too late. I've already promised the dog to Mayor Yorty."

Katzenelenbogen looks as if he'd just been stung by a wasp.

I get up.

"But if White Dog has some white puppies, I'll think of you."

He makes for the door with that furious, resolute walk which often takes the place of violence, verbal or otherwise, with people of quiet—or cowardly—disposition.

I had very little sleep that night. I was thinking, in my darkness, that Don Quixote was an implacable realist who knew that the familiar banality of those windmills was an illusion, and that they were there only to hide from view the monstrous and threatening dragon.

And Sancho Panza was a romantic, an inveterate dreamer,

incapable of facing reality, like one of those blind believers who went on thinking for over thirty years that Stalin was a loving "father of the people," and that the fake trials, the "purges," and the twenty million dead were just capitalist propaganda.

Don Quixote *knew*. With exemplary lucidity, that admirable realist clearly perceived the demons and genetic hydra who raise their filthy heads, at the slightest opportunity, from our inner snake pit.

I turn on my lamp and pick up Cleaver's autobiography. I hit immediately upon a quotation from Le Roi Jones: "Come up, black dada, nihilismus. Rape the white girls. Rape their fathers. Cut the mother's throat."

Shit.

I get out of bed.

My thoughts wander aimlessly, as I wander myself at the wheel of my Olds in this vague, hesitating city. I drive out to Malibu to listen to the ocean. Only the ocean has the vocal means needed to speak in the name of Man.

But my brother the ocean is sleeping. . . .

I drive to the ranch and go into Pete the Strangler's cage. He unrolls himself obligingly, then slips into his prudent triangle position.

We stare at one another.

When that python goggles at a man with his round beady eyes, he looks as if he had never seen anything like *that* or had even thought it possible.

We watch each other for a while, once again fraternizing in our total lack of comprehension, in our bewilderment. . . . We are exchanging our impressions, so to speak. And they can be summed up in one word: monstrous.

I visit Batka and get the same warm welcome that always delights the eight-year-old kid I shelter within me. He puts his head on my knees and dozes off, while I gorge myself on Russian pickled cucumbers and black bread bought at Hugh's Market. Then I doze off myself and wake up with Batka's adoring eyes watching me. The one place in this world where you are always sure to meet a man worthy of that name is in a dog's eyes.

Keys finds us like that, basking in brotherhood.

"Hi."

"Hi."

He feeds the dog. Batka whores around, jumps, licks the black hands, and wriggles his behind.

Keys glances at me sideways, grinning.

"Wow," I say, in the way of a compliment.

"Yep. He's coming along fine, just fine. . . ."

He straightens up and lights a cigarette, then watches me with an odd, almost mocking, look in his eye.

. . . The bastard. I shall never forgive him.

XIX

Back at Arden I find a message from Nicole Salinger. Bobby
Kennedy is taking two days off from his campaign against
McCarthy. He asks us to meet him in Malibu at John
Frankenheimer's home. I knew his brother when the latter
was a Senator, and had seen him again at the White
House a few months before the assassination, but I had
never met Bobby. The press says he can already count on
ninety per cent of the black vote in California, but Jean instantly begins to bubble with plans: if we could arrange
a meeting between Bobby, a moderate like Brooker, and a
radical like Red? She gathers her literature, complete with
the Montessori "school without hate" brochure and lets
Brooker know about the possibility. I phone Red in Wash-

ington and at first meet with refusal, then he decides to come and arrives that night.

I find him nervous and ill at ease, "insecure" as they say here. Since King's murder, the air is so thick with poison that a Black Power leader who agrees even to talk with the "white establishment" feels as if he were betraying, "collaborating," as the French Resistance referred to those who cooperated with the Germans. I have never seen him like that, studious-looking, his glasses pushed up on his forehead and a pile of papers in his lap. . . . He spends some time fulminating against the Kennedys, "who haven't done a thing and know nothing about us"; then comes up with some ideas that I found crazy at the time. I have since thought better of them, after reading a couple of well-documented books about the power, both financial and political, of the Mafia, with one of the authors, a distinguished professor, actually suggesting that the only way to preserve the political integrity of the nation is to negotiate with the *Mafioso* and draw up some kind of treaty with them. Red's words ring with a passion, a resentment that, for the first time since I have known him, fill me with the *malaise* I always experience when a man's voice is more like blood gushing from a deep, open wound. . . .

"The crime-and-union complex has always kept us blacks out of both unions and organized crime—same thing—which explains a lot about our situation today. The unions keep us off jobs and we don't have the financial power to exert pressure. The F.B.I. kid-gloves the crime-led unions because that keeps unions nonpolitical. You can bet they prefer a criminal leadership to a political one: it keeps any threat of 'socialism' away. Nobody is more conservative than hoods. The Mafia-union complex bars our people because that puts the Mafia right with the establishment and the unions, with the blue-collar class. The Italian, Jewish, and Irish minorities gained equality status by organizing pressure groups, but until then, poor immigrants—the white niggers—had to resort to organized crime, like all have-nots who aren't given a chance. . . . I think the moment's come to force the Mafia to give up its position to us, and we can achieve that without too much difficulty by striking at the top: there's nothing but old men up there, and the young ones are too fat. . . ."

I try to look at Red as if I were taking him seriously. But then there *was* at least one thing, truly serious, overwhelmingly so, in these ravings: a quality of despair. . . .

Toward two o'clock in the morning he admits:

"Bobby is the only one we might possibly trust. McCarthy is all rhetoric, blacks are a theoretical problem for him. . . ."

He gives it to me in French:

"*On est trop 'populo' pour lui.* We're too much 'a mass' for him. He can't see a face to it."

I yawn.

"Listen, McCarthy himself is strictly a theoretical issue. He can't make it. How's Philip?"

A flicker of a smile, but enough for me to catch the expression of pride.

"He's been made an officer. Got a couple more medals."

You would think you were listening to a "law and order" father, talking about his patriotic hero of a son.

He gets hold of himself, comes back to the "point":

"He'll be back home in a month or so. Before Vietnam is over, we'll have fifty thousand black fighters—the real thing —ready to make their voice heard, and oh boy! That's going to be *some* voice. Above all, what they'll give the revolution is *discipline*. That's what we need most. Too much individualism parading, jockeying for leadership positions, and nothing in terms of organization, coherent action. . . ."

"The big blow-up?"

"Not necessarily so. I'm thinking in terms of a political force, something like the unions fifty years ago, when they really began to get at the boss's throat. Marginally, a take-over of Mafia strongholds. If American-style political pressure fails, then we'll reappraise. It's equal rights or else. I don't say we can achieve victory by violence, that's poetry. But there are enough of us to make America impossible. And that ought to make America possible."

"Are you going to tell all this to Bobby?"

"Damn right. I'll give it to him right in the eye."

I couldn't take it any more. The "plan," the hope, the projects themselves, all right, it made some sense, and maybe more than some. But how the hell could he ignore the fact that his son was a genuine *American* hero? Was he pretending? Was he cheating on me, on his son, or on himself? Deliberate self-delusion to spare himself a break with the son he loved so much. . . .

When the moment of truth came a few months later, on that yellow lamp-lit staircase on Arden, I was to blame myself bitterly for my irritated, even hostile prying into the heart and mind of a man who, in a less insane world, would have been a magnificent American leader, second to none in our time. . . .

But right then, I was boiling with frustrated common sense. The man was deeply practical: a pragmatist, with a typical, traditional, grass-roots horse sense. Yet the rejection and the denial, the negation of his deep Americanism, of his devouring American dynamism and need for accomplishment, for meeting the challenge victoriously, was shifting him from reality into the realm of the imaginary, a Commander in Chief of an Army of the Future, consumed by an almost mythological dream of power and greatness, a dream bordering on the fantastic, with its roots deep within the very soul of Africa, with its magic, sorcerers, and legendary kings.

His face had that calm and self-assured mask so often worn by those who are much closer to a dream than to reality. Who was it who had first coined the expression "logical delirium"? I hesitate briefly, but then the urge to bring him back to earth, to sanity, is stronger than the wish to *spare* him. . . .

"You know that Ballard wants to come back to the States? He's one of those guys like Cleaver, who can't adjust to a life away from home. He can't take Europe. He's too American, I guess."

His face closes, lock, stock, and barrel. You can almost hear the key. All that is left is an air of disdain and detachment. He shrugs.

"*Un pauvre con.* . . . A jackass. One of those hippie types that mushroom out of this country's rot. We don't need freaks like him here, there're too many of them as it is."

A trace of uneasiness, and then he betrays himself:

"He's better off in France. Tell him that."

He doesn't much like the thought that Ballard will be treated as a deserter in America. . . .

He avoids my eyes, and repeats:

"For God's sake, tell that idiot to stay in Paris."

"I will."

Jean and I drove to Malibu the next morning.

Bobby Kennedy was in the ocean, and all I could see was his hair floating over the waves. The waves were rough, and he seemed to enjoy that.

He came into the living room a few minutes later wearing a pair of Bermuda shorts, his chest bare, and sat cross-legged on the floor.

Jean grabbed her briefcase and brought out her papers. He laughed, shaking his head, raising his arms before his face in a mocking gesture of self-defense. . . .

"Hey, I'm taking a day off. . . ."

He listened attentively all the same and promised to talk both to Red and to Brooker.

Then he squatted on the floor once more between Nicole Salinger and me. A few days earlier, Paul Ziffren, the former Democratic Party head in California, had asked me to write down my views on the Problem, as seen by a foreigner, an outsider's reaction. I didn't write the report because I am unable to feel an outsider anywhere, least of all in America. Neither do I feel capable of objectivity when I come face to face with injustice and race prejudice. Call me a naturally biased writer and leave it at that. But I was amazed by the idea of the Republic of New Africa, a "black Israel" in the South, a messianic dream that I kept hearing about.

I mentioned this to Bobby, who shot back immediately: "Unthinkable, absurd. This kind of intellectual defeatism amounts to a capitulation of democracy, yes, an unconditional surrender of the American democratic ideal. . . . Just good for today's usual apocalyptic talk. To reach that point, it would take a worldwide nuclear cataclysm, total anarchy for years, the sort of thing they had in Europe when the plague wiped out sixty per cent of the population. . . ."

He was sitting cross-legged, a glass of orange juice in hand. There was something about his body that made you think of the big clumsy feet of young dogs. The boyishness and the charm were so much more apparent than the supposed ruthlessness. . . . I was thinking that these features, round, fleshy, and delicate at the same time, these unruly locks, were in the mainstream of American faces, the Will Rogers kind, and when age and white hair come, he would look a bit like Cordell Hull, or Wilson of General Motors and Capitol fame.

Two weeks before, I had told Pierre Salinger at the Ziffrens':

"You know, of course, that your guy will be killed?"

Salinger froze, staring at me for a long time. Then he said:

"I live with that fear. We do what can be done, and that isn't much. He runs around like quicksilver. . . ."

Mickey Ziffren asked me:

"Why? Why do you think so?"

"Folklore. The emulation race, the competition. A taste for the 'happening' and the 'I-can-do-better.' Since Jack's assassination, Bobby represents an irresistible temptation for the average American paranoid personality. The psycho-contagion of deeply traumatic events, with its craving for more of the same. . . . And another thing. Bobby is *too much*. He is a constant challenge, a provocation for any man with a paranoid grudge tortured both by his desire to assert himself and by his feeling of nonexistence. Bobby is too rich, too young, too attractive, too happy, too lucky, too powerful, too successful. . . . He arouses in every 'perse-cuted' type a deep sense of injustice. He acts on such a person the way a luxury store window display acts upon a destitute Harlem kid, or in the way the exhibitionism of American wealth acts upon the underdeveloped countries. . . . Bobby is *too much*."

It would be grotesque if I patted myself complacently on the back for "predicting" it. I am compelled to report this incident because it raises an important element in any "spectrum analysis" of today's America. This country, which is in the forefront of almost everything, including excess, is also in the forefront of neurosis. This immense techno-logical distributing machine processes people's lives the way it processes other goods, with an over-all concern for pro-ductivity, usefulness and rentability, which is the best way to crush people into nonexistence, in terms of human values, personality, self-respect, and self-realization. Living becomes an empty bureaucratic ritual, endlessly self-repeat-ing, and the call of nature, never quite suppressed, becomes a basic, elemental one, that is, the call of violence. In such a situation, the need for self-liberation cannot become anything else but violence, as in all relationships between free-dom and a social strait jacket. The suppressed individual either transfers his individuality upon a group—the modern "group" tends to be more and more a sublimated, multiplied "I"—and then runs amok with the group, or if too much alienated for this recourse, asserts himself in the most shock-provoking way he can find, in the hope that the great-ness of the bang will assert and express the greatness of his "I." The threat of this American paranoia lay heavily on Bobby. In this country, where the cult of success accentuates more than anywhere else the feelings of failure and in-feriority, paranoia is perhaps no more prevalent than else-where, but certainly more apparent and dangerous, as the American temptation to prove yourself a "success" all too often seeks release in the dramatic, the shocking and the awe-inspiring.

I asked Bobby what precautions he was taking, after the "precedent," as he referred to it. He shrugged, shook his head.

"There's no way of protecting a country-stumping candi-date. No way at all. You've just got to give yourself to the people and to trust them, and from then on it's just that good old bitch, luck."

He laughed, toyed with the dregs of his orange juice, and that boyish forelock fell down on his forehead in the way America will long remember it.

"Anyway, you have to have luck on your side to be elected President of the United States. Either it's with you or it isn't. I am pretty sure there'll be an attempt on my life sooner or later. Not so much for political reasons. I don't believe that. Plain nuttiness, that's all. There's plenty of that around. We live in a time of extraordinary psychic contagion. Maybe the contagion has always been at work as far back as you can look, but with mass media, it's be-come instantaneous. Because a guy kills Martin Luther King here, some other type catches the bug in Berlin, and tries to kill that German student leader, what's his name. Someone should make a study of the traumatizing effect caused by mass media, which dwells on and lives by drama, and creates in turn a psychological need, almost an addiction, for dramatic events, until the whole thing keeps snowballing, on and on. A chain reaction. . . . And there's the overpopulation, the demographic congestion in cities, with people rubbing and bumping against each other. There's been an experiment with I don't remember what kind of animals, and it proved that when animals are not given enough living space, they go mad and jump at each other's throats. People feel so repressed—you can see that in the ghettos—they literally explode. With the young, the need for violence is often a creative urge, and if you haven't got a way to express it artistically, no talent . . . well, I guess you just make a 'happening' in the street. Not to mention the spiritual void. . . . Though you know, people can be murderous about their beliefs too. And there's Hemingway. I admired Hemingway as a writer but he's the one who started that myth about the 'virility' that goes with firearms and with the beauty of killing animals or enemies. It's been absolutely impossible to get a law through Congress banning the unrestricted sale of firearms. . . ."

We talk about the students putting colleges throughout the country in a state of siege. His first reaction is typical of a man who is first of all a politician: he begins to speak figures and votes. The impact of the new young voters won't be much felt in the 1972 elections. He says this with a half-mischievous, half-embarrassed smile, as if both slightly apologetic and yet "ruthless" in his realistic approach. Then he adds: "I can't help feeling a bit reticent toward students." Is it because they are by and large for Eugene McCarthy? I don't ask him this suspicion but he confirms it as if he had guessed my thoughts:

"I leave certain university circles to McCarthy. I don't

have much use for them, frankly. The sort of thing that's going on right now at Columbia, makes it out of the question for me to come out on the side of young people just because they are young. That's no specific kind of credit or reference in itself, it depends on what you do with it, with being young, I mean, what you're about. I'm all for dissent, if it means articulate, coherent criticism and debate, but at Columbia, as was the case in Berkeley last year, it is exactly the kind of behavior that starts all the things they are protesting against. Vietnam came out of violence, so violence is the first thing you've got to be against. They're tearing down the campus because they can't do a thing about freeing that writer Siniavski in Russia, or stopping the war in Vietnam, but that's like smashing glassware when you get mad. It's a release, not action."

There were ominous rumbles coming from the streets of Paris, with de Gaulle still on a state visit to Romania, and Kennedy asked me several concerned questions about France. Was de Gaulle letting the situation go deliberately out of hand, so that the opposition would be lulled into a false feeling of power and overplay its hand? I told him I had no answer, but in France, as almost everywhere, the young generation was refusing to fall like "insert one coin" into prefabricated slots of society, designed to "distribute" people from job to job, until old age or retirement. Discontented as the kids were with the "reception committee," that is, with the society awaiting them, and as sincere as they were in their desire for a change, what was important and apparent was their determination to build something with their own hands, a creative refusal to accept the world of others.

"Anyway, de Gaulle is the last of his kind," Bobby said. "There'll never be another like him. Do you think the way we treated him during the war explains his present attitude toward the Anglo-Saxon world?"

His brother had asked me exactly the same question five years earlier. It was true that Roosevelt and Churchill had given de Gaulle a lesson in power he had never forgotten. Through them, he discovered that the word "France" didn't have a magical ring in the ears of his partners, when it was no longer accompanied by the sound of power.

"Just how many attempts on his life has he survived, exactly?"

"Six or seven, I think."

He shook his head and laughed.

"I told you: luck. You can't make it without that good old bitch, luck. . . ."

It was over. Present were two of his aides, Dick Goodwin and Pierre Salinger, Salinger's wife, Nichole, Angie Dickinson and her husband Burt Bacharach, Alan Jay Lerner and Karen, Warren Beatty, the John Frankenheimers, the astronaut Glenn, three or four other people on Kennedy's staff whose names I didn't catch.

Before we left, he promised Jean to speak with Brooker and Red that very day.

He kept his promise.

Red called me that evening from the airport.

I asked him, rather nervously:

"How did it go?"

I can tell he's trying to sound indifferent, to play it cool:

"You can't trust any presidential candidate. They'll promise anything. Well, this being said, he's the only one. . . . There's no other. . . ."

He checks himself.

"But that doesn't mean a word more than I'm saying: there's no other. Period. We'll judge him on what he does, not on what he says."

XX

A friend whose profession is to know these things warns me that our telephone is tapped and that there are sure to be mikes hidden in the house. And why not? Let them do their job.

Nothing that is said there at Arden is more informative than what you read in the press. Endless discussions, an orgy of dialectics, with an addiction to phantasms and Talmudic abstractions, typical of all intellectual ghettos and of all people whose possibilities to act are reduced to a minimum.

I am saturated with American "negritude." Happily, sounds of thunder keep coming from France, more and more ominous, and it is like a breath of fresh air for me. Nothing more welcome to take your mind off *real* problems. The TV never stops. The Sorbonne has been stormed by the students and transformed into a revolutionary fortress: Saint Germain is becoming Cuba; thousands of students are manning the barricades; a general strike is paralyzing the country. That takes care of the blacks for me. My pulse quickens, I catch myself singing. There is just nothing like a good French revolution to put America in its place. They've still got a lot to learn over here. I take refuge in my study and watch TV, eating pickled cucumbers, while a "green power" meeting goes on in the living room. The purpose is to lay the bases of a new all-black capitalism, with black banks, black business, black management. The true capitalist revolution.

I make a brief appearance in the living room, where I find Jean signing checks, and come eye to eye with a guy dressed in a kind of mauve and pink toga, who wears around his waist something that looks like a chastity belt with a small copper Negro mask for a buckle: the hook comes through one eye and goes out the other. A huge peace cross dangles on his chest, a rabbi's cap is perched on his "Afro" and he has a gold earring in the lobe of his right ear. I feel like a perfect square in my flannels. He is talking. What he has to say is such fine writer's material that I simply can't afford to let it go to waste. Back in the study, after one quick look at the French riot troops on the screen, in their medieval knight's outfits complete with shields, helmets, and clubs—all that is missing is St. Louis, Joinville and Richard the Lion Hearted—I grab pen and paper and press my ear against the door, taking notes, so as not to lose one of the pearls dropping from the lips of Saïd ben Mektoub inch'Allah whom only three months ago I had known under the name of Peter Steward, a professor of creative writing at ——.

". . . and don't you come talk Mao, Lenin, and Communism to blacks here, because we say drop dead to any kind of integration into anything that's got white shit in it, and I mean *anything*, whether you call it proletariat or class struggle. Any nigger who talks of overthrowing American capitalism is a psychologically integrated son-of-a-bitch and a traitor. We don't want to let 'em get away with it. I mean, the blacks who talk get-rid-of-capitalism are idiots. They're being used. We want American capitalism to stick around until we get our money back, until we get back pay on those two hundred years, with eleven per cent interest. . . ."

I am puzzled. Why eleven per cent? The going rate is seven and a half per cent. I never did discover the answer to that eleven-per-cent mystery, how he got the figure and why, I guess I'll leave this world with a lot of questions unanswered.

"We want back pay for two centuries of blood-sucking, exploitation, blood, sweat, and toil while we were building this goddamn country for crackers, and we have no intention of letting them get away with it, they'll play no tricks on us, Marxism, Communism, or whatever. They aren't going to get away with it, without paying off their debt to us. And we have no intention of sharing it with any white ' proletariat.' Screw the proletariat and screw the class struggle. We are no proletariat, we are niggers, this is no fucking class struggle, this is the brothers' struggle. We've sweated, we've built, and now we want to get paid. Whitey is so fucked up he's capable of going Communist, just to get away without paying a cent. . . ."

How American can you get?

Peter Steward Mektoub inch'Allah, or whatever he calls his brand-new get-up, goes on, and on, and on, and I do hope creative writing won't lose him, he's made for it. His earlobe is still slightly swollen from the bad infection he had when he pierced it himself, the African way. I stare at the earring enviously. I have always wanted to wear a gold earring in my ear—the right one—but I've never been able to find a valid excuse. I am still a member of the French

Foreign Office and they tend to frown on diplomats who wear earrings. I could invoke my Mongol ancestry on my father's side. . . . Yes, but my mother was a Jewess, and though I am a Catholic, that still makes me a Jew. Thus I am on the horns of a dilemma. My ancestors on my father's side were pogromers, while my Jewish ones on my mother's side were pogromed. I've got a problem. If I don't have a valid excuse for the earring, they'll say I'm an exhibitionist. A famous French tongue-twister comes to my mind: *Mon père est maire de Mamers et mon frère est masseur.* Mind-twisters are everywhere. When I was in Israel, right in the middle of a broadcast press interview, a venerable reporter from the *Maariv*, who looked like Ben-Gurion, only much older, asked me: "Monsieur Romain Gary, are you circumcised?" It was the first time the press had shown interest in my penis, and put it on the air, too. There's a first time for everything. Jesus, I thought, I don't dare say No because I don't want to do that to my mother. I said Yes, and there was a murmur of appreciation from the audience which went on the air too, with the rest. And then I suddenly felt an odd prickling itch down there: the truth was protesting. I added lamely: "My son is circumcised."

"So you are bringing up your son as a Jew?" *Maariv* asked. Personally, I'm all for honesty, particularly when it's on the air. So I said: "No Sir, my son's great-grandfather was one of those stinking Cossack pogromers, his mother is an American of Swedish stock, his grandma was Jewish, his father is French of Russian origin, his native language is Spanish, his Spanish nurse has decided to bring him up as a Catholic, but when he was three, he had this slight inflammation of the penis and Doctor Bouter-Vasser—I recommend him to you, Sir, he's an excellent pediatrician—decided to remove the foreskin for medical reasons and without any sort of commitment on my part." And so my son's foreskin went on the air, too.

Racisms! I emphasize the second s.

I go back to my TV. The cobblestones, those famous French *pavés* heavy with history, are flying, and the riot troops, knights in arms, strike back with tear gas grenades, which in that orgy of chivalry have a curiously anachronistic effect. I settle down comfortably in my armchair and light a cigar. It's wonderful to be able to relax with the whole world served to you on a platter.

That night, I am a bit ashamed of my cowardice when I announce to Jean that I am going to run away from the Problem the next day.

She looks sad and miserable. Walking out on twenty million Negroes just to enjoy Paris in May doesn't exactly leave my image untarnished in her eyes. *Tant pis,* I am not going to pin my Cross of Liberation and Legion of Honor on my pajamas just to remind her of my warrior past. Anyway, they are twenty-five years old: in her eyes, I am a has-been. An *ex.* You can't really drag in the Battle of Britain as an excuse for copping out. The problem is right here, in America. In France, after all, you're dealing with whites. Which reminds me of dear Clara's remark, apropos of a mutual friend in Paris, whose wife had left him because he had lost his well-paid job. "What's he complaining about? He's white, isn't he? He hasn't got a real problem."

When you are young and you have to choose between love and tranquillity, you choose love, of course. When you are only five years away from sixty . . . I don't know.

To make it short, I decide to desert the battlefield, leaving my woman behind.

No more of those meetings during which I am supposed to close my eyes to the blatant fact that Abdul Hamid, who talks bombs and "kill the pigs," is an informer, or that the new group represented here by Bombadia, shaved head, *dashiki,* and that Desert King air, is more likely than not financed by the FBI, with the clever intention of (*a*) attracting the radicals for the purpose of easier identification and control; (b) sowing dissension and in-fighting among rival organizations. No more looking at their faces, wondering who's who, or why it is that almost half of the militants killed have been killed by other "militants." No more of those Mayflower Jews telling me patronizingly: "You can't understand, you don't have the Civil War on your back." No more sitting there hearing Jean grumble: "There ought to be some record kept as to where the money is going." And no more of that awful temptation to do a book with other people's blood and anguish, only to be through and done with it.

And so I come to the conclusion that my conscience is entitled to a vacation, and Paris in the spring, with its barricades in bloom and the shields and helmets shining, is exactly what I need in the way of a pleasant change.

The day of my departure, I take Diego to the kennel and we spend an hour with White Dog. My son is six, so we can make plans for the future, he and I. We'll take Batka to France and have him married to a nice French girl. My kid has always had black playmates and he doesn't even know yet that there's such a thing as a black. He has never once asked me why Kaba, or Jimmy, or Gabriel have black skin. He hasn't been trained yet.

There is a note on the table, when we come back. "Please don't go without saying goodbye. I have a meeting at Cranton. It's on the way to the airport. . . ." I shake hands with Sandy, who looks at me sadly from under his yellow Pierrot's eyebrows. Maï is sick. She jumps on my shoulder and rubs against my cheek and tells me a long, extremely complicated story about some birds and that other cat, distinctly vulgar and not at all nice to know, who lives across the road. Then there's that business about a piece of veal stolen from the kitchen table. She assures me she had never even heard of it.

I have never been to Cranton and I have some difficulty finding the house. I ask a bearded intellectual type for directions. Poor Lumumba has done at least as much for the beard as for the Congo. The name and address make the best of impressions. All smiles.

"You looking for Charley?"

"Yeah, I'm looking for Charley."

There are two guys in front of the house, in camouflage outfits, and you feel under the leather jackets what your eye can't see. I tell them I am Jean Seberg's husband and they almost go for their guns. I sure must have some reputation. I explain that it's my wife who asked me to come.

They let me in reluctantly.

It takes one glance around to realize that the meeting is not of the "green power" kind. It's the kind where there is a guy at every window scanning the back yard. The only man I know here is a Black Deacon, and in this company, he's a moderate. The general atmosphere is French Resistance during the war, berets and Cuban beards plus a certain Nazi touch in the leather. Castro almost made it with American blacks, until they finally began to realize there was not one person with black skin among Fidel's commanders, ministers, or friends, male or female. . . .

What's the matter, *barbudo*? Ain't there no more blacks in Cuba?

Some sight, that, Jean's blondeness against this dark background. She's speaking. Her voice is shaking a bit.

"The worst kind of publicity for you is a movie star hanging around. A movie star is always a joke. Knowing smiles. Big ha-ha. Columnists. The 'in' thing to do. Your skirt a bit higher, please. Everyone knows what a star is, right? Nothing but poses. Publicity buildup. I can only do you harm. Cheapen you. Glamorous blonde taming the wild beasts, could we have that once more, Miss Seberg? I've done all I could for the school and the rest, but every time you ask me to sign another manifesto, you're hurting yourselves. It's make-believe. We're not supposed to be human. Artificially. Pink marble bathrooms. We're a stone's throw from Hollywood. You know about Hollywood? That's the place where they're going to make the movie *Che Guevara,* with Omar Sharif playing Che. . . . In short, whatever I do, it will always look like ego and trash. . . ."

The two guys at the window watch the street and the back yard. Maybe you think they're afraid of a police raid? Come on. The police don't have to move in. They're already inside. There isn't a single black or radical group that isn't infiltrated.

Just take an "unsolved crime" and a suspect with strong evidence against him: you've got yourself an informer.

And poverty. And dope. And despair. And no longer caring a hoot about pride, self-respect or anything. . . . You've got yourself an army of informers.

The guard is there against rival groups. Two student members of this particular group have just been killed at U.C.L.A. by blacks.

"Gaming whitey" is running neck to neck with "gaming blacky."

I kiss Jeannie goodbye. I am the one who is going, but I feel like a weeping wife who is saying goodbye to a husband off to the crusades.

Maybe the best thing you can do for a woman when you love her too much is to leave her.

No, I can't truly say I feel sad. I no longer feel anything at all. I am all dead inside. Not even ashes, just nothing.

Besides, you know, there's not much chance there'll be another love in my life. You can't start from scratch when you're not that far from closing time.

I can't even say I lost her to something or somebody. I just gave up. Gave up on her and on myself.

Why? Because I can't put up with my eternal youth any

o

longer. You can put up with being young when you're young; not when you're old. You've got to have some dignity.

And then there is that age difference between us. It's a terrible thing, when you marry a girl who is several centuries younger than you. You've got Voltaire and La Rochefoucauld on your back; she doesn't go farther back than America.

I somehow manage to drag my sorrow to the airport and to put it on the plane.

XXI

I knew our phone on Arden was tapped, but the little incident I ran into at Kennedy Airport still was an unexpected delight. I had barely fifteen minutes to change terminals and board the plane for Paris.

Dear son of an ex-king of the Orient, if you read these lines, believe in my sincerity when I assure you the thought that it was the C.I.A. who had put you on my path never crossed my mind. I find it perfectly normal that, just as I make a mad dash to the exit, so as not to miss my plane and the revolution in Paris, I should be accosted by a handsome young man, who almost pushes me back into the waiting room and into a chair, explaining to me that he is responsible for welcoming international travelers at the airport. Very well, thank you, fine, just great, and yourself? . . . But you see, my plane is leaving in ten minutes and. . . . A royal reassuring wave of the hand. Nothing to worry about. You won't miss it. Sit down. Plenty of time. . . . I sit down again. Since one is to be welcomed, let's enjoy it, it may be fun. All the same, what with those thousands of international travelers around, why am I the one singled out for caresses? He introduces himself, gives me his card. A prince. A hundred per cent one from head to foot. The son of a late oriental potentate, I tell you. I even remember his exotic father touring Poland when I was a child.

What do you think of poverty in America, of the unbelievable misery of the black masses here? Just like that, straight from the hip.

My eyelashes flicker in amazement. My God, Prince, what is it you're telling me? Are you implying there is something wrong with America and with her black masses? And *what* black masses? Never heard about them. Listen, my plane is leaving in five minutes' time and I have to find a taxi to get across to the other terminal. With another princely wave of the hand—a noble hand, a kind of five-fingered aristocracy— he reassures me again. Have no fear, you'll get there in time. So you're not particularly interested in the black problem in the United States? . . . Prince, I say, I'm a Gaullist. That's about as far Right as you can get. Total reactionary. I spit on the masses. Kill the bastards, I say. Believe me, America can sleep in peace, as far as I am concerned. And apart from that, how are things in Kipling's country? Still perky? Gunga Din okay? So, he inquires, during your rather long stay in America, you haven't shown any interest at all in the black situation, or come to any interesting conclusions about it?

I look at my watch. The plane's just left. I've missed the revolution. I get up. He remains seated. The greatest of ease. Princely. Terrific style, you've got to be born with that.

"*Putain de merde*," I say, for there are moments when the popular flowers of the rich French earth blossom on my lips in all their splendor.

But these are truly aristocratic ears and they know how to remain closed to my peasant's lack of elegance.

"Do you believe in insurrectional movements in America?"

"Look," I say to him grimly. "Fifty-fifty."

"I beg your pardon?"

"Let's make a deal. Fifty-fifty. You get off my back and give me your address. Here's mine. You send me a full questionnaire, and I give you my word I'll answer it. My Gaullist's word. You know, de Gaulle doesn't horse around when it comes to honor."

He nods, gives me his card, scribbles his address. Some address, it is: he just puts care of Chase Manhattan Bank. Nothing showing.

I glance at my watch again.

"I missed my plane."

He rises with a superior smile, and with a wave of the hand dismisses the whole matter like a Lord and Master sure of his servants.

"No, you haven't. Go ahead. There's a car waiting for you. . . ."

The Thousand and One Nights, that's what it was. *The Thousand and One Nights,* a magical manifestation of super-natural powers. . . . *Because the plane had waited for me.*

Prince, if you read me, hear this: I write fiction. I am overly endowed with imagination. The idea that you are a paid snooper and provocateur is monstrous beyond all belief, and merely shows how low one of those writing liberals with a sick imagination and twisted mind can sink. You are merely the living proof that the Thousand and One Nights are still secretly there, dispensing their magic. You are the Harun-al-Rashid of the Kennedy Airport waiting room, a good genie benevolent powers put in my way so that the Paris plane would leave twenty minutes late, thus giving us time for a nice, friendly, heart-to-heart chat.

PartThree

XXII

I find Paris with its guts all over the pavement, overflowing with garbage in a display of sincerity unprecedented for that bitch-city. You feel the revolution has at last managed to get the truth out of it. Kravitz, the KRX correspondent here to whom I had lent my apartment, is away, but his tapes and recorders are on every chair and table in the house. I put on a tape and turn it on. Explosions, machine-gun fire, a voice screaming, "The bastards! Give it to him, come on, Danny." There's a ghastly groan, moan, yelp, it sounds like Danny gave it to him, all right. I stop the tape double-quick, pick up another one in the hope of something more entertaining, and hear a hair-raising groan: "My eyes! God, my eyes!"

God, my eye.

Kravitz is a keen collector of sounds. In his audiotheque in Pomona, I once listened to the last breath of a dying man, recorded in Vietnam, and the tape bore the words: GI DYING. TET OFFENSIVE. BATTLE OF SAIGON.

I put on a few more tapes at random: seagulls, waves, a woman reaching climax. . . .Funny guy, Kravitz. There are people who prefer to forget, and others who prefer to remember. All these coiled tapes around me remind me of "Noah" Jack's snake pit. Curled up in their black boxes, ready to hiss. The black round monsters are all over the place, curled on my writing chair and desk, perched on the mantelpiece. I feel they'll suddenly come to life and crawl.

I give it another try: I'd rather listen than to look at it and to imagine. . . . Nothing, silence. I look at the label: BIAFRA 1968. I listen to this total absence of voice or sounds, as the tape unwinds. . . . What on earth is that? A mass grave? Are those kids already dead or just too weak to cry or whisper? It does make your imagination work. . . .

The soft Parisian night is punctuated by explosions. The grenades have a funny way of exhaling after they blow up, a sigh, as if they were glad to get it off their chest.

I hear a herdlike gallop and go out on the balcony: a group of students jog along, singing:

> Les Bourgeois, c'est comme les cochons
> Plus ça devient gras, plus ça devient con!
> (The bourgeois are like pigs,
> The fatter they get, the dumber they are!)

That may be, but I find the thousands of graffiti and revolutionary slogans scribbled on the walls of Paris a tribute to advertising and a victory for the Madison Avenue type of high-pressure salesmanship. Whatever product these young radicals have got to sell, they go about it in the best marketing tradition of that "consumer's society" they rebel against. I can see Monsieur Blaustein-Blanchet, head of *Publicis* agency, giving a prize and signing up the rebel whose graffiti shows a real talent.

I go out for dinner to Lipp's, and on the rue de Sèvres, in front of that old bra billboard, I come upon B., one of my best buddies from our Faculté de Droit student days. He is a very famous lawyer now. A Communist in those long-gone times, now a stanch Gaullist. He is looking thoughtfully at the graffiti scribbled over the billboard:

> *Stuff de Gaulle!*
> *C.R.S.,* S.S.!*
> *Down with Fascism!*

B. doesn't see me. He stands there in front of the political slogans, his hat on the back of his head, his Cross of the Commander of the Legion of Honor in his lapel, his eyes lost somewhere far, far back, looking into our own rebellious youth. Then, furtively, after a prudent glance right and left, he takes a felt pen out of his pocket and begins to write. I tiptoe a bit closer, peep over his shoulder:

> *Set Thaelmann free!*
> *Franco no pasaràn!*
> *Hang Chiappe!*
> *Stuff Daladier!*
> *Disband the Fascist leagues!*

A wave of nostalgia overwhelms me. Thaelmann, as I am sure all you kids know, was our Ho Chi Minh, in the early thirties. I am so happy you remember. Chiappe, of course, was the Chief of Police who gave the order to fire on us during the dissent riots on the 6th of February, 1934. Seventeen dead. Thank you kids, thank you from the bottom of my heart, for your fraternal knowledge of our own struggles.

Compagnies Républicaines de Sécurité. Special riot police formed in 1947 during the Communist strikes.

I tap B. on the shoulder. He gives a little start—the cops were cops in our time too—then recognizes me. We shake hands. It feels good to be young again.

I take the pen from him and write:

> *Free Dimitroff!*
> *Vengeance for Mateotti!*
> *Hands off Ethiopia!*

I wouldn't have the *chutzpa* to remind you who Dimitroff and Mateotti were. I'm sure it's engraved in your revolutionary hearts.

He grabs the pen and scribbles, his hand shaking with excitement:

> *They've murdered Roger Salengro!*
> *La Roque drop dead!*
> *Stop the Fascists in Spain!*
> *Keep your hands off Prague!*

It's my turn now:

> *Death to militarism!*
> *Set Carl von Ossietzky free!*
> *Avenge Guernica!*
> *Planes for Spain!*
> *All to Teruel!*

There's a sound of tear-gas grenades approaching. The pigs are after us again.

We look each other deep in the eyes. It is a particularly moving moment. It isn't every day you're twenty years old.

A C.R.S. riot-troop bus slowly passes by. We assume an innocent "Who me?" air. B. has tears in his eyes.

"Madrid's still holding out," he whispers, "The International Brigades will save the day."

"Léon Blum will send them planes and arms," I assure him.

"Anyway, the German people themselves will stop Hitler," he murmurs. "The peace-loving masses will make war impossible. It's people who decide history."

I nod.

"We've got to organize, we've got to organize."

I reach for the pen again, but there's no ink left.

We shake hands once more with feeling and I leave him there and walk away proudly, my head high, the chin up. I have done my bit, I too have taken part in the fight. . . .

I hesitate between a *choucroute* at Lipp's and a *cassoulet* at Réné's, but since the revolution, the restaurants are packed, the Parisians are living it up. I manage to get my usual table at Lipp's and listen to a girl at the next table, who is explaining that the C.R.S. have already killed a hundred and three students and thrown the bodies in the Seine, so that no one can count the dead. It's a *fact*, she says angrily, though the families do not dare report their missing sons and daughters, fearing reprisals from de Gaulle; besides, some of those parents are bourgeois reactionaries who don't give a damn about their own children being killed, as long as law and order are assured. She treats herself to a *millefeuille* oozing with *crème Chantilly*, while giving no less oozing details of girl students raped at police stations with Perrier bottles, after which she orders a Grand Marnier. I long for a *millefeuille* myself, but I've got to watch my waistline. The girl polishes off her dessert and leaves with her friends: they are going to finish the night on the barricades. Each of my Parisian friends has his favorite barricade; the most popular one is near the Luxembourg, Boulevard Saint Michel, under the blooming chestnut trees.

I ask Roger Cazes, the owner, how the food situation looks.

"We're holding out," he tells me.

Reassured, I withdraw.

They have set fire to tar barrels in front of the Bon Marché, and against this gay background of flames, silhouettes are gesticulating, bouncing and running around, with the riot troops standing there, their shields raised, under a shower of cobblestones. The troops have weapons, but no ammunition, and they are scared stiff, which gives them the petrified appearance of medieval statues. In the smoke and stink of burning tar, I catch sight of a tall Negro in a *dashiki,* a Nigerian skullcap on his head and a Zambian *burdaka* on his chest, with the words SCREW YOU in bold black print on his back.

He is yelling:

"Burn, baby, burn!"

Hearing that war cry of Black Power here, at Sèvres-Babylone, warms my heart and fills me with a nostalgia that can be fully understood only by those who have left behind them back there, very, very far from everything, in Beverly Hills, a heated pool, an air-conditioned Olds and fourteen television channels, not counting the "educational" ones.

". . . Burn!"

Whenever I see a lone American in Paris, I feel a crazy longing for "home." Crazy, for a man who has never been able to find one in the world. He raises his long arms:

"Burn, baby, burn!"

He is at the heart of the matter, as close to the truth about the student revolt as you can be, this Yank looking at the French flames. For it is evident to me that when our riot troops surge forward, brandishing their clubs, what they are up against is Vietnam, Biafra, American blacks, they are up against the stinking injustice and madness everywhere. Thanks to television and radio, all intolerable local situations have become world situations, with the result that the whole world has become a local situation, here, under your nose, staring at you, and when your sensitivity is still alive and not dulled, that is, when you are young, if all you can do is stare back at it helplessly, you run amok, you blow up, you smash whatever is at hand, you *express* yourself, you seek a release. Thus Pompidou is paying for the murder of Che Guevara and for Vietnam. And in this strange way, French students renew the link with the tradition of French universal humanism which they claim to reject so vehemently; they pick up once more the burden of our *mission spirituelle*, giving it a reality it has always badly lacked. If it weren't for Vietnam, segregation, squalor and wretchedness in South America, Asia, and Africa, the French students' revolution would have looked very much like mice rioting in a cheese.

"Burn, baby, burn!"

I go up to him.

"American, I see?"

"You bet. Chicago."

I invite him home for a drink. He ponders, studying me severely from behind his steel-rimmed glasses.

"No thanks, I'll give you two reasons: you're either a fag on the make, or you're the kind of French pain in the ass who's got no real problem of his own, so he masturbates with us blacks. I've had my belly full of that. I'm thoroughly fed up with being exploited by liberal white sensitivities. Go get your kicks from what's happening in Prague. And aside from that, what do you do in life?"

I love the expression: "What do you do in life?" It always makes me think of those who are doing wonderful things in death, where everything is yet to be accomplished.

"I am a writer."

He looks nauseated.

"Oh, shit! I should've guessed. Me too."

It's my turn to be disgusted. We exchange knowing looks. We feel we suddenly know everything about each other.

I mumble:

"You've no doubt come to Paris to work in peace and quiet on your novel about the American blacks? A grant from the Rockefeller Foundation, perhaps?"

"Hey, how did you guess?"

"Because I'm doing the same thing. Who can afford to miss that literary gold mine."

He laughs. The only reason why blacks always seem a gayer, happier, and more laughing people than others is because they always seem to have more teeth.

"I've got a good angle," he tells me. "A white housewife who screws only with Negroes, because, you see, with Negroes it really happens in another world, so it doesn't mean a thing."

Am I mistaken, or do I really detect in his mischievous eyes that little spark of terroristic complicity?

I sound him out:

"Then I bet your white housewise goes off with a black, and sleeps around with whites, so that her Negro lover can get a wonderful feeling of equality with whites?"

A few grenades explode in front of the Lutetia. I feel we writers can do better than that. He raises his hand:

"Dramatic twist! The black receives an anonymous letter: his beloved is actually a transvestite. He had never noticed that, because it's the first time he'd ever screwed a white woman. He didn't know what they were like."

A soul brother. . . . We truly have something in common: we are equipped with the same brand of grenades. They are heartfelt, heartmade and heartsick—and as powerless as the heart itself. Their explosions do no damage at all to lives or property; they have been around since Mark Twain, and in the end they are merely to be listened to for enjoyment and for a personal feeling of relief and pseudo-vengeance. They are found in literature and Groucho Marx, and are about as capable of changing the world as either of them. Humor is a passive form of terrorism, of resistance, and of pseudo-aggression that has less to do with changing the world than with mental hygiene. It is self-therapy, and a typically "bourgeois" form of revolution which sets the world right only for the benefit of your own eyes, through an ironic, mocking way of looking at it, while actually leaving it as it is. It is so satisfying that it almost removes the need for action. . . . It is a comfortable rocking-chair terrorism—and I couldn't survive without it. And it explains the survival of the Jews, and why niggers and kikes are soul brothers, but why black and Jewish Americans will have less and less in common. . . .

The firemen's hoses are pissing on the flames, the tar crackles, burns, and smokes, evoking the image of Hitler's soul in hell, the night is yellow with lights, gray with drifting whiffs of smoke, tearful with gas, reddish with fires, and from above, millions of peeping Toms blink in appreciation, the oldest audience to the world's oldest clowns.

My brother in grimacing irony tells me he is actually here to write a novel about Laura and Petrarch. His glasses sparkle with amusement at the unformulated question he reads in my eyes.

"No, *not* a black Laura and Petrarch. The real ones, history. . . . There's an out-of-time permanence about them. I guess I'm a reactionary. Won't have many young readers."

We part, and I walk back home wondering how my America is doing, if Sandy and the cats look after her, if she misses me, if those exquisite features under the short-cropped hair are sad or serene, and if those sweet peepers still look at the world and people with the same belief in something that can never be world or people, and which has always had so much to do with prayers. . . . I miss my America very much.

I keep turning in circles in my huge and cavernous apartment, listening to the exploding tear-gas grenades.

This tough, callous city has never shed so many tears.

XXIII

I spend a few hours writing, then go up the service stairs to the fifth floor. Madeleine is there, in that tiny room which was part of the nineteenth-century servants' quarters. If you want to meet people who are truly alive and real, look for them in those tiny rooms under the rooftops of Paris.

I give her a fatherly kiss, and the kiss is a bit of a cheat. She is so pretty. . . .

She is expecting her baby in June. Her dark eyes have that strange expression out of time and place I have seen so often in the eyes of pregnant women, as if they were looking at you from another dimension. A psychiatrist once told me that with neurotic women, most of the psychological problems tend to disappear during pregnancy, through the workings of a physiological process as yet unexplained. But then Madeleine has never been in the least neurotic.

"*Comment ça va,* Madeleine? How are things?"

She smiles. It is a brave smile, so I guess things are not going too well. Many problems? No, not really. . . . Her family helps them out.

"It's just that Ballard can't get used to France. You know, he's so American. . . ."

"What is it he's missing? He can find racism here too, if he bothers to look for it."

"Oh well, it's hard for me to know, but there are lots of small things. . . ."

"The World Series? *Le baseball?*"

I become aware of a sudden aggressiveness in me. I am the kind of idiot who believes only the French have the right to dislike France. If some guy from Lyon tells me that France is *un pays de cons,* a shit-eater's country, I look benign and sympathetic. But if a foreigner comes up with the same compliment, I start boiling.

"He can't find work," Madeleine tells me. "He's finished his classes at the Institut de Coiffure, got a diploma, but no ladies' hairdresser will employ him."

"If it's a matter of a work permit, I can fix that."

"It isn't that. No hairdressing salon will employ a black. . . ."

"*In France?*"

She shrugs helplessly.

"Even while he was taking the course—women there get their hair done for free—there were *des bonnes femmes,* broads, who wouldn't let black hands touch them. . . ."

I let out a kind of smirking half-laugh of hatred.

The grenades exploding in the Parisian night suddenly take on a luminous meaning. I try to calm down. I remind myself that Stupidity is the mother of us all, it is great, all-powerful, and holy, the Mother-bitch of our essential nature. We must lower our heads piously before our human goddess. Slimey, ugly Stupidity, with gynecological complications. Those French floozies who refused to be touched by a black's hands remind me of a girl I laid thirty-five years ago, though why I should've done my best for her, I really don't know. As I was beginning the usual approaches on the sofa, she pushed my hand away and murmured, "No, no, if you touch me, I'll lose my head." In classical Greek, that's called an Invitation to a Waltz. You can just see what kind of effect a touch from a black man's hand had on them, and there were too many people around. Black African students have told me of white husbands approaching them in the Boul' Mich's cafés, offering to let them screw their wives while they themselves watched. You don't believe me? Go and ask. They wouldn't dream of coming up with that offer to a white student, but you see, with blacks, *its different, it doesn't really matter,* and everyone knows what those living sex symbols are after.

Do you think I am exaggerating? Okay, then listen to this. For it so happened that I was soon to be offered a chance to observe first hand the obsessional persistence and prurience with which these sexual fantasies feeding on racial antagonism gnaw at the American Dream. Jean and I were awaiting the birth of our second child in our house in Mallorca when, in the newspaper, a columnist reported that Jean was expecting a child and that the father was black. This appeared in other magazines and newspapers which caused an interesting little whirlwind of controversy.

Bon, as we say in France. Okay. I did wonder a bit what that nice, lovable, and God-fearing American Ed Seberg must think reading those items behind his druggist's counter, in Marshalltown, Iowa. Personally, the only tragically relevant thing I found in these two discharges of racial fantasy was their un-Christian un-Americanism. It seems impossible for a white girl to try to live up to the American Dream of her schooldays in her native Middle West, the Jeffersonian ideal of brotherhood, decency and equality, without being immediately accused of secret sexual appetites for black flesh, and her civic involvement is instantly publicized as vaginal vagaries, with total disregard for her family, for Christianity, and for the American Dream itself, once more reduced to sex mania and pornography.

And this little journalistic *intermezzo* didn't stop there. The best was yet to come, as Sheherazade used to say in the Arabian Nights.

A couple of weeks later, Jean, who was then in her seventh month of pregnancy, began to have cramps and a slight hemorrhaging. As she had almost lost our first baby, and fearing a miscarriage, I called for an ambulance and had her taken to a clinic. *Eh bien,* the teletypes went to work and within a matter of hours half a dozen "reporters" were buzzing around the house, wetting their pants with excitement at the thought that a Black Panther baby was about to be born to Romain Gary. Dribbling at the mouth, throwing at me through the gate tidbits of Miss Haber's and Earl Wilson's juicy pieces, standing on their hind legs and trying to jump over the gate, sniffing, smelling blood, they were eagerly trying to get hold of a morsel of that black fetus. . . . Oh well, bread and butter, I suppose.

I listen almost avidly to the exploding grenades, but that's make-believe. Tear gas. I long for the real thing. The May Revolution suddenly begins to look to me like a pastorale. Shepherds and sheep grazing.

I hadn't realized to what an extent that last month with Jean in America had shattered my nerves, I feel a permanent tension in my shoulders, arms, and hands. A physical emptiness that yearns to be filled, like some last echo of the tremendous physical craving of adolescence. I try to soothe myself by closing my eyes and remembering all the Nazis I killed during the war. I only succeed in getting depressed: you try to wipe out injustice, but all you succeed in is wiping out people. Camus said: "You condemn to the shooting-squad a guilty man, but you always shoot an innocent one." That old dilemma again: love for the beast and a hatred of beastliness.

I reach the point where I begin to look at Madeleine's big stomach almost with hostility: more of the same. . . .

"Ballard is homesick, *voilà*," Madeleine says.

I laugh sadly. Here is a black missing *his* homeland—the very homeland his black brothers feel is only a white man's one.

"He was brought up in Los Angeles," she goes on, "and obviously, things are very different and easier out there. . . ."

"*Watts, vous connaissez*, Madeleine? Does the name 'Watts' mean anything to you?"

"Yes, of course. Balard always talks to me about it. But he says he isn't a racist."

I almost bark:

"And what does that mean?"

"He thinks times will get better soon, what with the Chinese threat . . . ."

The Yellow Peril. I had forgotten that one.

"Jesus!" I groan with absolute despair.

"He says when America really feels threatened from outside, the color barrier will disappear. . . ."

I have to admit that kid has a point. There is some hard core of truth in it. There is one experience that is completely missing from American history: an experience of common suffering, of agony, blood and an elbow-to-elbow fight for survival, common to all, both black and white, which is the mold from which all European nations have emerged.

I am correcting these pages a few days after hurricane Camille ravaged the South, leaving whole towns destroyed in its wake. A relief center was set up near Hattiesburg, Mississippi, which is white-supremacy country. Well—oh sweet miracle!—this relief station was completely *integrated*. Blacks and whites who had been saved from the floods slept side by side, as if in some brotherly Auschwitz, and *Newsweek*, September 1, 1969, quotes an adorable sentence which may well be prophetic. A white, southern lady is speaking, and what she says is: "I don't think that in these circumstances you can stop and look at the color of someone's skin."

I think Ballard may be right. That is what is missing. The American people have never experienced in all their history a misfortune common to black and white, of the kind European countries have gone through. They need a fraternal cataclysm.

"Ballard is a real product of the American way of life," Madeleine says.

She smiles sadly.

"I've even bought an American cook-book. . . ."

I go:

"Fried chicken. Gumbo. Baked beans. Lemon and apple pie, the way Ma cooks 'em. . . ."

I hear footsteps in the corridor, and Ballard comes in. The last time I saw him, he was twenty-two. A nice-looking, boy-next-door type, with delicate features, like so many blacks of Jamaican stock, a very long neck with a big, protruding Adam's apple, a Basque beret. I don't see what Madeleine finds so special about him.

"Why, hello, hello there," and he sits down on the bed. He is wearing Army boots, denims, and one of those shirts that go better with Florida, cigars, and fat men under straw hats.

He keeps silent, beating the tip of his foot against the

floor, listening to things that go bump in the French night.

"Can you tell me what all this is about? What's eating these French kids? They don't even have a problem. It's all fat and juicy and all made out to them. So, what the hell. . . ."

Which means, translated into *American,* that for ninety per cent of the blacks there, their country could be the greatest thing on earth, if only racism didn't keep that peach away from them. The only flaw in that paradise on earth is that it won't let you in.

Ballard stares moodily at his feet.

"You know somethin'? They've lost me here. Those guys don't have any problems of their *own.* All their problems belong to other people. Vietnam, racism at home, Biafra, South Africa, Czechoslovakia. . . . They all hurt in other people's sores. . . ."

I say solemnly:

"That's France for you. Nothing that is human is foreign to us. We call that *la vocation universelle de la France*—the universal mission of France. De Gaulle is like that, too. That's our beauty, our greatness. I'm so moved I'm going to cry."

He gives me a pretty dirty look.

"Aw, I've had that kind of French crap. It's all abstraction with them. You should hear 'em talk about the 'black problem' on the Boulevard Saint Michel. Their faces light up, you'd think it's the greatest thing since hot dogs. They just love their 'black problem.' It seems that the 'black problem' is actually a class struggle. Capitalism. They don't have a fucking idea what they're talking about. You've got to be an American to understand."

I close my eyes. That's what I keep hearing from every white southern politician.

"Are you sorry you went A.W.O.L. for keeps?"

He glances at Madeleine and smiles.

"No."

She is standing near the hot plate with her back to us and she is crying. You know the kind of backs that cry? I long to get up and put my arms round her. . . . But she isn't mine. I look at him a bit critically. The Basque beret doesn't suit him. . . . Am I a little jealous, by any chance? Here's a woman who sticks to her man. . . .

He shakes his head in wonder.

"Have you heard about the 'consumer society'? They're all against that, whatever it is. They want to blow up the super-markets. In Watts, we looted them. . . . That's the difference between them and us. Rich kids."

I suddenly find something incongruous in the presence of that tall, black American in a Paris attic. He's all out of place. The very long neck and the prominent Adam's apple make his little Basque beret with its short pigtail look ridiculous. I'd sure like to know what Madeleine sees in him. I sigh, thinking of Jean. But you don't choose the person you love. You love her, and that's all there is.

"All the cats here are Communists," Ballard informs me. "The minute they see me, they start playing that violin of theirs. Always the same thing. All-out Communist propaganda. They become buddies with me just because my skin is black. All they see in me is color. They love it. I've never seen such goddamn color-conscious guys, in my whole life, not even back home. They're nigger struck. Jesus, talk about nigger lovers. . . ."

He says with that falsely mocking air of truth trying to pass for a joke:

"Say, what d'ya do when you're a black and you're home-sick? Crazy."

"As soon as the war's over, there'll be an amnesty."

He taps his foot.

"It can take years."

Madeleine turns toward us. There are some women who cry as if they're not crying. Their faces remain calm and resigned, and they speak to you silently of centuries of Christian forbearance and acceptance. I never was able to understand why a person like my mother wanted me to be a Catholic. I suppose because she was nonreligious and being a Catholic was for her part of being French. She wanted me to claim St. Louis as my very own.

"He wants to turn himself in."

Ballard keeps tapping his foot, nodding his head to the rhythm.

I must have one or two more electric outlets put in this room. It's too dark in here. Too gloomy.

We fall silent. The grenades are fading away in the distance.

Homesick . . . yes, of course. The black American is the most typically that: an American.

I have repeated this so often in these pages that it may sound to some whites like a kind of baiting whitey. Okay, I'd better come up with *facts*.

The American black has been "overlooked," to put it mildly, by education. He has been left out, with the result that he is by and large untouched by the process of intellectual oversophistication, with its natural grain of skepticism, its challenging of values, reappraisal, and even cynicism. The consequence is that the black masses still believe in traditional values, in the basic values they were permitted or forced to learn; their outlook is essentially traditional, as unrevolutionary as were the beliefs and values and dreams of Martin Luther King. How many of you, my readers, still believe without self-questioning or doubt, unshakably, in the American Way of Life, in terms of your grandfathers? Inasmuch as they are still the closest thing to "American primitivism" today, black citizens, particularly in the South, are what America has always been about, until it suddenly sat up and started to open its eyes. America has been invaded by the world more than it has invaded it, but the black masses are still closer to isolationism than any of its whites. The black masses are closer to the American past because that is where they have been left by neglect and by segregation. And this makes them, as anyone who has lived in the South knows, basically nineteenth-century Americans, with all that means in terms of a God-fearing attachment to traditional values.

That thirty to forty per cent of black people, mostly very young, are breaking away with this world of Abernathy, only underlines the sturdiness of the American outlook they are trying to break away from. The basic Americanism of the Abernathy type is of the solid kind that has as yet been left untouched by intellectualism, abstraction, dialectics, and sophistication, and there is nothing more "good guys and bad guys" than that.

Ballard laughs, and it is that silent laughter that always goes with shaking your head in wonderment.

"You wouldn't believe it," he says. "As soon as those cats set their eyes on me, it's who'll knock America hardest, a kind of contest. You feel like placing bets on the winner. It's all race talk, you'd like to kick them in the ass. You should see their superior smiles when the words United States of America come up. Blind hate. A real supremacy bit. And yet those kooks're blowing up everything *here*, or trying to, and they don't have 'the problem,' so why do they keep grinding at it? If we didn't have the problem back home, do you realize what kind of country we'd have? Who could do better? The French? The Russians? The Chinese? Jive! They make me sick. They keep telling you the U.S.A. is all rotten, just shit, and because I'm black, I'm supposed to listen and say Gee, thanks, *merci beaucoup*. You know what? *I'm not even an American in their eyes and all because I've got black skin.* Racist red shit-eaters, that's what they really are. . . ."

"How long is it since you left the States, Ball?"

231

"Eighteen months or so. . . . How's Dad?"

"It's tough over there right now."

"The backlash?"

"Well, yes, but the championship bit is almost as bad, if not worse. . . ."

He stares at me.

"The championship. Who's the 'heaviest brother' in terms of fanaticism and violence. Your old man begins to look like a moderate. . . ."

"Who's the champ right now?"

"In terms of talk, I'd guess Ron Karenga. . . . He's got pretty solid support, though where it comes from I don't know and don't even want to think about it. The Panthers are being blown away. All that's left of them is a few fists over the water. The sad thing is that to be the champ, you've got to get rid of competition. There are moments when the in-fighting smacks of Chicago in the thirties. And you never know who's pulling the strings."

He thinks it over.

"Well . . . at least, back home, everything makes sense You know what's wrong. You know the reason: the color of your skin. It explains everything. You know what it's all about. But here, nothing makes sense no more. Some kind of crazy game."

I think I know how he feels. Here, in France, he has lost his master key, the key that explains everything: his skin color. So nothing makes sense any more.

He listens to the grumbles of the French night.

"Crazy," he repeats. "What's it all about . . . ?"

"Open-nerve sensitivity. . . . Any news of Philip?"

"He's been made an officer. But he thinks everything's being fucked up over there. The Saigon guys don't want to fight. He says if he had fighters like the Viets with him, he'd be in Hanoi in two weeks. . . . He's a real soldier, Phil is. A real pro. Not like me at all. Funny, for twins."

"You really want to go back?"

He doesn't answer.

"Ballard will never get used to France," says Madeleine. "It's too . . . too *not* American here."

Small, almost fragile features, long black hair. . . . A quality of essential naturalness, the reassuring simplicity of bread and wine, it comes at you from her eyes, as if directly from some source of loyalty. You meet her eyes, and you say to yourself: you can rely on her. There is no greater beauty in a woman.

"It's all really my fault," she says.

I don't know if she is a practicing Catholic, but the tranquillity of her voice, barely touched with sadness, carries with it the mark of millenniums of Christian forbearance. . . .

"When he deserted to join me, I was so happy, I didn't really think about anything else. . . ."

I repeat automatically, without conviction:

"There'll be an amnesty."

I have never been able to change my way of looking at women. My eyes behave as if they were still twenty years old. Madeleine, you are so pretty. I have always been more vulnerable to a pretty woman than to the beautiful ones. Beautiful women always look as if they didn't need anyone.

She pours us some coffee.

"It's American coffee. . . . I've gotten used to it."

Ballard looks at her with such love that I begin to feel I'm an intruder. I catch myself thinking: that love is theirs, keep out.

It's high time for me to face maturity.

I'm going to go down to my apartment and write it out of my system.

Ballard gets up and takes her in his arms. That very white skin against the black confers to the couple a quality of perfection, of balance and the symmetry of contrasts seeking to complete each other that is one of the great laws of nature. My throat gets a bit tight and my mouth dry and my heart beats faster.

I regard the solution that is right there in front of me in the stomach of that pregnant white woman, and yet I doubt that history and nature shall ever walk hand in hand.

I get up. I mustn't stay here any longer. This is their planet. I go over to Madeleine and kiss her on the cheek, a fatherly kiss again, and it makes me feel like a fraud. I long to take her in my arms and to hold her lovely head against my shoulder. That soft dark hair has the fragrance of the forests of my childhood. . . .

Nothing looks happier than the happiness of other people.

I tell them, with that final, exaggerated authority which usually serves to cover up a total lack of assurance:

"It'll all come out all right."

I give Ballard a pat on the shoulder without looking at him. It is one of those unbearable moments when I feel envious and a hypocrite. I can't possibly allow him to guess I have a crush on his wife. They have enough trouble as it is. Fatherly, that's all, fatherly. . . . But I still can't refrain from throwing to Ballard, on my way out:

"You ought to give up that little Basque beret of yours. It just doesn't suit you."

I leave them there feeling crushed, with the sensation of being a perfect son-of-a-bitch.

XXIV

I hear there are still virgin atolls left in the tropical paradise east of Tahiti, but instead of catching the first plane, I settle for a dinner *chez* Lipp with Kaba, a student from Guinea who is one of those unlikely creations of our time, a mixture of African dream and Marxist dialectics, with Chairman Mao taking over from the witch doctors, and no less capable than the old magic of ordering rain to fall or raising the dead from the grave.

Things are pretty rough around Saint Germain-des-Prés, with students and riot troops swapping paving stones with tear-gas grenades. At Lipp's, Roger Cazes has the iron shutters closed, and to get out, we have to go through the back door. There is a thick and tense barrage of C.R.S. knights-in-armor right in front of the *brasserie*. One of them, red nose, red neck, red wine, full belly, full balls, full ass, looking like a Gargantuan king fallen on bad democratic times, with the shield of St. Louis in his hand, orders me back.

"Nobody goes through."

I looked around. The young intellectual elite is by the church, to our right. The rue de Bac where I want to go is to the left, and all is peaceful there.

"Listen, I'm going to the *left*. . . ."

Fatal word. Pavlov's reflex: the Rabelaisian face twists with hatred. He narrows his eyes. When Our Mother Stupidity narrows her eyes, it's quite something. They literally sparkle with imbecility, and *La Connerie's* small rosy little lips, which bring irresistibly to mind all kinds of other sphincters, twist in a well-informed smile. It's the smile of a man you can't fool, a typical fool's smile. The word *connerie* has no equivalent in English, it's a mixture of "cunt" minus delight, plus gross unredeemable idiocy, and you have to be French to have a birthright claim to it. The over-all impression is that of His Majesty the Carnival King in my beloved city of Nice, where I grew up. *Le vent de l'esprit*—here again you have to be French to have a natural right to this expression "the wind of the spirit," which is all too often more wind than spirit—*le vent de l'esprit* blows from the depths of French democracy, and I feel on my face whiffs of garlic and lousy wine, plus that extra something you can expect from sphincters.

"Oh yeah? Going to the left, huh? Here, take this, you bearded asshole. . . ."

I get a first-class blow from his *matraque* on the back of my neck. The effect is extraordinary: after a momentary blackout filled with Christmas candles and, for some reason known only to my subconscious, a brief, but splendid hard-on, I experience a wonderful impression of my rebellious youth welcoming me back with open arms, a prodigy of rejuvenation of the kind that only police can achieve. *La Connerie* then goes through my pockets and comes out with something that, judging from the expression on his ass, could well be an infernal machine, that is, my diplomatic passport with my rank of Consul General de France, assistant to the Minister of Information, *Compagnon de la Liberation, Croix de Guerre,* these last details marked on my "privileged treatment" high official's pass. I can almost hear *La Connerie* think, and the thought is: "Oh, shit! this is the end of my career."

I get up on all fours, helped by Kaba, then onto my feet. *La Connerie* is brushing my clothes. With that instant Groucho Marx buffoonery that has always saved me from jail for murder, I begin to take off my shoe to give it to him to lick, but suddenly think better of it. *La Connerie* only did his duty. He was defending the establishment, of which I am such a distinguished member. He was defending *me*. And I was asking for trouble. I have a beard, I am wearing blue jeans, high boots, and a red sweater, no tie, and to crown that typical "enemy of law and order" get-up, my companion is a nigger. *La Connerie* got his social classes mixed up. Understandable error.

But the important thing is: *I am defended.* I am not paying taxes for nothing. A wonderful sense of security. My bourgeois self almost wets its pants out of sheer excess of gratitude.

Tears come to my eyes, though the smoke from the grenades does help a bit. I grab my papers from my shaking and saluting guardian and go in search of his commanding officer. I show him the documents and introduce myself:

"Commander Gary de Kacew. Lieutenant, allow me to congratulate you."

He glances at my credentials, salutes smartly.

"I dressed up as one of those radical bums to test your

troops. They are remarkable. Your man gave it to me without hesitation. One look at my clothes and the *matraque* came down on my head. Never saw a better-trained animal. I myself have a dog specially trained to go after scum, I know what it takes to achieve this kind of efficiency. Bravo."

I shake his hand warmly.

"*Vive la France.*"

He beams with patriotic zeal. I go back to *La Connerie* and pat him on the shoulder.

"Carry on, *mon vieux*. Chow okay?"

He is still a bit worried, squints toward the lieutenant.

"Too many beans, perhaps? They make you fart."

"Everything is fine, *mon commandant.*"

"You'll get an extra ration of booze tomorrow. You fellows can do with a bit of stimulation. I'll see to that."

I depart, feeling I've done my best. Kaba trots along at my side, very worried. During my encounter with *La Connerie,* he had made himself invisible, although actually never moving an inch from me. A real piece of black magic. This kid is so used to riots that he has perfected a wizard's technique of turning into thin air on the spot, and then materializing again. That's what Mao-Leninism can do for you.

"Are you all right?"

"Couldn't matter less. The important thing is to know that we are well protected."

I make for home, disregard the elevator and gallop upstairs for the first time in years: my twenties are back with me, youth is singing in my blood, a terrific hormonal upsurge. . . .

And now comes that bit about *"Monsieur Romain Gary's incredible behavior, strange, to say the least,"* as the *Nouvel Observateur* was to comment, while other leftist papers also raised their eyebrows. . . . Here is my answer, though a bit belatedly, as the book is already out in Paris: the French could do with a little less *esprit,* and a bit more of a sense of humor.

Anyway, I put on my best striped pants, my *homme du monde* suit, all my medals, plant a Homburg on my head, custom-made at Gallot's. The final touch: an elegantly rolled umbrella. It's essential. A must.

I take a look at myself in the mirror: Jesus!

I am ready.

"Now Kaba, you be a good nigger and go home. You speakie-speakie pidgin Frenchie? You go fucky fast back your village, me white boss go-go alone. Me meet big white man all by self. You talkie-fuckie?"

Kaba shakes his head disapprovingly.

"What's mattie? You no likie-likie nihilists?"

He shrugs, shakes his head once more sadly, and leaves. Those Marxist-Leninist son-of-a-bitches can't stand real terrorists. Makes them feel they might get it in the ass themselves someday.

I walk over to Sèvres-Babylone, looking like the greatest thing that has happened to the bourgeoisie since the 1789 revolution.

In front of the Lutetia, there is quite a promising confrontation. On one side, students and workers, on the other, the riot police. The *pavés* are flying. The tear-gas grenades go bang! and expire, hissing. Smoke. Yells. Broken glass. Fires.

Three times, very politely, after saluting my striped pants and my umbrella, the C.R.S. warn me:

"It's dangerous here for you, sir. *Des gauchistes* . . . anarchists. They'll be after you with bricks."

"Out of my way, officer. I am an *ancien combattant*. A veteran. Libya, Ethiopia. The Normandy beaches. I can take care of myself." I show them my "special privilege" Ministerial pass.

One of those goddamn leftists catches sight of me. My Homburg and my umbrella have on him the instant effect of red on a bull. He goes for me with an iron bar. I step back heroically behind the line of the C.R.S. He stops. This is going to be an old-fashioned shouting contest, as in the epic days of Homer.

The bastard is one of those typical French proletarian types, a *Gauloise* in his mug.

"Banana!" he goes.

A terrible insult this, real hitting below the belt. Though a banana has the right shape, it's a notoriously soft fruit.

"*Cocu!*" I go, just as a warmer up.

"Go home and get your balls back from your wife!" he yells.

Tiens. That's rather American of him.

"You have a pair of balls back of your ass, all right," I yell, "but they're never the same pair!"

A direct hit, that one.

"Fascist!" he goes, which is cliché, weak, falling back on bare minimum, a Frenchman should be able to do better than that. Let's stimulate him a bit.

"You kike!" I go.

Funny thing, call a good French Communist worker a Jew, and you'll hear from him. That's about the worst thing you can say about his mother. They're staunchly non-anti-Semitic, of course, but that doesn't mean you can go around insulting them.

I didn't expect to get such quick results. A tidal wave of hollering, indignant pure Aryan proletariat starts rolling toward me. I carry out a rapid strategic retreat, leaving three lines of riot police between me and those true, good Frenchmen.

"Jews!" I yell once more from my bourgeois position, waving my umbrella, more heroic than ever.

That does it. The red scum rolls forward, the pigs stand their ground, there is a beautiful mélée, a delight to watch. I don't want to brag, but I sincerely feel I have accomplished something: I have poured oil on the sacred fire.

I light a Havana, and make another effort a little further

down in the rue de Sèvres. There's a nice little gathering there, but it lacks gusto, it's a bit tame and waning, the kids just stand there, bricks in hand. The point is, they have been fighting for almost a month and they haven't been watching TV or listening to the radio during all that time, so the World has receded a bit into the distance, they're losing touch with it, and the urge to smash and burn everything in sight has begun to subside. They need a helping hand, a bit of goading to get them back into action again. As my head still feels twice its size and full of broken rocks, I feel I am still in debt to the police.

So I step forward in my one hundred per cent conservative get-up, medals and all, I wave my umbrella at them and I yell:

"Down with Jews and *métèques*, down with foreigners, *La France aux Français*, France for the French!"

That does it. The sacred fire flares up again. Bricks fly, the police charge, the students hold their ground, there are at least three C.R.S. put out of action, while the kids retreat without casualties. I have done some good work there. Groucho would be proud of me.

And that's when, it seems, the left-wing press caught me redhanded, and that's how I became a reactionary for keeps. "Let us not forget," wrote Guy Dumur, in *Le Nouvel Obser-vateur*, "that M. Romain Gary believes only in force: he is a Gaullist all right." M. Guy Dumur, let me salute in you one of those left-wingers who keep breaking the traditional French right-wing monopoly on *La Connerie,* and are giving a stronger and stronger left-wing slant to it.

"France for the French! Jews to Israel!"

When I think that I lost my holy Russian fatherland because of kikes like me, I am unable to resist it:

"Kikes go home!"

There is not one Jew among those pure-blooded French Communists, so you can imagine the indignation and rage with which they go after me. Thank God, the cops recognize their own kind: they surge forward and I find myself back where I belong: behind them.

It's a good fight. A real pleasure to watch. I feel I have accomplished something for my fatherland, I mean, I have avenged the burning of Moscow by Napoleon, and all our Cossack dead. That son-of-a-bitch Kerenski. He had a hundred opportunities to liquidate the Commies, and now they have even taken over the Odean Theater here in my beloved France.

I am a born nationalist, no doubt about it.

I walk gloomily toward the Boul' Mich'. The life of a Russian refugee is a cruel one. It makes you Minister Plenipotentiary of France, a decorated patriot, a spokesman for the French delegation to the U.N., and then they give you the Goncourt Prize for literature. Heartbreaking. I take out my silk Hermès handkerchief and wipe away my tears. Grenades fill the streets with smoke.

I walk up the rue des Écoles toward the Sorbonne. The students take one look at my bourgeois appearance and move quickly away, holding their noses.

My most memorable experience of the May Revolution awaits me on the Sorbonne campus, where I go in a spirit of nihilistic terrorism I have inherited from my spiritual fathers, W. C. Fields, and the Marx Brothers, a desecrating hygiene, a puncturing of all pompous self-importance, of all the deadly grips of conformity and overseriousness. It is a form of terrorist attack on everything in sight, from which only *true* values emerge unscathed. Satire, irony, parody, and humor are the tests of true value. But go tell that to the French intellectuals. Like all messed-up, insecure people, they can't take the challenge of parody and are dying of seriousness. You have to be sure of yourself and know what you are really about to be able to laugh at yourself. That is how Jewish humor was born.

The students let me down. I am received icily but politely. They recognize in me a notorious Gaullist and an enemy of liberty, and we get involved in a political debate.

Paris in May, 1968, was the greatest debating assembly the world has seen since the Athens democracy: strangers stopped each other in the streets and compared their respective beliefs. There were thousands of such spontaneous discussion groups on the Left Bank streets.

I am attacked about Malraux: papers said that it was Malraux who placed me as his "tool," that is, as an adviser to the Minister of Information, in charge of the state-controlled TV. I tell them they are right. Malraux is clearly a Fascist traitor. As far back as 1936, he invented Che Guevara in his novels, and Tchen, the first "Red Guard," and Regis Debray, the French Maoist, Guevara's companion, now rotting in a Bolivian jail. As Minister of Culture he was responsible for the building throughout France of thirty *Maisons de la Culture*, the cultural centers out of which rolled the present tidal wave of student dissent. In short, as the sensitive Catholic writer and shit-eater Maurice Clavel put it in a *Combat* article: "André Malraux is an old reactionary pisser, and a bastard to boot."

The students really give it to me.

All my arguments are valid and yours are hot air, but I am wrong and you are right. I don't need your Marxist-Leninist arguments to know that. I have only to remember White Dog, or to look at the front page of *Le Figaro*, July 24, 1968. Under the headline: *Journey to the Limit of Horror*, you will find a soul-scorching article by Jean-François Chauvel on the starving children of Biafra. The article begins with the words: "Oh, Lord, hear our wrath . . ." and directly beneath the text, there is an ad, with a charming picture, headed: *The New Pleasure Port at Beaulieu-sur-Mer: a Reality [une réalité]*.

There you have it all. This is our society of provocation,

of callous baiting at work, raising its skirt and showing a piece of ass on a mass graveyard. That is what makes motives behind student dissent and violence God's own inspired truth.

And don't try to tell me there is no other connection than a typographical one between "the new pleasure port: a reality" and Biafra's dying millions, because this lack of connection is, precisely, the most frightening connection, out of which all revolutions are born.

I come out of the Sorbonne depressed, feeling I've left my own youth behind.

And it is then that beauty suddenly begins its reign in the rue des Écoles.

A lady stops me. A mother: the boy and the girl who are by her side both look like her. She is thin, gray-faced, gaunt and worn out, with her hair in a bun, and she reminds me of the Russian women around 1905, who were preparing the 1917 revolution and got themselves killed or deported to Siberia, so that one day their children and grandchildren might get themselves killed or deported to Siberia. A revolution won is a revolution lost. No? All right, friends, give me *one single* example when this hasn't happened. Give me one example of a revolution that didn't end exactly in that kind of "law and order" all revolutions rise up against.

"Monsieur Romain Gary, Monsieur Ro——"

She touches my arm.

"We need help . . ."

Who's "we"? I know her kind of face. It isn't the sort of face that ever asks something for itself.

"Who's 'we,' Madame? The students?"

There is a trace of irony in her smile.

"Oh, you know, the students . . ."

I know. And to share this knowledge with you, allow me to present to you, here and now, a real little jewel. The revolutionary lady with those eyes craving for justice can wait, here, on the rue Soufflot sidewalk. She's got plenty of time: she is immortal.

I had come across Alain L. on the terrace of the Deux Magots. An enlightened millionaire with a fine collection of paintings. I knew him only casually, but we have Walter Goetz in common. There are hundreds of people in the world who have nothing in common except Walter Goetz. Alain L. talked to me worriedly about his son, who was the driving force behind one of those Leninist-Trotskyist-Maoist groups which were popping up all over the place, like those succulent mushrooms that real connoisseurs of revolutions like Stalin and, today, Brezhnev in Prague, find so enjoyable in a salad.

And lo and behold, this revolutionary enemy of the establishment had come to consult his stinking-rich father. The anarchist members of his group had a problem. At great pains and by all possible means, they had acquired a considerable sum of money, capital to keep the movement going. But because of the revolution at which they themselves were working so hard, the franc was going down; there was talk of devaluation, and the revolutionary son had asked his capitalist father for some advice. How should the anarchist group go about protecting its capital, that is, its revolutionary nest-egg? Should they invest in American stocks, in German marks, in Eurodollars, or, should they buy gold? I told Alain L.:

"Tell him to invest in silver. It's going up."

"You sure? I don't want to give him a bad tip. If his Maoist-Trotskyist revolutionary group loses its little nest egg, he'll think I deliberately misled him."

"Why don't you send your anarchist to a good stockbroker? Valmy is a fine, traditional firm."

"I may do that."

This millionaire father and his anarchist son, discussing the best way of making revolutionary capital grow and prosper, represent something that explains political trials, the invasion of Prague, and generally speaking, the usual way in which all revolutions are betrayed. It represents the triumph of logic over ideas, which is characteristic of all totalitarian thinking.

And both the weakness and the pride of what Americans call "liberalism" and the French "humanism" lies in the exact opposite: with liberals, ideas are stronger than logic—that is, stronger than expediency.

I look at the lady with Don Quixote's face and recognize the fire in her eyes; it is that noble fire of all revolutions waiting to be betrayed.

"We don't worry about the students so much. It's the situation of the strikers at Renault that is really worrying. . . . The students can take care of themselves. They're all well off. But the workers at Renault. . . ."

She hesitates.

"The Communist Party wants to put an end to the general strike. The strike fund has run out and the womenfolk at home are getting fed up. . . . Could you and your friends . . ."

Yes, I did hear her say: *and your friends.*

". . . raise enough money so that the Renault workers can keep the strike going?"

I was looking at a human being armed with that holy naïveté which has assured the survival of our species since time immemorial. It would be easy to dismiss her as one of those "impractical dreamers, whose heads are perpetually in the clouds," as if realism, reality, *realpolitik,* total rationalism, were compatible with an adventure that began with a creature without lungs crawling out of the primeval sea, learning to breathe and becoming Einstein. To accomplish that, it took something other than logic and "correct thinking."

This woman knew who I was: a notorious Gaullist, an official of the "establishment," whom every right-thinking leftist had denounced as a "reactionary writer," and Moscow's

Znamie had once labeled "an enemy of the people." She was fully aware of my bourgeois ignominy, she knew that, by all the rules of the game, I was one of those against whom the May Revolution was being fought. But she also clearly knew that the "rules of the game" are a smoke screen for more cheating and falsehood and "tactical" fakery than any truth can possibly survive, and she was capable of looking beyond all convenient categories and dividing lines. And so she had run after me in the rue des Écoles and was now asking a "notorious Gaullist" to start a fund-raising campaign among his bourgeois friends, so that the strikers at Renault could continue their struggle against Gaullism.

The entirely irrational character of her request stemmed from the deepest and most instinctive sort of understanding, the kind that is denounced as "idealism" from the left and as "irresponsibility" from the right, but which is essentially something very humble that both these sides lack: a belief in human nature.

There is no logic, no rationalism in *that*. She was a typical liberal, of the undying kind.

I give her all the money I have on me. She begins to scribble a receipt.

"Come on, Madame, what the hell, I don't need a receipt."

"There are hoods around the Sorbonne who say they are collecting money for the students but keep it for themselves."

"Forget it."

"Please speak to your friends. . . . If you could raise a few million francs. . . . The wives of the workers can't take it much longer."

My left shoulder and forearm begin to shake: that is as close as I have ever yet come to a heart attack.

I look at the woman for the last time. I feel I am standing in a street in Moscow, back in 1905, with the troops firing at the workers.

There are no more women like her in Russia today. The victorious revolution has taken care of that.

XXV

Back through the smoke and burning cars of the Boul' Mich',
through the milling crowds of Saint Germain-des-Prés,
I watch the last stand of anarchist students from the
Beaux Arts Academy with their black flag raised over a
mini-barricade of overturned café tables, garbage cans, and
cobblestones. The May Revolution often looked like a release of long-accumulated hatred against Paris traffic, with
its stinking stream of mechanized garbage cans called
automobiles. As I reach the door of my apartment, I hear
the characteristic hiccuping ring of transatlantic calls. Jean
is on the line from Beverly Hills and I am almost immediately aware of the deep anxiety in the slightly trembling
voice and of her favorite way of reassuring me, which con-

sists of using words as a cover up for the real meaning. . . .

"I'm just calling to tell you I'm sleeping out for a night or two. . . . If there's no answer, please don't worry. . . ."

"What's wrong?"

"Nothing, really. . . ."

"Come on, Jean! What is it?"

"There've been a few telephone threats and then . . . then . . ."

Her voice breaks.

"They've poisoned the cats. . . ."

"Who, 'they'?"

No answer.

"Who, 'they'?"

She repeats:

"They've poisoned the cats. . . ."

"Maï?"

"No. . . . Chamaco and Bang. . . . And after that another threatening call of the 'next time it'll be you, white bitch' type. . . ."

She adds, in a tone of voice that sounds a bit more hopeful:

"Obviously, it's a provocation. Some white racists doing their usual best. . . ."

Yeah, whites. Miss Seberg and her usual American optimism.

I can almost see some black Saleh Ben Yassef Rakhat-Lokoum on that phone, threatening her, and his words ring in my ears:

"Don't you stick your nose into our affairs, you white bitch. . . ."

During the past year alone, this particular white bitch has given away to various black groups the better part of her earnings. . . .

"They sabotaged my car, too. A wheel almost came off. . . . Then someone fired through the kitchen window, while Celia and I were out. . . . I'm going to stay with friends, just a few nights. . . ."

It was then that I heard my voice say coldly, somewhere outside of myself, speaking in another world, that of the great common denominator of beastliness:

"Get Batka from the kennels. You won't find a better guard. He'll take care of those bastards."

At the other end of the line, a shocked exclamation of disbelief:

"What? It's *you* saying that?"

"Yeah, it's me, dammit. Cut the soft stuff out, Jean. Call Carruthers and tell him to bring the dog there immediately. This very minute. Take the dog with you wherever you go. I'll sleep better."

"You want *me* to be guarded by a dog trained to jump at black people's throats? *Me*?"

"Self-defense. Don't be a goddamn racist, Jean. A stinking, shit-eating son-of-a-bitch is a stinking, shit-eating son-of-a-bitch, whatever the color of his skin."

She yells, and that is a very rare thing with her:

"Never. Do you hear me, Romain? Never!"

"Have you told the police?"

"You want me to go tell Reddin I'm threatened by blacks, after all our protests about police brutalities against them?"

I swallow a few profanities, the usual sign of helplessness, then slowly catch my breath, a few dollars' worth of transatlantic silence.

"Jean, the most sacred right of a person is to refuse to be manipulated, handled, cheated, and then kicked in the ass——"

She cuts in:

"I didn't call you for help or advice. My friends will take care of all this themselves. I just want you to know you won't be able to reach me at Arden. . . . That's all. Don't worry, please."

She hangs up.

During the next hour, I run round and round in circles at the end of my leash, with the other end held by some unknown hands out there in Los Angeles. I keep telling myself that people who threaten usually stop at that, but there are too many kooks, dope addicts, and paranoids of all colors in my sunny California for any threat to be taken lightly. At about four in the morning, I decide to pull some strings and, thank God, some of the best strings are my friends. I put a call through to one of them, a young black leader, a real one, not merely a "blackmaker," that is, a black who makes it on the backs of blacks. He is the kind of militant lawyer who gets *all* his questions answered. When I have him on the line, I explain the whole ugly business to him and on the other side of the Atlantic there is a long, expressive, millionaire's silence which costs about ten dollars, or so it feels.

"Okay," he tells me at last. "I'll see what I can do. I have a feeling it won't be too difficult."

It took him thirty-six hours to give me the information I was asking for—and it turned out to be so sad, I wished I had never asked for it.

"Is it serious?"

"Right now, it's only depressing. I don't think this will surprise you, either. Just human nature, like it or leave it. I think you know the bit: the beautiful, happy, famous, 'rich' movie star who *stoops* to be part of things, *our* things. . . ."

"Go on."

"Well, it's *too much*. Jean Seberg, for our womenfolk, it's *too much*. . . . You get it?"

I am silent. Yes, I get it. It's human, to say the least. And it makes sense, yes, all the sense in the world. . . .

"It wouldn't be right to speak of jealousy or envy. . . . It's a great deal prouder than that. Our women live in a state of siege, the militant ones, I mean, and all they have is poverty, fear, and unrelenting pressure . . . but you see, all the same, *it's theirs. It's all theirs* . . . the fear, the agony, the struggle. It's their pride, their only riches. So, you see, Romain, when a beautiful movie star steps *down* to get into *that,* she suddenly gets all the attention and all the lime-light . . . and our women feel they're being robbed. They begin to feel a movie star is taking their riches away from them, she steals the show, she's robbing them of their suffer-ing, of their anguish, of their blood-soaked sisterhood. . . . You get the picture?"

"Yeah, I get it."

Silence again. I feel him as heavy-hearted as I am, but it isn't the same weight. . . .

"That's why some of their boy friends organized a little intimidation campaign to get Jean out of the way. So that our women could keep their misery and anguish and their privilege of suffering and of injustice all to themselves, without sharing it with a movie star. You see?"

"I see."

"You know what a movie star becomes when she sud-denly comes down into the small besieged world that's all their own, a world of black dignity and black courage?"

"*She* becomes a star. She takes it away from the others."

"That's right. You got it."

"I got it."

"So, the girls decided to get Jean out of their hair. . . . Now that they've done just that, they're once more the stars of their 'negritude,' of their blackness, and of their besieged black fortress. . . . That's all."

"Thanks."

"Right. Be seeing you."

"Be seeing you, yes, yes. Thanks again."

"That's the way things are, Romain."

"Yes. That's the way they are."

I hang up.

Talk about black capitalism. . . . They sure want all of it for themselves. Now, at least, I understand why black intellectuals were so hateful and resentful and often beastly when Bill Styron's *Confessions of Nat Turner* turned out to be such a success. Although their arguments sometimes bordered on delirium, *yet they were absolutely right*. It was not a matter of a good book, bad book, truth, fiction. It was much more final than that. *It was theirs*. It was a matter of black ownership. Bill Styron had robbed them.

You can't say capitalism is dead in America.

The doorbell rings.

It is three in the morning. I am a man who needs his eight hours' sleep, but for the last few months, it has been nothing but nights of fire, nights of thunder, and something within me has begun to give into a lassitude close to indifference, dangerously close to acceptance and surrender, with the pain and suffering of the world rapidly becoming something of a bore. I guess this is the truest and worst judgment I have ever passed upon myself.

The doorbell rings again. *Them*. Let them stay outside, their hands full of their jealously guarded negritude. Keep it all to yourselves, brothers. I am too weary. When I was young, the world was my oyster, but when maturity sets in, you realize that all the time that you thought you were swallowing the oyster, the oyster was slowly, mercilessly, bit by bit, swallowing you.

But then I get up and open the door. I am cursed with something that I can only call *expectancy*. Something, sooner or later, will appear, reveal itself—though it takes an incurable hope addict to believe it will actually knock at the door. . . .

It's only them, of course.

Since my novel *The Roots of Heaven*, I have become a kind of Left-Bank Foccart* for Africans in Paris.

I glare at them darkly. It is one of those racist moments

---

* Foccart was special adviser to de Gaulle on African affairs, and now carries out the same duties under President Pompidou.

when the sight of a black skin has the same effect on me as the sight of a white one.

We all go into the kitchen and eat hard-boiled eggs. There are a couple of Americans in the group, among them the usual type of Parisian-based black American creep on the C.I.A. payroll, plus a poet from Tennessee who keeps up a nonstop political anti-everything tirade he probably began twenty-four hours earlier in one of those Latin Quarter cafés where students drop in for an ideological refill between tours of revolutionary duty on the barricades. His voice is so hoarse, one longs to pour oil down his throat.

"We'll never get anywhere politically as long as we are not represented at the center of all political power in the U.S.A., that is, inside the crime-union complex. Hoover accepts crime-controlled unions because *honest* unions would mean the end of capitalism in America." He spits that out between two hard-boiled eggs. His glasses sparkle with dialectical inspiration under the wild bush of his Afro hair, which looks like electrified barbed wire. He pauses, an egg in his mouth. And why is he wearing a woolen scarf around his neck in the middle of May, and indoors?

He looks like the picture portrait in black of Zinoviev, one of the Bolshevik leaders hanged by Stalin. And at four o'clock in the morning, after many a sleepless night, the hard-boiled egg stuck in the middle of that dark face looks like a quick repair job awaiting a coat of paint.

"Right," the creep says, "abso-lu-tely right. So what's the Black Maoist-Leninist Guard* intend doing about it?"

I say:

"Watch your answer, Pogo. The son-of-a-bitch'll take it directly to the C.I.A."

The creep laughs. Since this is a routine crack among black American *émigrés* in Paris, he can shrug it off.

* The name is fictitious, for obvious reasons.

"The answer is obvious—and we don't look for precedent in China or anywhere else, because there is no precedent. We are acting within a highly organized society, and it requires specific, creative thinking. The U.S. is the most sophisticated technological structure the world has ever known, and the most fragile. Remember the east coast electricity blackout? You know what three pounds of LSD in the New York water supply can do? The States has the most expensive, complete, and sophisticated military protective 'shield' around the country, and its efficiency is a matter of minutes —fifteen minutes for counterattack. But the vulnerability of the inner technological power structure is such that you can have what is known in physics as an 'implosion,' with the whole military complex both intact and harmless, sitting there, looking *outside*. . . ."

I see the creep's eyes taking notes, while there is a thoughtful silence full of hard-boiled eggs.

"Why is it that the Algerian freedom fighters always cut off the French soldiers' balls and stuffed them in their mouths?" Saad Ibrahim asks.

I put my hard-boiled egg back on the plate.

The bell rings.

I am going to put a sign on my door: *Foccart-Left Bank, open till 2 A.M.* I am so tired I envision myself surrounded by hard-boiled eggs eating black faces.

I open the door. It is Cosso, the prettiest and tallest Malian girl in Paris.

I announce:

"I am closing down. Go back to Mali, for chrissake."

"He doesn't love me any more," she informs me.

"Go to the Elysée Palace and tell it to Foccart. I can't do a thing about it."

"Maurice says we're through. He doesn't want me. What am I to do?"

"Go eat hard-boiled eggs in the kitchen."

I go to bed. But I can't sleep. I think of Jean. America

is a country where the most senseless things can happen, as the Sharon Tate murders were later to prove. It's a country where the crushed, maddened individual becomes a mad group. It is quite possible that within two or three generations, this process will become a life-saving one: the *constructive* breaking down of monolithic societies into a cluster of infra-societies, thousands and thousands of Renaissance societies, united by their specific creeds and ways of life and independent within a mega-structure of economic lifelines. But right now, the groping for something else, something radically different from both mind and soul, takes the form of sickness of both mind and soul.

I book a seat on the next plane to Los Angeles, but postpone my departure when a friend calls me to give the news of a final Cross of Lorraine march on the Champs Elysées that afternoon. The last remaining Free French of World War II, the last of the Cross of Lorraine militant anti-Nazis, anti-Vichy troops of 1940—there are a handful of us left today—will march down the Champs Elysées that afternoon.

A "last stand" is something I've never been able to resist. I have a profound dislike for majorities. They always become crushing. A majority may sound like a democratic force, but there is usually more force than democracy.

So it's easy to imagine my horror when, upon reaching the Champs Elysées at the Arch of Triumph, instead of being greeted by a few hundred true *minoritaires*, I am confronted by a yelling, thundering, flag-waving mass of something like three hundred thousand Gaullists who exude such a stink of total, self-satisfied, superior unanimity that it gives me gooseflesh.

Gaullist or whatever this howling, grinning, stamping mass begins to smack of brute force, of "final solution," and shows all the unmistakable signs of *La Connerie*. No matter on what side you are, this kind of sheer demographic outpouring sooner or later gives it to you in the ass.

To say that the French word *minoritaire* simply means "a member of a minority" nowhere near expresses the history of the term, the millenniums of slavery, massacre, suppression and beastliness combined with self-satisfied, self-righteous superiority it conveys.

I am a born *minoritaire*, and I shall never be anything else, so help me God.

XXVI

I fly back to Beverly Hills the next morning and as soon as I reach the house, I hear a sad, desperate miaowing inside. Siamese cats always sound unhappy, but when they are in pain, their voices are heartbreaking.

The house is empty.

Maï is a little gray skeleton staring at me with her pink-glowing eyes. She is dying.

Those black sons of bitches have poisoned her, just as they poisoned Bang and Chamaco. I take her in my arms and with all those sleepless nights and tension behind me, my "iron" nerves snap and I begin to cry out of sheer hatred and frustration.

She speaks to me, looks at me intently, tries to tell me

something, yes, I know, I know, you really had nothing to do with it all. . . .

I can't stop my goddamn tears.

I stay there for an hour or two or three, hating. Jean comes back from work and finds me trying to feed Maï with an eye dropper. I stand up and look at her with the kind of face I have when I am no longer trying to hide the kind of face I have.

"Why didn't you tell me they'd poisoned Maï? Just who are you protecting, exactly, and from what? Are you shielding those black bastards, or my sensitivity?"

"But . . ."

"There's no 'but.' A brute is a brute is a brute, whatever the color of his skin. I've had enough of these black skunks being treated like fragile china just because of their color. . . . That's blackmail. . . ."

She is crying. Her face always seems to revert to childhood when she hurts and burns inside with a feeling of injustice, and she looks utterly exhausted and lost.

"Jeannie . . ."

"Leave me alone."

The Middle West all comes back in that nasal "aloone."

"Maï hasn't been poisoned. She's sick. . . . It's got nothing to do with them. . . . I take her to the clinic every day. . . . The vet says it's a degenerative liver disease, he can't do anything about it."

"Where's the kid?"

"With my family."

"Degenerative disease, my ass. They poisoned her."

"They haven't touched her!" she yells and runs out.

I hear the car pull off full speed with a furious screeching of tires and remain alone with the cat on my knees.

I feel I am touching the rock-bottom of loneliness, a record of some sort, though when it comes to breaking the records of loneliness, each of us is a champ.

I phone Pan Am and book a seat for Mauritius in the Indian Ocean. I have a friend who went to live there twenty-five years ago. Maybe he is still around.

Then Jean comes back, sits next to me and holds my hand. She has very small hands.

I spend the next few days watching Maï die. I can't stand that voice, that *protest*. Katzenelenbogen shows up and explains in that rational, no-nonsense, doctoral tone that no one has the right to make such a fuss over a cat, while the whole world. . . . I kick them out, both him and the world.

Maï is no longer a cat. She is a human being in agony. Every living thing that suffers is a human being.

She is cuddled in my arms, a small ball of lackluster fur, which gives her a horrible stuffed air already smacking of taxidermists. Every now and then she raises her head, looks at me inquiringly and miaows a question I understand, but am unable to answer. Our vocal chords are totally inadequate there.

What goings-on about a mere cat, huh? I hate your guts, you antisentimental, antiemotional, hardheaded rationalists. You are the ones who have raised the going rate on sensitivity. You have put all your emphasis on ideas, and ideas without "emotions" and without "sentimentalism," that's the world you have built, *your* work.

All the pseudo-people who have the Nazi arrogance to be reading this book make my hands ache for a grenade. I don't think I did enough back there in Paris. I could've poured more oil on the sacred fire. Dear God, I do hope you'll give me another chance.

Maï dies on June 7, at half-past three in the morning, and we bury her in Cherokee Lane, under the most beautiful trees in the world. She was a great tree-climber.

There is at least one person who will understand.

Dear André Malraux:
Maï, the Siamese you met at my house, died this morning
after a long illness. We buried her under the eucalyptus
trees, at the corner of Beaumont Drive and Cherokee, off
Coldwater Canyon. I thought you ought to know.

Yours,
R.G.

Around seven in the evening, a dark blue Chevy stops in
front of the house; another car pulls up behind it, with two
blacks who remain in the front seat, the engine running,
while a third gets out, stops in the middle of the sidewalk,
and stands there, smoking, with that falsely relaxed, un-
concerned air of a professional bodyguard. Then the driver
of the first car gets out and starts toward the house. I watch
this stranger through the bay window, but it is almost dark
and it is only as he raises his hand to ring the bell that I
recognize Red.

He has changed beyond belief. Physically, to begin with:
he has shaved his head completely, and his bulging skull
gives him a curiously oriental look. But it's the eyes that
have changed the most. I don't quite know how to describe
this change: his eyes seem to have lost their ability to see
the *outside* world, they seem to be looking inside, with only
whatever is purely mechanical in our vision still registering a
bare minimum of the world around them. It is something
quite different from blindness, exactly the opposite, in fact:
it is as if everything that really mattered, the true world,
the real vision, was all inside, and the rest was only steps,
staircases, objects, a routine of opening and closing doors.
Seen from outside, his eyes do no more than function in a
kind of elementary bureaucracy of living and motion.

He walks in without a word, sits down. The face is ex-
pressionless. The shaved head bulges in a weird symmetry,
with a slight recession in the middle. He has grown a small

moustache. The necktie is undone. The silence is an invitation to more silence: I am unable to utter a word. The square, broad-shouldered hulk of a body is as impressive as ever, yet its immobility no longer carries the suggestion of pent-up, hidden, burning energy, but of petrified matter. This is a statue that would have stood one day in a Washington square, if America knew how to recognize its own greatness.

Jean comes down the stairs to greet him and he says *hello* quietly, with a trace, a bare flicker of the old smile.

"Can I spend the night here?"

"Of course."

He waves away the glass of Scotch, looks at me:

"I better warn you it might get you in trouble with the police."

"That's all right, I can't keep the police out of my life forever, there's a limit. . . . Red?"

"Yeah."

"What's it all about?"

"Nothing, now. . . ."

"Nothing?"

"Yeah, Philip's been killed."

It's the hour when the rooks get noisy up there in the trees.

"He was leading a patrol in Vietcong country, and he got caught, killed, that is."

He looks at the opposite wall.

"He was a lieutenant, you know. His C.O. wrote me a personal letter. The best officer he ever had. That's what the letter says. . . . The best."

There is a strange expression of surprise in his eyes, as if he had suddenly remembered something. . . .

"Well, you know, of course, why Philip was doing all this. Don't get it wrong."

"I won't."

"The best officer that Colonel what's-his-name ever had the privilege of having in his command. That's what the letter says. Philip sure had what it takes. The right kind of rage, I mean. The kind that lifts mountains. The youngest black kid to be made a full lieutenant out there. He was training hard. Just the fighting kind we need here. Two stars on his D.C., they gave him all the medals. They taught him real good and he'd learned good and he could've done quite a job here. . . ."

He lapses suddenly into French, speaking words he had learned from me years ago, Foreign Legion slang:

"*C'est un sale coup, mon vieux. Un sale coup pour la fanfare.* A real, mean blow."

I keep my mouth shut. It always comes easier than words. Night has fallen. The waxen yellow glow of a lamp with orange and red birds painted over yellow silk. Jean is sitting on the staircase, her head low, her hands clasping her knees. The rooks have buried the day and are quiet. The seven P.M. sound of traffic from Santa Monica. . . .

He will never know. He will go through life proud of his militant son. He will never know it isn't the black army that lost one of its future guerrilla leaders, but the U.S. Army that lost one of its young American officers who had decided to make a career serving under the star-spangled banner.

"It's been months since I last got a letter from him, and now this. . . ."

He asks absentmindedly, almost as if out of courtesy to me:

"How's Ballard?"

"You know how it is for an American living in Paris. . . . He feels uprooted over there. Wants to come home."

"He shouldn't have deserted. He should've stayed in the Army. That's where you learn all you need to know when you're black. But then Ballard hasn't got it in him. Not tough enough. Well, of course, I can understand that. He's against the war, like a lot of black kids who aren't highly motivated enough."

He is lying. Not to me and Jean: he is lying to himself. He knows Ballard didn't give a damn about Vietnam. He deserted to be with the girl he loved, the most natural way in the world of *not* deserting, and because he was a young man of his generation, and this means refusal to submit, refusal to carry the burden and the dead weight of rotten traditions on his shoulders; he was like many of our kids, young enough to feel the times, while condemned to be part of them.

Pools of yellowish light stagnate on the shaved head and around the cheekbones of this totally immobile face which seems hacked out of shadows, and the eyes remind me of the last time Maï looked at me.

He is lying. He can no longer face reality and he is seeking refuge in his fantasy. One of the best, the most remarkable Americans that America has ever destroyed has been condemned to an imaginary world, to a mythical black realm, to dreams and unreality, like one of those oldtime African kings. . . .

I can't take it any more. *I* can't take it in *him.*

"What they really want is for me to show resistance—you know, an excuse for shooting me. The old routine. Cops specialize in legitimate self-defense. *Mais à part ça, j'ai tué un mec.* I killed a guy."

"A cop?"

"Yes. . . . Well, no. A black provocateur. Same thing. They don't sign receipts for the pay they get, you know. We can't afford the kind of money it takes to get at the F.B.I. files. All we know is that some niggers showed up at one of our meetings and gunned down three of our young brothers. Students. I got one of the murderers the next day. It wasn't a matter of revenge, you know. I don't believe in that. But there comes a moment when you have to show you have blood on your hands, or you're back where you started, a nigger. And never mind the fact that this is exactly what our enemies want us to do. We still have to do it. It's not a question of choice, like it, dislike it. It's not about me, or Karenga, or Rap Brown, or Huey Newton, or any of us, good or bad. It's about that fourteen-year-old kid sitting on the ghetto sidewalk and watching us with those big attentive eyes."

"Red, how many militants have been killed by blacks?"

"Not by blacks, by guys who *look* black."

There is a trace of the old, ironic, almost Pigalle smile again. . . .

"Some of us are just *painted* black, you know. You rub the paint off and what d'you see? *Du pognon.* Money."

"What are you going to do?"

"I don't know. I just have to see into what position they'll maneuver me, the morgue, the chair, jail, or exile. Well, exile is out. I'm not going to leave the country. It's mine, and it stays mine. Let 'em bury me, that'll make one god-damn piece of earth mine for keeps, period. I have nowhere to go, anyway. I've been to Africa, you know, and, man, I was a total stranger there. Castro's out: Cleaver's been there—and it's not the answer. I'll try to find a good lawyer, one of those guys who give the police so much trouble and make such a stink that the heat prefers to leave you alone. . . ."

His voice sinks deeper in, down and down, as if in search of the very depth of his rancor.

"The game consists of pushing us to a point where we'll side with the a-b-c enemies of America—Castro, Peking, Moscow—and lose our American character in the eyes of our own people. When the Panthers turned Maoist, that was a great all-white victory. Or else, go into exile. But of course what they really want is to encourage a power struggle within the black movement. That's real cream for those F.B.I. cats. We just off each other, the old Chicago way. But there's an even better way, and it works, man, yes, indeed. We're walking right into it, and that goes for me too, because there's no way around *that* trap."

The voice rises again out of its subterranean ashes, it is once more the strong, deep voice I know so well and his earthy "manpower" hands lock, almost biting into each other.

"The pattern is very clear, all traced out, you know. The point is, no matter how clearly you see it, you can't avoid following it, because the kids don't listen to words, they want heroes, and they want to know and remember their names. Up to now, we mostly *talked* violence. But there comes a time for all people in a state of siege and who feed only upon themselves, a moment when the words first destined to remain just that, words, begin to convince the very people who keep uttering them, by the sheer process of repetition. The result is either action or a feeling of falsehood and devirilization. You either go out and kill or you begin to feel you're just making soul music, your incendiary speeches become the equivalent of New Orleans jazz and Negro spirituals: in both cases, you're a loser. That's how the white establishment is turning a few thousand hard-core militants into a new "lost generation," condemned to a few murders and more and more fantasies. . . . We can raise our voice to a certain pitch, but higher up, it becomes the voice of impotence. It becomes empty words, fake thunder. The truth of the matter is that as long as the black minority keeps raising its voice, it's nothing but soul music, the second it resorts to terrorism, it becomes easy to eliminate, but if I say all this openly, I'm washed up in the eyes of our kids in terms of leadership, and I won't be able to accomplish anything for them. We have to choose between heroism and practical accomplishment, but accomplishment is the most unheroic thing in the world, and it's contrary to the nature of youth. It means painstaking conquest of local political power through legal methods, pressures, boycotts, strikes, and clever use of voting power. . . . This isn't the kind of program you can come up with to a sixteen-year-old kid in the ghetto. . . . And so even the most realistic among us are condemned to romanticism."

I remember asking reluctantly, for there was something almost shaming in challenging him:

"And what about that black guerrilla army back from Vietnam?"

"We *have* to think, talk and act that way, *mon vieux*. . . . If the moderates are going to get anywhere, we have to keep the fire burning. I'm not nutty enough to start raising a black army in this country. But the veterans back from Vietnam are our only chance to organize ourselves and to get out of our present bag of individualism, with every leader jockeying for a kind of political Jackie Robinson-Cassius Clay superman position."

The voice fills with weariness.

"When, every day, you get your dose of prejudice and injustice, and when you learn more and more about the past, as our kids are, it's easier to give in to heroism and romanticism, with violent speeches becoming either dead bloods on the pavement or soul music than to organize, maneuver, use, tactically and strategically, your voting and consumer power, and force America either to use genocide and thus sign the death warrant of Western civilization, or save itself. . . . Only blacks can save America, man, because everything that refuses to give us our American chance refuses to give a new chance to America, and how many times can you put all your stakes on the same old number? Personal heroism in such a situation is almost a form of laziness. . . . But then, youth never has time to wait. . . . And they're the ones we get our orders from."

He gets up, and so do I.

"I'll show you to your room."

We walk upstairs.

"What if the police come banging on the door?"

"I don't think they'll show up. They'd rather hold the threat over my head. That's supposed to make me discreet, you see. Less conspicuous."

"What about your three guys outside? They're conspicuous as hell."

"They're there against the competition."

"I wish you dumb bastards would stop killing each other."

He is a few steps ahead of me.

"What's she really like, that *môme,* that chick in Paris?"

"I wish you could meet her, Red. She's the best thing that can happen to a guy. The very best. The baby is due any time now, I think. I do wish you knew the *môme . . .*"

"Well."

"Red . . ."

. . . I shouldn't have done it, but this was a moment of truth, and after all, he himself was the one who had spoken to me about the end of dreaming, of self-delusion.

"Red, I'm sure you know Ballard deserted for that *môme's* sake. For no other reason. It had nothing to do with Vietnam, with ideology; it was love, the best, the only valid reason in the world."

He is standing in front of the door with his back toward me. A light brown, checkered suit. I can see it now.

"Yeah, I know, *mon vieux.*"

"And Philip . . ."

He lowers his head a bit and waits. He waits for it with all the strength of his broad, massive back, with all those centuries of "manpower" in that back. . . .

He waits. But the load of truth is on his shoulders, and I have seen it.

He knows.

He goes into the room and closes the door behind him.

I go downstairs into the living room. Jean's hands are ice.

It can be pretty fatal to love animals. If you are capable of seeing a human being in a dog, you can't help seeing a dog in every human being, and then you've had it. It's love again, and brotherhood. You are caught.

Red was killed on November 27, 1968, in Detroit. A machine-gun burst fired from a car.

Ballard gave himself up in February, 1969, six months after his son was born.

XXVII

I came back to America and that house on Arden six weeks later, after a few more zig-zags across the world, from Paris to Khartoum and from Spain to Somaliland. It is almost impossible for me to stay away from America for long, because I am not yet old enough to lose interest in the future, and in what it holds in store for us. America is living *us* intensely, violently, sometimes ignobly, but compared to the great cadaverous rigidities of the East, it is a continent in an acute state of aliveness. Something there, painfully, gropingly, tries to give birth and to be born. It is the only maximum Power in history to summon itself to account for its own crimes. This has never been seen before. That is why even in the depths of its desperation, it is a country that does not give in to despair.

I saw White Dog again. I shall have to live to be very old if I am ever to forget our reunion. My son will have to grow and become a man among other men at last worthy of that name. Our civilization will have to emerge from prehistory, and as there is not time enough for a change of such magnitude, if only I could catch a glimpse of a more human world before crossing the shadow line, something of what my life has been about will never vanish entirely.

After my homecoming, I kept trying to reach Keys on the phone. But a recorded voice repeated soullessly, "You have reached a disconnected number." Every time I hear that message, I think of this whole alienated, disconnected generation. . . .

I called Jack Carruthers at his home, only to learn that Keys wasn't working for him any more.

"He's gone into business for himself. I don't have the address here. . . . Call me at my office. No, wait. . . . It's in Corinne Street, behind the football field, a green house, in Cranton. Take Florence Avenue, it's the third or fourth street on the right."

Lloyd Katzenelenbogen comes to talk business with Jean, but she is out. He offers to drive me a Cranton. He knows the neighborhood.

"I did some work there after Watts."

We go down La Brea, take Crenshaw. . . .

"I went through here a few weeks ago on my way to see an Italian movie, *The Battle of Algiers*," Lloyd tells me. "And over there . . ."

He points to a half acre of nondescript vacant land, waiting there for real estate prices to go up.

". . . there were about twenty kids dressed up in camouflage suits, and carrying wooden rifles and mock hand grenades. They were training for street fighting, Vietnam type, you know, with grenades thrown into windows and doorways. The black guy in charge of the outfit was obviously a former G.I. and he certainly was seeing to it that they learned the job properly. All this with two white cops in their car, at the intersection, just sitting. . . . Then while I was watching the movie—it was banned in France, you know, for showing the heroic fight the Arabs put up against the French oppressors . . ."

I wince. There is no reason why the words "French oppressors" should make me wince, but there you are.

". . . while I was watching the movie, the same bunch of kids and their instructor come in. It was part of their training, apparently. The picture is in Italian neo-realist style, and every time a *fellahin* brought down a French soldier in the street, there was applause, laughter, and yells of delight. . . . How about that?"

I take careful aim, right between the skunk's eyes—as you may have guessed, I don't like the guy.

"Just imagine the applause and delight if the picture showed the heroic struggle of Palestinian Arabs against the Israeli oppressors?"

He winces.

We drive along in a silence heavy with hostility.

"I think it's here," Lloyd says.

It seems to be the only green house around and there is a football field a bit farther down, just as Jack had told me. But then I notice another green three-story, dilapidated house, across the street, next to a wired-up oilwell. We get out of the car.

"See if Keys lives here, I'll ask at the other house."

I cross the street and take a few steps on the lawn under the plane trees. I reach the green clapboard structure when I hear a scream of terror behind me, then a long animal howl, followed by a burst of short rapid furious barks and another silence, while the animal has his mouth full. . . .

I spin around and run toward the house.

There is no one in the back yard, the door is wide open, and I can hear children screaming inside, and the throaty murderous growls of a dog at his quarry. . . .

Lloyd is on the floor, his face and hands covered with blood, and he is trying to push Batka away. The dog's bared fangs are aimed at Lloyd's throat and he mercilessly plunges them again and again into Lloyd's outstretched hand.

There are several children in the room, and the biggest, who must be six or seven years old, is trying to pull the dog off by his tail. Another kid with a pink doll in her arms is crying, in a small, high-pitched wail. The other kids—it seems the room is full of them—just stand there, paralyzed, watching.

I throw myself on top of Batka and instantly feel his fangs in my hands, again and again, like deep slashes from a knife. The dog keeps growling, still trying to get at Lloyd's throat. I roar and swear and try to get my fingers into the beast's eyes, and feel another deep bite, a burning pain, the fangs tearing at my flesh, right in the middle. . . .

I let go and roll away. As the dog plunges with maniacal persistence at Lloyd's throat again, I manage to kick the animal in the balls with all the might I can master, but as I am lying almost flat on my back, the kick misses, the dog is still at it. . . .

And that is when I catch sight of Keys.

He is standing on the stairs almost naked, wearing a narrow pair of black underpants.

And he is laughing.

. . . How long had he been standing there, with that smile on his face, his hands on his hips, victorious enjoying his *equality*?

"Black Dog!"

Even here in Djibouti, by the Red Sea, where I am writing this, alone with the horizon, except for a few Arab *dhows* with their oblique masts and narrow sails, I can still hear my raging, hysterical voice, in which I now clearly recognize the echo of some ghastly feeling of relief and liberation, almost of joy, as if I had at last succeeded in getting rid of hope, as if I had at last learned the secret of giving up. . . .

"I see you succeeded, you dirty bastard. It's Black Dog now!"

Batka was coming at me. He had bitten me several times, but they were blind bites, in the thick of battle, and with Lloyd finished and immobile, his arms folded limply over his face, the dog had now singled me out for attention.

In a second, he was on me. The first two rapid bites were for my wrists, and then, kicking, I rolled away, the back of my neck hitting the wall. . . .

I waited, with my face hidden in my arms, my eyes closed, my knees up. . . .

Nothing happened.

I raised my head.

What I saw in front of me were my mother's eyes, the eyes of a loving, faithful dog.

Batka was looking at me.

I have seen friends wounded and dying next to me, but whenever I shall try to recall what an expression of total human despair, incomprehension, and anguish, the expression at *the end of everything* is like, I will be looking for it in my memory of that dog's eyes.

He raised his head high and gave out a soul-rending howl, full of all the sadness and hopelessness of the earth's darkest nights.

Then he was gone.

Lloyd was unconscious. He had to have fourteen stitches, and the deepest cut was only a fraction of an inch from the carotid.

Keys was still there, standing above us on the stairs, and in his nudity he looked like the figure-head of a slave ship.

"Is that what you wanted from the beginning? That was the goal, the motivation, the only reason for that tireless dedication and pursuit? White Dog was to become Black Dog! You've made it, you win. Hurray and thanks, brother! At least now we aren't the only ones to have discredited and debased ourselves!"

"Yeah, we've learned a few things from you all right," he said. "Now we can even do the teaching."

My shock and nervous exhaustion took on the form of resentment and rage, childish in their lack of all sense of measure or restraint. I remember that, while looking with hatred at that all-black symmetry, the only coherent thought that found its way to my consciousness was that he was truly one of us, and as such, contemptible. He'd made it. He had joined the club.

And yet that was not how it came out, when I spoke to him at that moment. It somehow came out all by itself, out of my bitterness and racist disillusionment—yes, racist, for how else should I label my belief that blacks were better, and therefore different from us?—and Keys didn't miss the clumsy emphasis and rhetorical snootiness of my words. They were the most sincere I had ever uttered, but they came out overdressed.

"Listen to me, Keys. Blacks like you betray their brothers, because by joining us in hate, you're losing the only battle worth winning."

He shook with silent laughter, his arms crossed over his bare chest.

"I know. I know you are a noted writer, Sir."

"Drop dead. White Dog, Black Dog, is that all there will ever be?"

"Well, we have to begin somewhere," he said.

"Equality in beastliness?"

"Self-defense, that's what it is."

"You bet. But I find it pretty sickening when Jews start dreaming of equality in terms of a Jewish Gestapo and blacks in terms of a black Ku Klux Klan. . . ."

Suddenly, there was an expression of extraordinary pride on his face. His voice freed itself from baiting mockery, expanded, while at the same time deepening, as if coming from under his feet, from the very earth, and I could no longer recognize it. It was the first time in all those eight months since we had first met that the voice no longer sounded American to me, and it brought to mind instantly all my years in Africa, among its painted warriors, tribal chiefs, and hunters.

"The man's killed nineteen of us over the last two years. We'll get even in every way we can and there's no such thing as a small way, when it comes to getting even. We're building our own black community, with our own *black* dogs. Not watchdogs. *Attack* dogs. That's my job and I'm the best at it. The very best, as you've found out."

A grin . . .

"I hope you'll recommend me."

I hear the police and ambulance sirens, though I shall never know who raised the alarm. Keys's wife upstairs? Perhaps. I watch Lloyd's bloodied face as they take him away on the stretcher, in a state of shock, his eyes wide, glassy, terrified. . . . I look at Keys for the last time.

"Pity. You're about to blow the only real chance for black people: that of being different. You're taking a lot of trouble to be exactly like us. Thank you for the compliment, but it's more than we deserve, and it can only help you become the white man's best joke . . . the best he ever played on others. It seems we've been so successful that even if our lousy breed vanishes, nothing will change."

He laughs and nods good-naturedly. Those teeth . . .

"That may well be, but don't let that stop you from vanishing," he says.

The cops listen, shuffle their feet, can make no sense of it all. They want to know if the dog had his shots against rabies. I tell them the vaccine has to yet be discovered.

He ran through the streets, and along his way police patrol cars were flashing the message: "Watch out for a mad dog." There was in his eyes all the incomprehension and all the despair of a faithful believer whom his God of love had betrayed and forsaken. At the corner of La Cienega and Santa Monica, the patrol car driven by Sargeant John L. Sallen tried to run him over, but missed. By then, he was almost back home at Arden: he had only two hundred yards more to go. . . .

I found him in Jean's arms, twenty minutes later. There was no trace of blows or wounds on his body. The eyes were open and peaceful. He had reached the house, rolled up on the mat in front of our door, and died.

They kept me two weeks at the clinic, after the first few days and nights of drugged sleep. There were, however, moments of twilight, when some almost coherent thoughts would slowly come together in my mind, and with the first light of consciousness would stir in me and raise again the strange, undying, and invincible hope that never fails to get the better of me and, in a manner closer to some deep survival instinct of our species than to my own will, forever compels me to see in all our lost battles the price of our future victories.

I am not discouraged, and those deep peaceful sands of despair remain as inaccessible to me as ever. I have been defeated once more, but after so many defeats there comes a moment when you begin to feel invincible. My excessive love of life makes my relations with life very difficult, as difficult as when you go on loving a woman you can neither change, nor help, nor leave.

When I woke up for the first time, she was leaning over me almost eagerly, as if all this time, while I lay unconscious, she had been waiting to give me the good, the wonderful news.

"You got it all wrong, Romain. A terrible misunderstanding, but of course, it all happened so quickly. . . . I had a long talk with Keys. He didn't train that poor dog to attack whites. He just trained him to attack any strangers who entered the house. . . ."

It didn't come easy to me, loaded as I was with narcotics, but I made it all right:

"*Et avec . . . les oreilles . . . tu ne fais rien?* And with your ears, Jean, don't you do any tricks?"

"Honestly, Keys assured me. . . ."

Honestly. Mercifully, my mind went blank again.

Then I woke up once more, and she was still there—but then I often see her even when she isn't there—but this time she didn't have any more wonderful news to share with me, only a smile, before I slipped back into oblivion.

The next time, she was still by my bedside, but also Madeleine, with her three-month-old son: François Gaston Claude. I don't know at all how it will come out in America.

"How's Ballard?"

"You know he's given himself up?"

"I know."

"His trial comes up very soon now. He might get five years."

"What about you, Madeleine?"

"They have to give him back to me, sooner or later. . . ."

Her voice was calm, self-assured, the voice of quiet certainties. It made me think of Chartres Cathedral, I don't quite know why.

"I'm going to look for a job. . . ."

She smiled. I smiled too. The easy way out. . . .

But it is such a relief to be able to respect someone, at last.

"I'm just waiting to know what jail it'll be, so that I can be near him. I have the right to two visits a week."

Nigger lover. Nigger lover.

Andraitx, September 1969
Djibouti, August 1970